Revenant
Legends of the Starborn

STEPHEN PHILLIPS

DEDICATION

For all of those who look up at the stars and wonder, are we alone?
And for all of us who see adventure in the darkness and grasp at the
starlight. And thank you to everyone who has given me feedback and those
who have enjoyed the stories I've shared.

Contents

Chapter 1
One Step Closer

The engine's hum filled the background as Eislie piloted the ship. She and Jace had finally finished the new hull installation and were testing its effect on the ship in hyperspace. It had been nearly two months since they'd started the modifications, and it felt good to be ready. Most of their testing was complete; after this final run, they both knew the next step would be to test within the filaments themselves. Their remaining time on Yata Beta had been, thankfully, uneventful and surprisingly quiet, allowing them to refine the systems for flying within the filaments. The environment they had now was also nothing like months earlier. Eislie thought back on the dark memories of being taken to Arlain and tortured by the Hurmonn. Jace and Eislie suspected, however, that there were others in the background waiting for them to finish what they were working on so they could steal it. Using the filaments to travel could be far more lucrative once they found a way to do so safely. How or where these others would distribute the information afterward, neither really knew.

"The ship controls still feel solid," Eislie said before asking the computer, "Are you finding any issues, Ed?"

Several seconds went by before their computer answered, "My diagnostics have not found any errors in the installation. The new shell material also seems to allow us to move quicker within hyperspace."

Jace looked up from his monitor. "He's right. The ship's quieter, too." He looked around. "I keep thinking something's wrong."

Eislie scoffed. "Let's hope our luck holds out."

"Maybe we should head back."

Eislie sighed, then said, "Yeah, maybe we should. My parents have been asking us to come home since they headed back to Gilese."

Jace raised his brow, then remarked, "I meant go back to Yata, but I'm getting the sense you're feeling a bit homesick." Eislie, looking apologetic, nodded, and Jace continued, "Eh, you're right, we probably should. Besides, having to wear a protective visor every time I leave a building is getting annoying."

Eislie chuckled as she exited to normal space before setting a new course and heading back toward Yata Beta.

When they arrived back on the planet, Miriz met them outside her home. "Well, you didn't blow up. That's a good sign."

1

Eislie mockingly reached out, tapping their friend. "Miriz? I'm surprised. It's not like you to wish harm on me."

Miriz laughed. "Well, when it comes to you two, I think not blowing up is a good day. Can you blame me?"

Eislie looked surprised as Jace chuckled. "She kinda has a point."

Miriz reached out, putting her arm over Eislie's shoulders. "The ship looks good. It looks like a proper spaceship, not that grungy grey-green from before."

Jace feigned being offended. "How dare you insult our ship, Mirizali Elysse? You might hurt Ed's feelings."

They watched Jace try to stop himself from laughing. Miriz leaned in to Eislie and asked, "How do you put up with him?"

Eislie pondered briefly before answering, "One, I love him. Two, you get used to it. He's Terran. They're naturally sarcastic."

There was a bit of laughter from everyone before they headed back toward the house. As they closed the door, the computer's sensors picked up movement nearby, within some plants that lined Miriz's property. They seemed to be moving in an unnatural way, the branches seemingly bending toward the house, but there was no reason for it. "Peculiar," Ed said. "I detect no life forms except for the flora."

The house was a flurry of activity as Jace and Eislie started packing. Miriz invited them one last time for lunch. As they ate, they talked. "I can't believe you're leaving already. It's only been two months," Miriz said with a solemn look on her face. "My best friend is heading home again. Along with her cute partner."

Jace knew Miriz was chiding Eislie again. They seemed to always tease each other. He said, "You know, one of these days, one of you is going to have to tell me what it is between you two. You're always messing with each other, like it's some sort of competition." He felt their stares, making him look up from his food. It took a moment before he yelled, "AHHH! The beams are burning through me! You've vanquished me." Jace then leaned back in his chair, his tongue hanging out, before he held up his napkin, waving it like a flag of surrender.

Miriz nearly spit out her drink as she laughed. The sound of Eislie's laughter also bellowed through the room. When Miriz regained her composure, she said, "I'm going to miss that when you're gone, both of you."

"You know, I really am curious about what this whole competition thing is with you two," Jace continued. "But I'm also smart enough to realize I probably shouldn't press the matter." He walked over to Eislie, kissing the top of her head. "My survival instincts are telling me I should walk away from this. Well, at least for the moment." He leaned down, putting his arms around Eislie. "But I'm just so damn curious."

Eislie put her hands over his, feeling his warmth. "When you're older, I might tell you."

Jace sighed. "Then I guess I'll never know. I plan on never growing up."

There was laughter again throughout the room until Eislie began focusing on the large glass door. Jace noticed and looked to where she was staring. He became focused, too, before whispering, "You see something."

Noticing the interaction, Miriz turned to look in the same direction. Was there something behind her? Her senses were heightened after recent events, the previous poisoning and the discovery of the quantum recorders in her offices now flooding her mind. "You see something?" she whispered.

Eislie shook her head. "I had the feeling we were being watched."

* * *

The sound of someone running echoed as the plants on the outside of the property moved from the footsteps appearing within the moist dirt. They disappeared into a vehicle as its door opened. Inside the cabin, there were two others.

"Taylyn, did you find out anything?" the driver asked.

Next to the woman in back, the head of another woman appeared from nowhere before the rest of her body revealed itself. "There's no filament signature on that ship. They didn't travel using it. The readings were all the same as when they left." She turned to the smartly dressed woman, who seemed disappointed, before continuing, "This quantum suppression and prismatic unit worked flawlessly. I must hand it to your division, Loren. This new tech is useful. But I think Gilese sensed I was there."

Loren nodded. "Gilese and other planets can be difficult, or where there's a greater level of empathic senses. We've been working on it since we started using quantum recording. The suppressor and prism suits are useful. But the power system still needs work."

Taylyn looked concerned. "What do you mean?"

Loren looked to the driver. "Paren, let's go. We don't want to be caught here if they're following." The man hit the accelerator, and they were off. Loren turned back to Taylyn. "The system uses a lot of energy. Right now, it's stable. You were briefed on the usage limits, weren't you?"

Taylyn nodded. "Yes. It has a limit of three standard hours, then it needs to be shut down to regenerate power."

Loren looked to the floor before looking away. "It's not regenerating power. It's repairing itself. It's a micro-spide inversion system. We've stabilized a slow reaction to suppress the local light and quantum fields. That's what allows the suit to become essentially invisible." She was then quiet for a moment, lost in her thoughts, before unceremoniously pushing Taylyn forward. "Relax. I need to check something." She tapped the controls on the slim backpack before pulling part of it away from the top, inspecting the part before saying, "Good, it's still stable."

"Stable?!" Taylyn yelled. "You weren't the one with a spide reactor on her back!"

Loren said confidently, "Relax. Since we've upgraded the systems, there's only been one inversion that injured anyone." She leaned back. "Besides, you have those two you were watching to thank for the system working. If it wasn't for their ship's reactor upgrades, we couldn't have made this viable."

"You mean this was a field test?!" Taylyn yelled.

"Calm yourself," Loren replied coldly. "Yes, this was an active field test. All the lab tests have been perfect since we upgraded the system."

Taylyn crossed her arms. "Next time you need a test subject, forget my name."

There was an audible sigh from Loren. "You were the only one who was able to get close to them. Those two and that ship of theirs has been a thorn in the Grand Matron's side since they arrived."

"Wait? What do you mean? I thought she was willing to help them," Taylyn said, confused.

Loren straightened the seam on her pants leg and said, "The ministry of intelligence cannot look at this situation in that way. Yes, they have been given Yata citizenship. Yes, they have been allowed to work on their vessel while they stay here. We all know what they're doing, but the full reason and mechanics on what they're doing are still eluding us. Right now, there are several planets working on filament travel. None have been able to perfect it, at least for traveling as far as those two have." She tapped her comm. "Central command, set up a meeting for me with the Grand Matron."

"Yes, director. What time would you like to meet her?" the voice on the comm asked.

Loren looked toward the driver. "How long till we arrive?"

The man looked back. "About thirty-five standard."

Loren gently pushed Taylyn's arm, causing her to turn so she could access the thin pack again. She pulled out a memory core, handing it to Loren, but she refused to take it. "That memory will corrupt itself in a minute," she said. "Pulling the recording core does that."

Taylyn looked at the small device, its small screen now displaying characters that didn't make any sense.

Loren said, "It's a failsafe. Just in case the suit operator is caught and captured. You need to disable the scramble code, then the quantum core can only be read in a resonant reader." She smiled, looking forward. "It keeps things out of the hands of our competition." She could see the look of disgust and dejection on Taylyn's face. Loren tapped her comm. "Make the appointment for one hour from now."

"Acknowledged, director," the operator responded before her comm went silent.

An hour later, Loren walked through the front office of the Grand Matron. She waited to be announced. In her hand was an information tablet she held with an assured grip. She watched as the assistant went to inform the Grand Matron of her arrival.

There were several people inside. This was a general meeting, and it didn't seem to be going well. Included was the Ternen representative from Arlain, Farh Celos, who was again asking for permission to head home. "Grand Matron," they were saying, "it has been months since we have taken control back on our world. We need an answer from your people about if you'll lend more aid, and if you will aid us against the Duggor threat. They have been moving closer to our world."

The Grand Matron looked toward the man. "We have offered what we can for now, Farh. It is understandable that the toxin used to enslave many of your lower class is difficult to undo. We have been dealing with a similar issue from our people returning from offworld, from both the Karazon and yours. Even with our capabilities, there are limitations."

Farh lowered his shoulders in defeat. He was about to speak but was interrupted when the Matron's assistant walked into the room. She had left the door open, and he could see a woman on the other side, smartly dressed and deploying a very enigmatic stare at them. He watched as the young assistant whispered something to the Grand Matron, causing her to stand. "Thank you for coming, everyone," she said. "We can continue this debate later. For now, I must ask you all to leave. I have another appointment."

The Matron's assistant gently but firmly pulled him from his chair. As he exited, he passed the woman standing outside. He recognized the woman from the intelligence reports of the current Yata government. Loren Diur, head of Yata Ministry of Intelligence. *What is she doing here?* he thought as he walked past. He noticed that her eyes never deviated from her target, yet somehow he knew she could see him staring. As he crossed the threshold, the doors to the Matron's office closed.

Before anything was said, Loren tapped her pad, causing a bright flash of light to be emitted into the room. "We have five minutes on the scrambler, Matron," she announced without moving. "I have the information on the two you asked me to watch."

The Grand Matron asked, "Any evidence of them traveling?"

Loren shook her head. "Our initial reports show they haven't moved forward. They may not have found a solution yet."

The Grand Matron sighed. "I fear their recent abduction and other events may have slowed them somewhat."

Loren nodded.

"Anything else to report on our two resident starborn celebrities?"

Loren shook her head.

"I see." She held her hand out, and Loren gave her the information pad. "Any other bad news you wish to share?"

Loren smiled. "No, ma'am. But I'm pleased to note that the Arathea systems seem to be functional thanks to their unknowing efforts."

The Grand Matron smiled. "That is good to hear. Let me know when you have more information." She made it clear that Loren was dismissed.

Chapter 2

Unknown Enemies

Farh returned to his quarters and activated a secure comm. He had been informed of the recent information regarding Yata Beta. He updated the data on the two starborn known to be working on a way to travel the filaments and their involvement with the deaths of most of those who had held his world under the old reign. The new government now worked to secure their world for everyone on Arlain equally. They had co-opted the information already in place by the former rulers of the Tas and Hurmonn.

He was apprised of the situation and knew the reason they had taken one of the starborn in the first place. He read the file on Eislie Licessien and what had transpired under the hands of Malik, the Hurmonn who had taken her. He knew that one of the Hurmonn had tortured her to make her compliant and ready to serve another master. But her partner Jace Tucker risked his life and that of another Arlain to get her back. He also knew that both Jace and Eislie were known starborn who had previously exposed the enslavement of other starborn.

Currently the two were spending some time on Yata Beta to retrofit their ship, known as the *Wolfhammer*. It was an old Takloh vessel they'd modified with different technologies. It was also a ship that had proven formidable when attacked. It was confirmed as the one that had disabled and destroyed a Duggor planet cleaver over two years earlier. In a way, he felt sorry for the captains. He had met them and seen the condition they'd been in after they'd escaped from his home world. One of the ruling Tas had set a bounty on their heads, as well as an army of assassins. They were all destroyed when the ship the starborn were flying activated its tunnel drive while on the planet's surface.

He saw in the report that the two were attempting to outfit their vessel to presumably travel the filaments safely. Farh had only recently become aware of the project the Alliance had taken from the two starborn months ago. Reading further, he realized that the Tas had implemented a network of spies and monitoring equipment throughout the Yata and Alliance systems. He, like many, had wanted to take back the rule of their world from the Hurmonn. He had never cared for them; they were more a hybrid of their people and the Karazon, resilient and difficult to kill. All Arlain were able to resist injury due to the engineering that was part of their culture. However, the Hurmonn took it to extremes, enhancing themselves to the point of almost absurdity in order to push themselves to the physical limits of organic life.

Farh returned to the information before him, his eyes squinting as he concentrated. One section made him lean his head back in frustration. He read it again.

Update: Wolfhammer

Information gathered: Although the modifications to the ship have been confirmed, all Arlain retrofitted vessels have been destroyed upon attempting to travel the filaments. Actions will be necessary to secure the starborn vessel once it has achieved stable filament access. Status indicates that the ship can travel within the filaments for a limited time, but modifications and programing are still needed to update current projects for the filament program on the planet.

"Wait a minute," Farh muttered. "There's no filament program on Arlain. Where is this report from?" He scanned the page and found his answer, his mouth uttering words he never thought he'd say: "Yata informants confirm configuration but were unable to secure programming."

He leaned back into his chair, his shoulders heavy. "They're spying on them. So much for Yata being friends of starborn." He leaned forward with a realization. "That's why director Diur was there." Farh had deduced the reason he had been rushed out of his meeting with the Grand Matron. And why was the head of Yata Beta's Information Ministry there? He realized they're trying to steal the secret to filament travel.

Farh shook his head. He remembered how the two starborn had been battered and near death when they had been rescued. The toxin he knew all too well was flowing through both of their bodies. The Hurmonn had tried to break them, but the two starborn were more resilient than they'd anticipated. The entire Tas and ruling class had paid with their lives.

Farh smiled and said, "Good for them." But he also knew that his world needed to know that the Yata ministry was involved, and that the people of Yata couldn't provide the additional supplies to help undo what the Hurmonn had used to enslave them.

He tapped his secure comm and waited for the screen to respond. "This is Farh Celos. I'm calling with a report for the Ternen council," he said, sounding weary.

Moments later, a new image appeared. "Farh, I see they've been keeping you busy. Any word on the additional help from the people of Yata Beta?"

Farh shook his head. "Oslin. When did you get back? I thought you were offworld." Farh watched as the man waved and motioned for him to continue. Farh felt the burden of his position as he continued, "It took me several hours to process in after I arrived. It seems that there are many people who have been affected by the Karazon and our former leaders. My meeting with the Grand Matron did not go well."

The man on the screen bowed his head, and a metered sigh could be heard. "We were afraid of this. It seems that even though the people of Yata Beta are willing, they may not be able to help us quickly."

Farh nodded. "It would seem that is the case."

The man on the screen nodded, then looked to the side. "I wanted to let you know that the rioting has mostly stopped. Any remaining Tas and Hurmonn compounds have been emptied of their riches. It is surprising how many were willing to use that very wealth to help rebuild and heal those under the control of the Hurmonn." Farh smiled as he nodded, but that quickly disappeared as Oslin continued, "I understand that your meeting was interrupted by the intelligence minister."

How did you know that? Farh thought.

"We need you to continue to stay on Yata for at least a few months longer. We've sent some additional orders for you. You are to meet with a Representative Mirizali Elysee to procure access to more Sotiral systems."

There was a look of confusion as Farh read the additional orders. He could understand the negotiation for more of the Sotiral systems, but that could be done through standard channels. His confusion lifted as he read further. He found himself muttering as he read, "You are to meet with the designer of the Sotiral systems and negotiate for offworld production. Please see enclosed information on Eislie Licessien."

A look of disgust was prominent on Farh's face as he crossed his arms and stared back at the screen. His words were laced with distaste as he asked, "How did you know my meeting was interrupted by the intelligence minister, Oslin? I was calling to tell you that very information."

Oslin gave a practiced smile before responding, "Farh, they trust you. You were the one who informed them they weren't going to face charges for taking action against the Tas and killing most of the Hurmonn." There was no movement from either man before Oslin shifted back. "Are you aware of what those two starborn are working on?" Farh nodded, and Oslin smiled. "Then you understand the importance of the orders we sent. If we have the information on filament travel before anyone else, we can undo centuries of wrongs the Hurmonn have inflicted and finally be able to compete throughout the galaxy."

Farh felt the bile in his chest rising. He knew his friend was right. If Yata Beta had filament travel before anyone, they would drive the market for trade. And since Yata was no longer a member of the Alliance, now only an ally, Yata Beta could control everything.

Oslin moved closer to the screen. "Farh, we need any information that can help us rebuild."

Farh focused his eyes on his friend. "We've been fighting to do what is right. To free our people. You're asking me to betray others."

Oslin shook his head. "We do what's needed. Besides, we have the backing of Eshea Alon. Her songs have become popular since she returned home."

"Who?" Farh asked.

Oslin chuckled. "Sorry, you probably know her better as Queeks Maco."

"The one who was doing concerts all around the galaxy to help stop the Hurmonn?" Farh sounded surprised.

"The very same. She created the persona to hide her identity. You should hear the songs they're singing now. They're so much better than what they had previously. Trin Laln was a former arena slave. Zarlin Gala is the writer, and if I may say, a very talented one. Queeks was the creation of a former slave who had escaped and helped them both. Although their former leader, Ralla Metious, has been helping the council."

"A former fugitive is now helping? I guess I've heard of stranger things." Farh was dumbfounded at the news but looked at the screen. "I'll do what I can to get any additional information on the filaments. Anything else?"

Oslin shook his head. "You have enough to keep you busy. Besides, we have a lot to do here. Keep us posted." The screen went blank.

Farh leaned back. The apartment provided by the Yata government was well established. It even had food delivery daily. He turned his head to see a bottle of something he had always wanted to try. He read the label, muttering, "Tauren Spirits." He huffed. "These people seem to enjoy poisoning themselves when things get troublesome."

He grasped the top of the bottle, saying "I wonder if it'll help?" before cracking the seal and taking a long drink. He felt its burn as it made its way down his digestive tract.

* * *

A lone Duggor female moved down the stark hallway. Her pale skin was accented with pale blue veins in a filagree pattern, only seen while her sleeves moved up as she walked. The silence was only interrupted by her footsteps, a sound of organic hardness, like talons on steel. The information about their intrusion systems on Yata Beta was still visible on her pad as she entered the room at the end of the hall.

As she entered, a computer's voice stated, "Subjects have resisted implantation of neural connections. Controls have not been accepted."

Almost as if in unison, all Duggor nearby responded, "Starborn subjects T671234BN and T671271WN will need repair. Harnessing of bioenergy was unsuccessful. Continue with current mission plan."

The female placed the information pad into a slot, and its contents began uploading. "Current information regarding starborn subjects T974561JT and G970189EL has been received," the computer announced. "No new update to filament protocols required."

The Duggor waited as the others worked. If this was any other world, it would seem as if she was waiting for orders. However, the Duggor were of one mind but many bodies. Their society functioned like cells in a hive—all part of the same, but each with specific functions. What one knew, all Duggor knew. Their people had been this way for all their known history.

The woman watched as the pad ejected from its base. She immediately reached for it then waited for instructions. Her function was that of a courier who transported external information to and from access their combined minds couldn't physically interface with. Her thoughts were of nothing until she heard, *Return to monitoring. Come back when there is more information.* She turned and moved through the door again, noticing a small vessel landing in the area outside, before disappearing into the long darkness that was her place.

Many floors above, several Duggor sat in a circle, their bodies connected by organic tethers that glowed. Several other Duggor walked around dispensing nourishment to those seated. There was nothing but silence as all interlaced, their minds connected by physical and unseen forms. The bustle of activity slowed as the eyes of each within the circle opened. When all the others serving them were gone, they spoke.

Outside, a man wearing long robes was escorted to the door before being stopped. The entire group waited. The man reached up and tapped the side of his ear. Within moments he could hear everything inside the room before him. "Information on filament travel without Lyri bioenergy has not been achieved," he heard. "The method the Tharak use to harness the energy that is required, we are unable to duplicate."

Now only a single individual spoke. "Neural control of Lyri subjects has been attempted for thousands of years and nothing has been achieved. Once neural control has been implemented, the subject either terminates or begins to lose the ability to function."

The Duggor two from the left of the one who just spoke retorted, "Those of Lyri are tenacious, fragile, and difficult. We cannot afford any terminations. Recent subjects have not been of sufficient Lyri ancestry to exist on this world."

Yet another spoke. "Information from Yata Beta on subjects T974561JT and G970189EL has been promising, although our tests from gathered information have ended in the destruction of the vessels. More information is required. Apprehension of subjects T974561JT and G970189EL, known as Jace Tucker and Eislie Licessien, should be made a priority."

There was a silence before the first one spoke again. "The Tharak representative has arrived. We will speak with them."

There was again silence as the attendants returned, introducing a figure dressed in a long-hooded robe who entered the chamber. Four of the attendants placed their hands on the stranger, stopping him before reaching the circle. The individual stood in his place. He had experienced this treatment from the Duggor before, during previous exchanges in trying to circumvent the difficulties of filament travel. He waited until being addressed before moving.

"Representative, what is your designation?" he heard from all the Duggor around him. If the man had not experienced this on many occasions, it would have been unnerving. His mind was smug as he thought, *Ah, one mind, one voice, many bodies working as one. Genetic perfection. It's too bad they haven't found their lost yet, although they do pay well.*

"I am Kertol Al'mem," the man said before removing his hood to reveal light hair, his origins appearing of Gilese descent.

The Duggor's reaction was one he anticipated. "You are not of Tharak. Explain."

The man smiled, raising his arm before tapping his wrist, causing a holographic display to light up before him. It showed a lanky, almost insect-like creature. "You are mistaken, allies," Kertol said. "I am wearing a fabricated bio-suit. My actual form is not immune to the effects of spide radiation, such as yours." The man had a slight lisp and his voice sounded hollow, as if he was talking from inside his own body. "My crew do not currently have similar augmentation. That is why they have not accompanied me." Kertol knew well the effects of spide radiation on organic material that was not resistant.

Several seconds passed before the Duggor spoke. "This interior form is smaller than your original form. Explain."

Kertol nodded, tapping the device on his wrist to cause the display to change. Now appeared an image of a compressed form of his, inside the humanoid shell. "Allies, as you know, we can travel the filaments to some degree, although we do need those of Lyri biological ancestry to remain in connection with the systems. This prevents the inversion of the crystals."

There was an annoyed tone from the Duggor. "You have not provided a more substantial means to travel as promised."

Kertol nodded. "There are limitations to our technique."

"Explain."

"As you know, we can currently travel for approximately seven standard hours at a time using our current methods. We are still evaluating the information you provided on the ship composition. However, all incidents have achieved the same result—the destruction of the vessel." There was an acknowledgement from the Duggor. Kertol smiled. "As you can tell, we modify ourselves and use a genetic copy of the host as protection. This bio-suit is a copy of the same Lyri descendant I used to travel here. If I were to be out of proximity for longer than three cycles, the radiation would penetrate, and I wouldn't survive. That has been the issue since we discovered the connection."

"Explain."

"All Lyri may travel the filaments. This we know. Even those with minute traces of their genetic base are capable. However, to survive the entrance and exit of the filaments, the energy reaction can only be regulated by them. The reason is still unknown to us." The man paused. "Our limitation has to do with the individuals themselves and the use of the bioenergy, along with the reactor and drive systems. The further we travel within the filaments, the weaker the individuals become. You have noticed this, have you not?"

The Duggor took a moment before responding. "Yes, their bioenergy does not regenerate after augmentation. It is a problem we have not been able to overcome."

"Our findings are the same. Currently, to survive the effects of spide radiation, we share the energy by mimicking the bio-entity. The drawback is that we need to restrain and encapsulate the individual to share such a connection."

"You restrain the Lyri? How?"

Kertol paced a moment before answering, "We restrain them. But keeping their minds active has caused problems. To keep them compliant, we use a method to allow them to enter a dream-like state, essentially shutting down all higher functions and will. This allows us to share their bioenergy using the genetic copy. If we were to allow them to be awake, we have learned that our method becomes ineffective." The Duggor all looked at him with the same confusion, prompting Kertol to continue, "Restraining starborn, my friends, is a bit complex. This may take a while to explain.".

Chapter 3
Uneasy Alliance

A couple of hours later, Kertol found himself explaining how they grew the bio-suit copies for use and the compression they put themselves through to wear them. The Duggor, even though they have been augmenting starborn for centuries to serve them, seemed appalled at the methods the Tharak used to harness the abilities of starborn. "Right now, we have only enough starborn with sufficient bioenergy to limit a crew of one per vessel," he was now telling them. "It isn't ideal. Perhaps you could spare some of those you're caring for?" The Duggor, now knowing what the Tharak do with the starborn, declined.

Kertol looked around the room as an alarm from his armband sounded. His time away from his starborn donor was nearing its limit, and he had to return to the ship. He didn't want to risk the ravages of the radiation. "My friends, I have one more update to inform you about," he told the assembled group. "Recently you asked us to visit a nearby planet. I believe from the Alliance information I know that it is called Reothis. I regret to inform you that we were not able to procure any information on the entity you spoke of. It seems that it is quite capable of slaughtering any who land."

"Many Alliance and starborn have landed there without incident," the Duggor responded. "Explain."

Kertol almost felt terror but complied. "All our teams were attacked when they landed, although the ones wearing bio-suits seemed to be left for last. We have yet to recover anything from the encounter. We have only the video feeds to know what happened."

"Were the starborn you held alive?" the Duggor asked.

Kertol sighed. "Unknown. As I mentioned, all our crews were attacked. Could you perhaps tell me what the entity is?"

"The schism, a revenant," the Duggor all said in unison. "It was created. It serves a purpose."

Kertol chuckled. "And what is its purpose?"

The Duggor only repeated, "It serves a purpose." There was a long silence before they spoke again. "Continue with your efforts to access the filaments. Return to your ship. We will contact you regarding any additional information that may be relevant."

Kertol shook his head before saying, "And the starborn? We could use a fresh shipment of them for our use. Perhaps we may find a way to travel further distances."

His words were met with several Duggor pushing him from the room. He was not rushed, but he met resistance as he tried to turn and speak. The Duggor holding him only replied, "We cannot spare any starborn. The recent descendants have little to no Lyri linage. We are protecting them."

"Then you can spare some. You've taken many prisoners and possibly bred some with a purer Lyri linage, haven't you?"

His words caused the Duggor escorting him to push much more forcibly. "We do not harm starborn without reason. We only seek to control them to aid us."

An arrogant smile appeared on Kertol's face. "You are weak. Starborn are a resource you haven't tapped for thousands of years. We all know too well that once you start to use a starborn, without compensation, they will take a different path. The Tharak have found a way around that. We use them until they are no longer viable."

Kertol felt the pressure on his back much greater now, his feet almost tripping as the Duggor moved him more quickly toward his ship. His people knew all too well the difficulty in enslaving starborn. Although the Alliance had found a way to subjugate them for a time, starborn always found a way to escape, if through no other means than by death.

He felt the final encouragement to leave as he was pressed forward. He slightly stumbled before turning to see two Duggor remaining as the others left. He looked over his shoulder toward his ship before saying, "Your people have been suffering for over ten thousand years, and yet you lack the stamina to do what's needed."

The Duggor continued to stare at him, their glass-like white eyes contrasting with their dark grey skin. The bioengineer saw his reluctant allies as only something to dissect. He heard his own voice, arrogant, as he muttered, "Many bodies, but only one mind between them all. No wonder you've been like this for so long. If you weren't so unique, it would be pathetic." He paused, then said loudly, "I will return in a few weeks. Depending on the viability of this form, you may see me in another." He turned, walking toward his ship. "If you change your mind, you know how to find us."

Kertol closed the door and hit the spide extractors before he ordered the crew to lift off. "See if homeworld can extract any more information from that recent batch of starborn before they process them," he said. "Maybe they have more knowledge on what those others are working on. Head toward the filament point. We have several jumps before we arrive home. I don't want to be stuck out here without a spare. Inform homeworld and have them access the Duggor database. Find the information on subjects T974561JT and G970189EL. Perhaps they might know something more."

Another one of the Tharak's spindly arms worked the comm as Kertol strapped into his seat. He was given a device to place into his mouth as they prepared the ship to enter the filament. He bit down on the mouthpiece as he was further restrained. His hands touched two plates on the arms of the chair. As they neared, the filament point was displayed and estimated by the ship's optical sensors, and Kertol was heard mumbling, "Engaging filament access in ten."

There was a bright flash as the Duggor watched the Tharak vessel disappear into the filament. There was silence before a low murmur was heard from all seated in the main chamber. "When the filaments open, we can still hear them. They are calling to us. We feel their agony. We must end this."

* * *

Farh exited the vehicle and waved the driver to move down to the parking area. He turned to see the now shining ship he knew as the *Wolfhammer* docked along the far side of the property. He turned as a person approached. The woman gave a slight bow before standing tall. "Ambassador Celos, we welcome you to the home of Representative Mirizali Elysee. I am the representative's assistant, Yeesen. The representative will arrive momentarily. She apologizes that she did not greet you in person. She is currently busy with her other guests."

The woman showed Farh her credentials. He pondered the name; it was spelled "Yeesen," yet she pronounced it as "Eesen" without the Y. Farh knew of the pride the Yata people had in their names. The strong will that made them a formidable force outside the Alliance was part of their culture. He paused before responding. "That's quite all right. I understand the representative has a business to run. I'm here for a similar reason."

The ambassador looked toward the ship on the property. He could see people walking toward it, along with a small cargo vehicle. He watched as several crates he knew as Sotiral systems were loaded on board, along with other supplies. He then saw one of the other individuals walk up, noticing her longer light-blond hair blowing in the breeze before noticing the man walking beside her. The other woman followed them both. He recognized her as the representative.

Farh started walking toward the ship only to find himself with Yeesen again standing in his way. Her deep grey eyes stared at him with purpose, her expression one of authority and protection. Farh glanced away from her, his eyes toward the people now clustered by the vessel. "I see the representative is over there," he said to her. "Perhaps you can take me to meet her. Also, I suspect the second woman is the other person I'm here to speak with."

Yeesen glanced back slightly before tapping her comm. "Representative, the ambassador wishes to speak with you and one of your guests. How do you wish to proceed?"

There was silence as he watched the people in the distance turn to look in their direction. He looked down. "Why do you ask for permission?" he asked her. "You seem to be very capable."

His remark barely phased Yeesen. She placed her hand on her sidearm and responded, "I am charged with the protection and well-being of the representative. If she speaks with you, it will be by her decision, Ambassador." The woman's tone implied a subtle threat, and he gave a bow, apologizing.

Moments later, her comm came alive. "Yeesen, please escort the ambassador over. I was informed of his arrival, and I have confirmed that he is here to meet with our guests as well."

Yeesen responded, "Acknowledged, Representative. I will escort the ambassador over to you now."

Within moments they were at the *Wolfhammer*. Yeesen turned to notice the driver walking a short distance behind them. Miriz stood on the loading ramp as Jace arranged the crates. She heard him grunting as he tried to force the pallet, which was much heavier than he was, onto the locking clamps. He growled, "Get in, you stupid clamp."

Miriz chuckled. "Just use the grav-loader. That weighs more than the five of you." She turned to Eislie and rolled her eyes. "Terrans. Always wanting to do things the hard way."

Eislie glanced at her friend, then shook her head before saying, "You don't get it, do you?" She headed over to help Jace push the crate into place.

Miriz huffed, "You like doing things the hard way all the time, don't you?" Eislie smiled back and watched as Miriz looked back over her shoulder. "Listen, someone's here to see us. Finish helping Jace, then meet me outside."

Eislie acknowledged her and watched as Miriz hopped off the loading ramp and toward her new assistant, Yeesen, escorting the person toward them. "He looks to be Arlain," she said to Jace. "I think that's the same man we met when we arrived. Back when we were in the hospital." She was referring to when Jace had rescued her after she had been tortured.

Jace looked back. "It does looks like the same guy." He started moving toward the door but Eislie stopped him.

"I'll go. It's probably the one who wanted to speak to us about making the suits offworld." Jace again moved forward, but she stopped him. "No. You finish securing things, in case we need to lift off fast." Jace could feel the seriousness in her expression and nodded before working again to secure the cargo.

Eislie walked down the ramp to see the Arlain speaking with Miriz. She overheard him saying, "Representative, perhaps you have some sway with your government. We were hoping to have more aid from your people." He then turned to Eislie. "Ah, Captain Licessien. You're looking well. Much better than the last time we met." The ambassador was referring to when Jace had escaped with her from the Arlains who had been holding her. The pain of the torture she had endured was still fresh in her memory.

Eislie gave him a smile, then looked toward the driver who had followed the ambassador but remained a short distance away. "Hello." She turned slightly, keeping her eyes on the man in the distance. "Everything alright, Miriz?" Eislie kept her eyes on both men. Neither appeared to have weapons.

Yeesen looked back at the driver before quietly saying, "Is there an issue, Captain?"

Eislie slightly shook her head. "Isn't it unusual that a driver accompanies their passenger?"

Farh looked back to see his driver standing a short distance away. He nodded, saying, "Please forgive me. The driver was provided by your defense ministry."

Eislie gave an "ah" and nodded. "It's Ambassador Celos, isn't it?"

Farh nodded. "But please, call me Farh. I'm happy that you're both here and doing well. It makes my job much easier."

Miriz said, "The ambassador is here to proactively procure more of the Sotiral systems and to ask for permission to produce them on Arlain."

There was a short discussion before Jace exited the ship. He hadn't heard anything from Eislie but could still hear the dialog happening. It seemed civil, so he continued to work on securing the cargo. Eventually he started toward the group, but as he moved closer, the man behind the ambassador also moved closer. That made the hair on Jace's neck bristle. *Who is this guy?* he thought to himself. *He walks like he's military.* Jace may not have been empathic like Eislie, but he was good at reading people.

Jace neared them, then turned to walk toward the man behind them. "Hi," he said. "Name's Jace. Who are you?" The man seemed surprised to see Jace between the ambassador and himself.

Eislie turned and saw Jace readying to fight. She pulled her comm to her face, whispering, "Ed, get ready, just in case." Miriz looked toward Yeesen and nodded. Her assistant rushed beside Jace, now standing with her weapon drawn, demanding, "Identify yourself." The man looked at Yeesen and then back to Jace.

Jace smiled and said, "Oh, this guy's some form of special forces. I can tell that just by the way you move, bud. Who are you?"

The man looked at the ambassador. "I was provided by the ministry for the ambassador's protection."

Jace chuckled. "No, I get that. But who do you work for? You don't seem like the regular security I've seen."

Back in the control room at the ministry of intelligence, the operator at the console watching the entire exchange called out to the director, "What should we instruct the operative to do, ma'am?"

Loren's face retained a practiced expression of patience. "We've always had an issue with Terrans being able to pick out our operatives." She sighed in frustration. "Open a comm line to the operator."

"Line open, ma'am."

She spoke in her mic directly into the ear of the man there at the scene. "Desep, tell Captain Tucker your first name and that you work for the Ministry, but tell him nothing more. Terrans know when someone is lying."

Desep said what Loren had instructed him to. Jace replied, "Makes sense. I mean, tagging along with a former agent from an aggressor world. Working to make things better?" He motioned to the man. "Come on, I'm sure whatever mics they've got on you are straining to hear. Why don't you move closer?"

The noticeable sarcasm from Jace's words made Loren's eye twitch. She ordered the operator to comply with Jace's request. She then placed her hand on the console operator's shoulder. "Keep recording. When they're finished, send the information to my office."

She began walking away when another officer said, "It's hardly standard procedure to tell people that you're intelligence."

The director looked at the man. "There's a reason Terrans are feared, commander. Even if they have nothing to lose, if you don't take them out quickly, they will fight until either you're dead or both of you are. Admitting the truth is better than losing an operative. I'll inform the Grand Matron of any information we find useful. Carry on."

Chapter 4
Slight Delay

Jace was piloting their ship when Eislie walked in drying her hair. He looked up with a smile and said, "What, the showers at Miriz's weren't working?"

Eislie rolled the towel up before whipping it at Jace. He started laughing as he blocked her attack. Eislie huffed, "You know those supplies we brought on board?" Jace nodded, looking apprehensive. Eislie sighed before continuing, "I decided to put away some of the food she gave us. You know the actual food? Well, there was a Juliberry pie and wine in there. The pie was good, but when I went to get some for you as a kind of romantic gesture, I hit the bottle of wine and knocked it over. It got punctured and then exploded."

Jace looked at her, concerned. "You okay?"

Eislie nodded. "Yeah, but the galley's a mess. Didn't you hear me cursing?"

Jace nodded again. "I figured Miriz put something in there to mess with you."

Eislie sat down, the towel over the arm of her chair and draping down onto the floor. "We do like to do that with each other. But she wouldn't do anything harmful."

Eislie looked somewhat sorrowful, and Jace noticed, asking, "You sure you're okay?"

She sighed, leaning forward. "The wine is kind of a gift from her, for both of us. It's because she wasn't there when we decided to become aligned. At least officially. The wine is an apology for not being there to see when things changed for the better for me. And it's supposed to welcome you into her friendship as well."

"Got it. Like a wedding present back on Earth."

Eislie nodded but added, "It's more a wish for happiness beyond what we've found. I'm just upset I broke it. Not that I'm superstitious, but it's supposed to be bad luck."

"You know, the kind of luck we have is a bit unique. I mean, come on, there's people hunting us, trying to steal our stuff, kill us, enslave us. It's not like we've had the easiest time. Besides I've been thinking about Farh's offer. I'm thinking it might be something good to do. I mean, I don't fully trust them, but maybe they can do some good instead of slaving people out."

Eislie tilted her head back. She had been thinking the same thing. Producing the Sotiral systems might convince the people of Arlain to try trading something else other than slaves. It could help the process a lot. The downside is that it might hurt Miriz's enterprises. Eislie had discussed the possibility of allowing the Arlain to produce the systems with Miriz, and she suggested it might be the best course of action. Besides, if they negotiated everything right, most of the profits would go to them, and Miriz could focus again on her existing business for ship parts. Miriz also volunteered to Eislie that she may be forced to build a new facility to keep her initial contracts in good standing. After all, in her business, reputation was your brand.

"Maybe we should tell them they have permission to build the Sotiral systems. Then Miriz won't have to put up any investment for her to keep her original business," Eislie said before looking forward again.

"Yeah, it may be the best option. We're sort of busy trying to figure out the filaments." Jace paused in thought. "I mean, the money's good from the suits, but think about when we figure things out." He motioned to the space before them on the screen.

Eislie nodded, her eyes still forward. "We could go anywhere we want. Hopefully no one looking to chase us down."

Jace nodded, seeing the subtle smile now on Eislie's face as she sat a little prouder. The whole time he'd known her, she'd always wanted to help others, even him. Jace knew what he had done before while on Earth. He had resorted to stealing just to keep people fed. He was surprised how little he cared for those who held everything, even if it hurt a few of them in the process. To him, those few being inconvenienced, especially for a greater good, was a bit easier than what Eislie was asking.

Eislie leaned back, the towel draped over the arm of her command chair now shifting a bit. Jace could see her staring off into the distance, reflecting on what happened. He was silent for a moment before saying softly, "Maybe it's a sign that things are going to change." Eislie turned to stare at him, annoyance in her eyes but found humor in his words. He continued, "I've seen things go really bad back on Earth, and out here… I, I almost lost you, Eis. There's no way I'm letting a broken bottle and a mess in the galley get to me." He sighed. "I'll go clean it up if you want."

Eislie stood, then leaned over, kissing him gently. "Nope. I made the mess, I'll clean it up." As she was walking back to the galley, she added, "Besides, you do your best thinking staring out into space."

Jace chuckled. "You know, Eis, you're right."

It was only a few days later when they finally returned to Gilese. Arren had been working on retrofitting the *Solace Star* since the *Wolfhammer* now had its new plating. Jace was surprised when Arren told him that the *Solace Star* didn't need much modification. "What do you mean you didn't have to change anything?" Jace said with a mix of pleasure and annoyance.

Arren waddled over, cleaning his hands with the same purple rag Jace remembered from before he left. "You did a thorough job of fixing the drive systems and updating the computer, but you only patched the hull. You never did an analysis on it, did you?"

Jace shook his head. "We didn't. It looked and sounded good when I hit it."

Arren slowly looked up. Jace could feel the condemning aura of his friend's stare as Arren shook his head. "That hull is one of the cheapest I've ever seen. I have no idea how that damn ship passed inspection in the first place."

"You mean we'll have to reclad the entire hull? It's five times the size of ours." Jace sighed. "How much is this going to cost us?"

Arren chuckled, then tapped the hull of the ship sharply. Jace looked curiously at the spot his friend hit and tapped it himself. "It sounds different. Not hollow. What'd you do?"

Arren smiled with a sense of pride. "Polyceramic plates bonded to the inside. The structure was good; it's the hull that was the weak point. I've already installed the updated tunnel coils."

Jace looked across the length of the *Solace Star*. "You think it'll work with a ship this size?"

Arren sighed. "I have no idea."

There were a few moments of silence before Jace spoke. "I guess it's comforting to know that if we get into trouble, someone might have a shot of getting us out of it."

Arren agreed, but then moved closer to Jace, whispering, "You should still let your other friends know when you're going to test your ship, just in case."

Jace gave a sly smile. "Oh, I'm sure they'll know. Probably watching us right now." He turned to look off in the distance, but saw no one there, although he had a feeling his joke had more truth than he meant. Since they had left Yata Beta, they hadn't encountered anyone looking for them. It was odd, but Jace found it a welcome change.

He looked back at Arren to see his old friend looking over the ship. "You want to try it, don't you?" he asked with the tone of already knowing the answer.

Arren nodded quickly. "You two—well, and maybe those others who screwed up the test last time—are the only ones who have traveled for a decent amount of time. I'm a bit envious."

Jace slapped Arren's back. "It's a little different than hyperspace. It's…" Jace paused, his eyes searching for the words. "It's a strange sensation. It's like you can feel the space around you. To be honest, it feels…I don't know, natural. Not like hyperspace."

Arren looked up skeptically before saying, "Feel? You can feel the filaments?" Jace shrugged his shoulders and Arren scoffed. "Well, I don't think everyone's going to feel their way through the filaments. Not like you two, anyway."

"Yeah, Eis and I kind of fly by the seat of our pants. It's just our thing." Jace smiled, then watched as a contemplative look appeared on his friend's face. "I know that look. You've got something in mind."

The short round alien leaned against the ship. "You know, I decided to buy my own ship, since you two have been working all over the place. Just in case I needed to make a run out of the system."

Jace seemed shocked. He'd never taken Arren for the type to run from anything. But he quickly understood when Arren continued, "Not many people can get you two out of trouble, and last time I didn't do enough to stop what happened to either of you, especially Eis."

Wait, is he blaming himself for what happened to us? Jace thought. From the start, Arren had helped Jace while he was imprisoned on Charon. And he knew that Arren hadn't gone after Eislie when she stole supplies for the bar while she was also imprisoned. He knew Arren felt responsible for when Eislie's sentence was over and Bosh had kept her there under additional false crimes. "Arren…" Jace said, but went silent when Arren held his hand up.

"I know what you're thinking. Your Terran brain has figured out I could have gotten her out of there. The truth is, I was afraid of being killed by that bastard Bosh. I've lived a long life. I knew what Bosh was doing was wrong. What he did to you, her, and the others. I can only try and make things right with those I finally helped."

Jace's brows raised, but he remained silent as Arren continued.

"Most of my people work until we die. That's our way. What you don't know is that later in life, we track down the things we harmed the most and work to make things right. That's also our way. From what I did and what I'm doing, I wouldn't blame you if you didn't trust me."

Jace said with a surprised tone, "Wait, are you dying?"

His friend smiled. "You and her are a lot alike, you know that? You care. You help when you can. You're both survivors. From the first day you arrived, I knew the two of you would be together. Don't ask me how; I just felt it. Whatever the creator saw in me, I knew at that moment I would help you both, even if it killed me."

"You're worrying me, Arren. What's going on?"

Arren chuckled. "Just a realization, and a pledge. Jace, the Alliance, the pirates, and whoever else knows wants what you two are doing. You've put up with me since I met you. I want you and Eis to know that you can ask me to do anything to help you. It doesn't matter what it is." Jace stood silent, his mind empty, and Arren continued, "Listen, do you think you could delay your test for a few days?"

"Sure, I guess. Why?"

Arren looked back at the *Solace Star* before saying, "I want to finish retrofitting my ship with the same hull components. I suspect the Alliance might try and corrupt the crew. Call it a hunch."

"Arren, that crew is family. What would they do?"

His friend moved closer, placing his hands on Jace's arms. "I know most are family, but it only takes one to make everything go wrong. I want to make sure there's at least one more ship we control that can make the trip if this works."

Jace's face filled with surprise as he realized that Arren was right. *Oh shit.* "Yeah, sure, I can delay," he finally said.

Arren smiled serenely before asking, "Can you get that computer of yours to run some simulations on this ship? I'll give you the specs on mine later. It's a hauler. Slower than yours and this one, but it's got power."

Jace nodded and tapped his comm. "You get all that, Ed?" There was no response. "Ed, you awake?"

He was relieved to hear, "Yes, Captain, my apologies. I am nearly finished decoding the rest of the database from that Lyri vessel. I was not monitoring your comm. Please repeat the request."

"Everything alright, Ed?" Jace asked with more concern.

"Yes, Captain. I apologize for the delayed response, but I am 98 percent

21

finished with the decoding and thought it might provide us some additional information on how to navigate the filaments."

Jace shook his head. "That explains why he was quiet the entire time we were heading back. Eis and I were getting worried about him." Arren nodded in agreement. "Can you run some simulations on the *Solace Star* but with a similar hull to ours? Arren has another ship he'll provide specifications on to see it if will work as well."

"Of course, Captain. Shall I inform the other captain of your request as well?"

"Only about the *Solace Star*, okay, Ed?"

Arren seemed annoyed. "You don't trust her?"

Jace snapped his head toward Arren but calmly said, "Oh, I trust her with my life. But I just realized I'm talking on something that might be bugged." Arren looked at him confused, and Jace smiled before shaking his head. "Earth expression for something being monitored remotely without the person knowing."

The computer responded, "Of course, Captain. I will inform the other captain of your request for the *Solace Star* as requested. The simulation should take approximately fifteen hours. However, if we include the additional specifications, it will take longer."

Jace nodded. "Understood, Ed. We'll get the additional specs to you in a bit. But get started on the *Solace Star* right away, please." He turned to Arren. "How long will it take to modify your ship?"

The old alien replied, "Only a day or two. I've been working on it since finding out that this one was easier to modify. If I have help, it'd be a day at the most."

Jace nodded, "Okay. I'll give you a hand. I'll let Eis know we're delaying the test and will now be going in three days."

He turned and stared out into the early-evening sky. "What are you looking at?" Arren asked.

Jace looked around. "I'm just thinking about what you said about the Alliance. How they might convince one of the crew to betray us."

Chapter 5
Helping a Friend

Jace was chuckling as Arren said the name of his ship, the old engineer griping, "Damn Terran doesn't get the subtleties of different languages." Arren's vessel, the *Ciaimose*, was only a day away from its retrofit being finished using the updated materials. Jace had convinced Eislie that they should wait a couple of days before giving the *Wolfhammer* its final test run into the filaments.

"Is it *chi-ai-mosey*, or like *chia-mo-say*?" Jace asked in a light tone. The old engineer sent him off to get more of the bonding agent for the internal plating. The name meant "blue-star light" in Rosta, where Arren was from. He had chosen the name to bring back some light into the things he had done in his past. All his people used the latter part of their lives to make things better for others, even if they had caused them previously. He wasn't superstitious, but he did have some faith in a higher power.

Arren placed the last plate against the inside of the hull, using the last of the bonding agent he had beside him. As the plate adhered, he felt as sense of accomplishment. "Well, that's done," he muttered. "Once I get the aft section finished, Jace and Eis can try out what they put together." The small, round, rabbit-like alien wiped the sweat from his face.

He reached up, removing the heavy gauge control wire so he could jostle in the plate. He complained that this was harder than what Jace had done to the *Wolfhammer*. He was jealous; the *Wolfhammer* had a shell all around the outside, since its hull was a full polyceramic composite. The *Ciaimose*, however, was like the Lyri vessel. Its metallic hull was theoretically better suited to the discharge the filament produced; but when Arren did try accessing the filament, his drive system would nearly blow out the entire reactor. If it wasn't for taking Eislie's suggestion, he would have atomized himself. He waited a long time before telling Jace what he'd attempted. There was a dialog that seemed to be inside Arren's mind as he muttered, "Only starborn can travel inside the filaments, so far," his tone filled with a humor hinting of jealousy.

He pulled at the power line, almost grabbing the end before remembering it was still connected to give him lighting in the cabin. "Don't do something stupid, old man," Arren chided himself as he tugged at the cable. He felt it snag on the framework down a few sections, so he did what he always did, shake the line up to send a small wave down the wire. However, as he focused on the other end, Arren didn't watch where the end he held was at. There was a bright flash, and Arren briefly heard a loud arc before the world went dark.

Arren felt the pain in his arm as he opened his eyes, the large round pupils focusing on the small drops of midnight-blue blood now flowing from his sleeve. He could also feel the rhythmic pressure on his other shoulder before the ringing in his ears subsided enough to realize Jace was yelling his name. The sense of pain subsided as fear flowed into his mind. Jace was yelling, but he couldn't understand him. The old engineer rolled over to look at him, hearing what he knew as Terran English, but his translator wasn't working. He pushed Jace away before placing two fingers next to his ear.

Jace watched as Arren moved his fingers several times. He finally said, "Say something in Terran." Jace did as he asked and watched as Arren nodded. "It's working again. Must have surged my translator."

The look on Jace's face was one of concern. He had only been away for a few minutes, getting the additional bonding agent. He had come back to a hallway filled with smoke and Arren unconscious on the ground. "You alright?" he asked.

Arren lifted his arm to see the scorch and the slowing blue blood before saying, "Yeah. Did something stupid. Wasn't watching where I was swinging the hot end." He looked up to see the genuine concern in Jace's expression, but then smiled, saying, "Not like you pull stuff like that all the time." Arren watched Jace smile.

"Yeah, it's inherent in all Terrans to do things the dumbest way possible. I think it might be genetic."

Arren chuckled before wrapping his arm in the rag he had been using. "Yeah, I should probably hit the med bay. I'm getting too old to bounce back from things like this easily."

Jace let Arren lean against him while they walked through the smoky hallway, its density making Arren sigh before complaining, "I've blown out that panel before, I believe. It's a bad design for the power lines. It's an auxiliary system, mostly external. I should really run them differently. Or at least increase the capacity so it can handle the loads better."

"I'm surprised you haven't," Jace replied.

Arren looked annoyed. "I had planned to, but some young Terran and his mate wanted to rush things."

"I'll let that go. You're just mad because you did something dumb." He paused for a moment. "Wait, is that the same panel that you said blew when you tried the filaments?"

Arren stopped walking. "How in Tarsus did you know that?"

Jace raised a brow. "Eis told me. I'm surprised you even tried a filament run."

The old engineer looked up in disbelief. He had told Eislie about his attempt but no one else. Arren felt a bit hurt that she'd told Jace what he'd done. But seeing that Terran stare back at him told Arren he wasn't done hearing the last of it.

"Look, Arren, Eis worries about you. Hell, she worries about me all the time. She was just making sure you're watched out for." Jace sighed. "She worries about us both, alright. In fact, just now she was making me look again at the navigation strings for the test tomorrow. I've checked them like fifty times."

24

The old engineer smiled. "I think she's ahead of her time with becoming empathic."

"Hey, she's not the only one who cares, old man." Jace gave him a wink. "C'mon, let's get you patched up. We can work on the panel later."

Later, in the medical unit of Arren's ship, Jace finished healing Arren's injuries. He took a look around the room. "This has some space in it," he remarked. "Not like our ship."

Arren wrapped a cloth around what remained of his sleeve before answering. "That ship is much smaller. It doesn't usually handle a crew of more than five, so the med unit can only handle four max. This was meant for a much larger crew." He looked at his arm before turning back to Jace, muttering, "I haven't had a chance to make things right yet. Time for time. That's the way of my faith. Always has been, always will be. I haven't made things up to you two yet."

Jace shot his friend an annoyed glare. "Arren, you owe us nothing. You did your best keeping us out of trouble when it counted."

The old engineer shook his head. "I shouldn't have let it go on for as long as I did. Eis was badly hurt from my not doing anything. If you hadn't shown up and thrown a wrench in the works, I'd probably still be there with the two of you."

"You *are* alright, right?" Jace said with concern.

Arren nodded. "Yeah, just feeling sorry for not doing more."

Jace understood that all too well. "You need help with that panel?"

"No. I'll take care of it later. I want to connect that feed line first. Besides, you should probably take another look at those navigation strings." He gave Jace a sly smile.

Jace rubbed his hand over his face. "You know, it probably couldn't hurt. Besides, we have to make sure our other friends know where we're going as well." He winked.

Arren knew he was referring to the pirates. Arren's own recent interactions with them, especially their queen, had been profitable. With their help, Arren was now about to find a way to retrofit other vessels with the alloy the Lyri used. "Let them know," he said. "I'll get things patched up here." He placed his hand on Jace's back and gently pushed him out, laughing and saying, "Go. Spend some time with that love of yours." Jace was about to protest when Arren continued, "You're both about to attempt something no one has done in centuries. If something goes wrong, at least you can say you didn't waste any time beforehand."

Jace opened his mouth, then paused. He looked at his friend. "Getting wise in your old age?"

Arren laughed. "Get out of here. I'll finish up, you uncivilized Terran."

He watched Jace walk down the corridor and wave with a smile before exiting the ship. He turned, looking at the other end of the hall. "Let me connect that feed line first and I'll see what I can do with the panel," he began saying to himself. "I should probably replace the whole damn thing, but I'm too tired to do it all today. I'll just reset the breakers."

* * *

Kertol felt the searing pain of the power as it flowed back through his body. He let out a howl of agony as the mouth of the bio-suit bit into the mouthpiece he had when they started. Even though the mouth wasn't his, he could still feel the feedback from the pain endured by the synthetic bio-suit.

He released the clamps on his chair, allowing his body to roll from it onto the floor. He groaned as he attempted to raise himself from the deck. Several Tharak attempted to help him up, but he weakly swatted them away before ordering, "Check the host for this suit. What's its status?"

One of the Tharak crew tapped heir insect-like tendrils against the bio pod that held the original for the clone's suit Kertol wore. She yelled, "Indicators show light movement and neural activity! Bio-energy is nearly depleted!"

Kertol struggled to stand, his own legs currently immobile because of the suit's control system. He motioned for another Tharak to help him up. He walked toward the bio pod and asked, "Brekel, what's the level?"

"Nine. Its biofunctions are questionable. This one's depleted. He won't be able to make another run."

Kertol growled before saying, "The Duggor were short-sighted. We could have used some new starborn." The commander stepped back. The body he was wearing seemed to lengthen before the skin around its neck tore away. Kertol's reduced body then wormed its way out of what was left of the bio-suit. His arms and legs extended, and he stretched his thorax to elongate himself. His stature was shorter than his counterpart's. Several cricks could be heard before Kertol said, "Take this suit and the host for recycling. We can use the raw materials for making new ones."

"But this one's still functioning. Are you sure you want to recycle it?" Brekel asked.

Kertol stretched again before saying, "Terminate it. We can't store its bioenergy anyway."

Brekel nodded, then tapped a few controls before the pod dimmed, and there was no sign of activity. Kertol tapped the bio-pod. "Shame, really. I was able to use this one for quite a few runs." He paused. "Any word on our two primary subjects? Have they found a way to access the filaments without starborn yet?"

"You mean subjects T974561JT and G970189EL?" Brekel asked.

His commander nodded, then sunk into his own thoughts again. He then moved to the nearby console, barely able to reach up and look over the controls. "They're using an old Takloh vessel, if my memory serves me correctly." He then moved to his command chair and hopped up onto it. "Get me the information on the model. I have an idea."

Chapter 6

Can We Do This?

After leaving Arren's ship, Jace met up with another friend of theirs, a woman named Callie, the former starborn head of the filament project. She still had the ability to procure some of the more difficult items they needed, and the crystal memory cores were something he needed quickly. He held the small, padded pouch in his hand as he walked into the door of the *Wolfhammer*.

Once there, he heard Eislie asking, "Ed, are you sure the numbers are correct?"

Jace paused to hear the ship's computer reply, "Yes, Captain. I have now gone through the calculations 327,428 times. There have been minimal simulations to prove otherwise. And all the counter simulations are well within the margin of error. The data you and Captain Tucker have provided show that the filament stream would be stable given the new hull composition. The charge build-up would be dissipated upon exiting the stream."

Jace stood silent as he waited for Eislie to respond. Instead, she silently turned to him. No one said anything for almost a minute before Jace remarked, "You know, Ed would usually have said something by now. He's not dumb or crazy." He smiled. "Well, no crazier than us." Eislie had a hint of concern in her eyes as Jace moved toward her. He placed his hands on her arms, gently pulling her closer. "I'm guessing he's doing a few more calculations."

He felt the warmth of her as she leaned against him. He could feel her tension as she softly pushed against his side. She held up the info-pad. "I don't see anything wrong, but we're going to be doing this at full throttle. You know, I'm just, uh, worried."

Jace looked at the info-pad as she scrolled through the information on the screen. "Yeah, I'm worried too," he admitted. "We've only done short runs, and nothing since we coated the hull."

The computer interrupted, "Captains, I have now completed an additional 182,776 calculations, and the data seems to point to the surge being dissipated successfully. There are several worrying factors, however. Although the data we have currently points to the charging being dispersed by the ship's new hull, the function of the navigation control from the Lyri ship has yet to be explained."

Eislie looked to Jace, her eyes wide. "He's right. Even Jana hasn't been able to explain the controls."

Jace nodded. Even Jana, someone who understood starborn and the Lyri to a much greater extent than them, didn't have an explanation for the control system from the found ship. All they did know was that it was designed to block power feedback from the reactor and drive systems. Other than that, it appeared to have no other purpose.

Eislie watched as that Terran look of working on a problem started to creep across his face. "I'm hoping it's not something we'll know about right away. But I don't think we should do a long flight. Do a short jump, let whatever charge build, and then go for the long haul."

Jace sighed, and Eislie didn't resist as he pulled her close. "We should go an hour. That'd be double the twenty standard we've been doing. Give the system a chance to really build up a charge." He gently nuzzled into Eislie. "We punch out and see what happens. Who knows, we might discover that we need to slowly back out of the filaments or something."

Eislie kissed him softly, then nodded.

"That's an excellent idea, Captain," Ed said. "May I suggest also procuring some additional sapphire cores? I wish to back up my systems before the testing."

Jace held the padded pouch up. "Already ahead of you, Ed. Don't want anything to happen to you. You're a good friend and saved our asses enough times. Can't leave you out in the dark, you know."

"That is very thoughtful of you, Captain. I appreciate your forethought." They could almost make out a choked-up sniffle in the computer's reply.

Jace placed the cores into the secondary system. "Ed, back up everything you have. Do everything up until we test. We'll pull the cores just before we enter the filaments. That way you'll have all the information needed if something goes wrong."

The moment was interrupted as the ship's comm came alive. Jace groaned before silently growling, "Nothing like the phone ringing to kill the moment." He then lightly pounded the comm. "This is the *Wolfhammer*, how can we help you?" His voice was mockingly cheerful.

There was a response of, "Must be talking to a Terran," before they then heard, "I have a relay message for Captain Jace Tucker and Captain Eislie Licessien from Captain Wehen."

Both Jace and Eislie's ears perked up. The last time they'd heard that name, they'd been on another ship, being informed that their former jailer was still alive. The memory of Bosh trying to capture them again a few months ago was still very fresh in their minds. "This is Captain Tucker," Jace replied. "Captain Licessien is here as well. What is the message?"

The person paused. "Message is as follows. I am to inform you that my original mission has traced the person we discussed to be located on an outer world colony. He is suspected of being on Gravut or Telen. I am on my way there. If I do find him, I will contact you. I'll send you the files we have on your former jailer."

They waited for more but nothing else was given. "Is that the entire message?" Jace asked.

"Affirmative. Over and out."

Both Jace and Eislie tensed before Eislie said, "If they find Bosh, I want to go see him."

Jace nodded. "Me too. I have a few things I want to hit him with. Mostly my fists."

Eislie gently touched his face. "I plan on using something hard." She then reached into the small bin near where they were standing and pulled out a heavy metal rod.

Jace chuckled. "Now that's gonna hurt, you know that."

Eislie nodded, then pointed toward their cabin. "We still have that other matter to attend to as well." Jace knew she was referring to the promise they'd made to the Slasta and the assassin's guild to bring back the bone blade with Bosh's blood on it. "We're not killers," she continued, "but I want to hurt him so badly. I want him to pay for what he's done too. Not just what he did to us, but the others before."

Jace pulled Eislie close. "I don't want to kill him either, but the deal with the assassins was too good to pass up. The thought of never being hunted by them for as long as we live, and all the people on the worlds they were a part of, is a very tempting prize." He sighed heavily. "Maybe we can find a way to not kill him but still make the Slasta keep their promise. I don't know. Maybe we can figure out something." He thought a moment. "I did a quick read on that file Wehen sent. Bosh's assistant is much more than she seems. She might be a handful."

"Which one?" Eislie asked.

Jace pulled up the file. "Halli, that's all she's called. Apparently, she was trained in espionage and assassination."

Eislie looked at the file. "Maybe I should read this, then."

The next day, Jace was walking around the *Wolfhammer*, tugging on the feeds for the coil connection. His actions confirmed that no one had added any devices between the connectors. The last few had caused control problems. Even though they were minor, Jace wanted to take no chances. As he checked the last one, he looked up to see the sunlight reflecting off the shell they had installed recently. He reached his hand out to touch it. "This is gonna work. I know it's gonna work," he muttered.

Arren was nearby at the workstation he had set up previously, watching Jace looking over the ship. The old engineer tapped away at the keypad before closing the entire screen. "I'm worried about you two as well. If this works, you'll help billions. That is, if someone doesn't try and kidnap the two of you again. Having second thoughts?"

Jace shook his head. "Nope. Just trying to think positive. I know what's at stake."

The old alien agreed. If these two pulled off what they were trying to do, it would make space travel even faster for everyone. And it might change the minds of those who thought starborn were lesser beings.

"It'll work. You two are going to do something that's been lost for over ten thousand cycles."

Jace scoffed, then smiled. "Don't jinx us, old man."

The old alien shook his head. "Eh, you two will find a way to get in trouble even if it works." He looked back over the ship. The shiny material showed some hazing from the environment. Arren dragged his hand along the surface, then inspected the dust that had collected on his fingers. He held them up to show Jace.

The captain of the *Wolfhammer* snickered. "You implying I need to wash the ship or something, Arren?"

The engineer joined him with a laugh. "Nah, just showing you that you've been on the planet too long. The ship's collecting dust."

Jace seemed to think for a moment before answering, "Wait, are you telling me to hurry up and test this thing already?"

Arren took a moment before answering, his eyes glancing over the ship that had protected his friends. The old engineer looked back at Jace. "I just want to see you two do what everyone thinks is impossible. That and make everyone who thinks starborn are lesser beings rethink that opinion." He hit Jace's arm with a friendly punch. "It's about time someone did. You and that mate of yours are just the people to do it."

Jace turned with an almost angry stare. He was about to say something when Arren interrupted.

"For the love of Tarsis, you think I'm being species-ist? I've seen pilots from many planets, many of them vaporizing themselves from the simplest of mistakes. But you two are tougher than anyone else I've ever seen." There was a pause. "You two protect each other. And this ship of yours does too." He looked back at the ship. "Ed, I know you're listening. You need to hear this too."

Almost immediately, Jace's comm came alive. "Yes, Arren. I am listening. But your statement does not make sense."

The engineer smiled. "It doesn't, does it?" He grabbed Jace's arm, pulling him around the side of the ship and pointing to the stabilizer. "You've been hit by space debris, antimatter, quasi-space, and a spide reactor explosion from a massive ship. You've slept inside a star and traveled the filaments, all in this old, tiny, beat-up ship. And all of you have made it back alive. You were all being tested."

Jace looked confused. "Tested? What the hell does that mean?"

Arren gave him a smile, then stood tall. "I know the two of you don't believe in fate or deities or anything like that. But you have to ask yourself why. Why is the universe putting you though all of this?" Jace looked skeptical, but kept listening. "You two—sorry, you three and this ship—are destined to do something that no one has done for centuries. The universe itself is testing you. It knows, like I do, that you are the ones who are going to achieve this, rediscovering what was lost to everyone. It wants you to do this."

Jace yelled defensively, "Bullshit!"

Arren moved closer. "It isn't, and you know it. You've told me about the hard life you've had before. How you barely survived. But you did. You found her from across the galaxy. You found this ship. All of you were lost, like what you're chasing now. This was what you were meant to do. This event, this achievement, this is what all of you were meant to do. That's why I know you'll be able to do it."

Jace was about to protest, but Arren wasn't hearing any of it. "You three are the only ones I believe can bring back what was lost. Every one of you was lost. You know what to do, even if you don't know what that is yet." He turned, looking at the ship. "If something goes wrong, you'll figure it out. No matter how impossible it is, you, she, and that crazy program will figure it out." He chuckled. "I'm a being of faith. I know you don't subscribe to that, but I do. I'm asking you to have faith in yourselves, because I do. You'll survive. It's what you all do, you survive." He looked around. "Speaking of your mate, where is she? She should be hearing this too."

Jace stumbled over his words. "Uh, she, er, went to medical. Just a checkup. Some unusual things happened with her empathic abilities on Yata. She was, uh, just making sure she's okay."

"And you didn't go with her?"

Jace shook his head. "Nope. She insisted I didn't. And when she says something like that, I listen, because I'm not a fool. Like you said before, we're survivors, Arren."

There was a subtle laugh before Arren responded, "See, that's what I'm talking about. I'll tell her the same thing. At least when she gets back, I'll have that better in my head. It won't be so drawn out."

They laughed as they rounded the corner. The computer responded, "Arren, I could play the entire conversation back if you prefer."

here.

Chapter 7

Almost As If You're Terran

In the medical facility, Eislie waited for the results on her tests. On Gilese there were specialists on empathic abilities and biology, since most people had an increase in their empathic abilities as they grew older. Eislie was much younger than most there and felt a little out of place.

She looked around, resisting looking at her comm to see if Jace had finished the checks. They had planned to test in the next couple of days, and she was concerned about sensing someone watching them back on Yata. She had told Jace, and he had agreed with her that it felt like someone was watching them, but neither of them saw anything.

She had been waiting for almost two standard hours before she saw the doctor she was working with appear from the closed doors, and heard her call her name. As they walked toward one of the side rooms, Eislie overheard someone they were passing say, "That's her. That's one of the people who broke the story on the starborn." Eislie felt her muscles tighten as she continued to follow the doctor

She felt a little relief after the doctor closed the door, but then a peculiar thing seemed to happen as the woman moved toward her; her actions felt familiar. The doctor had dark hair, but her eyes were light with a greenish pupil, almost like Jace's but slightly darker. Eislie watched her as she typed on the info pad. She was startled when the woman said, "You don't have to stare. Your results are fine. They're in line with someone your age. Although your neurotransmitter levels are a little higher than most." She lowered the pad and looked at Eislie. "They're not unexpected for someone with Terran linage."

Eislie felt offended, but she continued watching the doctor. Eventually, she leaned forward with a curious stare and asked, "Are you Terran too?"

The doctor leaned back. "My father was Terran. So yes, I am partially Terran."

Eislie leaned her head back. "Sorry, I don't mean to sound stupid. I'm just nervous."

The doctor smiled back. "I've been called worse things than Terran. But I can understand your trepidation." The doctor tapped the info pad, bringing the results up on the screen. "I have good news for you, though. You were complaining about sensing as if someone was watching you and no one being there. Your neurotransmitter levels are a little higher than average, but that may be normal for you. You did mention you sometimes had trouble sleeping. That would be in line with the higher levels."

Eislie then asked, "Then why would I feel like someone was watching us?"

The doctor tapped the pad, closing the screen. "It could be nerves. Maybe concern over something that's bothering you. Or..." The doctor looked to make sure the windows were frosted over before saying in a more hushed voice, "Maybe someone was watching you from a distance, and you were just able to sense them further away. Empathic abilities are nearly impossible to interfere with. You mentioned that your partner was there as well, didn't you?" Eislie nodded. "Terrans tend to have a more advanced empathic response than most Gilese early on, although they tend to ignore it. It's part of their survival mechanism. Someone with Gilese and Lyri linage might be even more advanced. Did your partner show any signs of sensing anyone there?"

Eislie looked around the room for the door, just in case she needed to escape. "He asked me if I saw something, and he looked right where I was looking. He was very quiet when he asked me, too."

The doctor sighed. "My guess is that your senses were probably correct, if your partner also seemed to sense your discomfort and mirrored your actions." Eislie suddenly felt fear roll down her spine. The doctor smiled and continued, "I don't see any indication of runaway empathic abilities. Your results are mostly normal. However, I would recommend forgoing any additional neural implants due to your higher neural transmitter levels. It may cause a neural offset event. They're not fun to come down from."

Eislie tapped above her ear. "No, I don't plan to get anything additional. My translator's it. I don't like anything messing with my brain."

"That's a wise choice. We can regenerate most cells, even brain cells, but the memories in them would be lost."

Eislie looked concerned before asking, "So, I'm normal?"

The doctor nodded. "For someone with a mix of Gilese, Terran, and Lyri DNA, yes. Although I can understand the Terran and Gilese part more."

Eislie smiled and said, "Okay," sensing the snarky attitude in her remark. "Now I get why they ask you to handle most of the Terrans."

* * *

On the Tharak home world, Kertol was floating in a vat of biofluid, undergoing a reintegration process. Brekel continued to monitor the readings, watching over his master. The Tharak had a hierarchy of a type. They reproduced using a brood tank with many similar to themselves. One was always chosen to be the leader for each brood. Similar to most insects on Earth, there was always one the others followed. Brekel was of the same brood but followed Kertol as second in command.

"How long till his full functions are restored?" another Tharak named Gahl asked as he approached.

Brekel turned. "A few more semi-cycles. His genetic patterning is more resilient this time. The overlay process has hardened his genetic structure to twenty-four. Another few and he'll surpass thirty."

Gahl looked in the tank at the unconscious Kertol. "The great ones will accept him hopefully. He'll be strong enough to join the collective."

Brekel nodded. "Indeed. He will have access to the Choral Engineering protocols and hopefully enact his plan for us to host starborn bodies."

Gahl stepped back. "The chance to explore and be outside in the radiation fields, to be within the filaments and feel the universe travel around you." He brought all four of his arms together to grasp each three-fingered hand. "To feel the power that these people touch."

Brekel nodded in agreement. "It would be a blessing to sense what they do. The wonder and power they grasp at." He shook his head in an unforgiving dismissal. "They are such unworthy beings. Not much more than genetic fodder."

"Such power to such little beings," Gahl agreed. "They are truly unworthy."

The two debated for a short while, expanding on how the Lyri lost their ability to travel the filaments, and how the others were driven away from this galaxy. They mused that now only starborn, the remnants of what was left of the Lyri, had any ability to travel, but hadn't retained the knowledge.

Suddenly a "process complete" alert displayed on the screen. They both watched as Kertol opened his eyes. As the fluid drained and the chamber opened, he expelled the fluid from his lungs. Brekel handed him a towel to dry himself off. Kertol wiped his face and asked, "Were you able to retrieve the recall codes for the Takloh vessel?"

"Not yet, master. I have been overseeing your reintegration. I have delegated that function to another. They should return shortly with the information."

Kertol growled with impatience. "How long was I in reintegration?"

Brekel calmly said, "Two point none cycles, master. The other has not been gone more than one cycle. Central archive for Takloh is not online locally. It will take five cycles at least. We will have the information shortly." He then placed a thin exoskeleton on Kertol's back. "Administering local mechanical attachment."

Kertol gave a graveled cry as the interface fibers connected to his brainstem. Brekel filled the small tank on top with a different biofluid and said, "Retraining muscles in gravity. Regrowth in atmosphere will take two cycles. You will be in recovery until that time." He turned to Gahl. "Was there anything else you needed to inform us of?"

The other Tharak stood at attention, looking away from Kertol. "Yes. Master Jun has asked you to meet with him. He wishes to debrief you on the Duggor interaction and to inform you that the recent batch of starborn have been somewhat difficult to integrate."

An audible groan was heard from Kertol. "How difficult?"

"Over two-thirds have failed integration. They were sent for genetic resequencing and dismantling."

Kertol swiped the towel down his face in annoyance. "The Duggor have set us back by not providing us additional starborn." He looked to Gahl. "Inform Jun that I will meet with him in four standard for debriefing." Gahl acknowledged his response but continued standing at attention. Kertol sighed. "You may leave. Inform your master that I will be there."

"At once. Thank you for allowing me to be of service." Gahl then rushed away.

Brekel took the towel from Kertol. "Master, your treatment will only be for an additional two standard. Why not meet then?"

"I want to explore the other information I requested first. The hive may not like hearing that the Duggor have decided to no longer provide us with starborn. Unless we can duplicate the genetic access to the energy they have, we will become limited to standard tunnel travel once again."

"We are in the most distant part of the galaxy. It will take us months to travel to any habitable world, and even longer for any that may contain starborn."

"We only have less than four hundred of the starborn to use as surrogates, and even those are minimal in quality. We need others with a higher percentage of Lyri DNA to continue using the filaments." Kertol knew the filaments were something they now required more than ever. The Lyri were currently the only race that could access them. There was another, though, the Ha'ak, and that was also why the Tharak homeworld had been moved to its current location. When the star that had held their original planet had gone nova, they had needed a way to move quickly. Their sister race, the Takloh, had offered to help, but paid the price when the Tharak used what remained of them for genetic material. The only things left of the Takloh was the meager knowledge that had been retrieved before the Tharak left the system.

"Brekel, have them deliver the codes to me in my office. I have a plan to use them to procure something possibly better than starborn. But I want to keep this secret from the Hive masters for the moment. If I'm correct, what we seek will come to us when I command it."

.

Chapter 8

Are We Ready?

On the Tharak home world, Kertol met with Jun and the council. His failure to procure more starborn from the Duggor was a new hindrance to his ascension into the council of the great ones. His displeasure with their decision now sat like a stellar fragment stuck in his throat.

"They've had no luck with the Duggor, but yet I'm the one at fault?" he griped as he swiveled in his private command chair. He had been studying the specifications of several Takloh vessels, now realizing that the one with the starborn he was looking to bring to their world was one of over a dozen models, all with AI integration. The additional fact that there were variances depending on where it was manufactured complicated the recall command line issue.

Brekel knocked on Kertol's door before entering. "Master, it is mealtime. I have brought your sustenance."

Kertol's stare never left his screen. "Do you know that there are over twenty-one different models of the Takloh stellar mining ships? They had different functions, but our former brethren made them all look the same on the outside."

Brekel placed the tray on his master's desk before answering, "They were practical. They probably did that to simplify the resources needed to manufacture them during their expansion."

Kertol grabbed a food stick from the tray. "It's a practical decision, but it makes it difficult to reverse-engineer which model's in use." There was an audible crunch as he bit through the food. "It may have been a security decision as well. We had just started a war with them. We knew they used command codes to recall and deactivate ships. The only problem now is that if I enter the wrong code, it'll do a temporary reset of the systems." He looked at Brekel. "They did that so that if a recall attempt was made, they could reset or disable the command protocols. It's actually quite clever. Cause a system fault so everyone knows you're being taken over."

Brekel took a food stick from his own tray. "Do you think the starborn have disabled the system?"

Kertol thought for a moment before shaking his head. "That ship has been modified, but if the AI's running, they probably never changed out the operation system. With its interactivity, they probably think it's adorable or something."

"Adorable?" Brekel asked, looking confused.

Kertol shook his head. "It's a term the Terrans use to describe the child forms of creatures. I'm attempting to see if I can think like them. Maybe I can figure out what they've done to the vessel."

Brekel looked at the screen. "Have you narrowed down the possibilities?"

Kertol nodded. "I have two solid options. The only issue is if they've allowed the AI to expand. It may not allow us to simply take the system. But if we reset the system while they're in flight, it may disable the control systems temporarily, which means we would lose them altogether if they're destroyed."

"When no action is ventured, there is no reward," Brekel said.

Kertol smiled. "You've been keeping up on your studies. Are you looking to replace me?"

Brekel shook his head. "I would never. You are a brood mate master. It's not in my programming."

There was silence as Kertol took another bite. He tapped the display. "This one. We'll send that and see what happens."

Brekel looked concerned. "What would be their arrival date if it is used?"

Kertol tapped a few times on the screen. "Nearly three standard months if they're using tunnel drive. But I have a feeling they've now implemented a filament system, or at least one that's partially viable. That would only be a few hours."

"How will you have the ship access that?"

There was a satisfied smile and huff from Kertol as he answered, "Easy. Those vessels use a fully integrated AI system with redundant overlays. We simply tell the ship to return at fastest possible speed." He picked up another food stick. "Hurry up and finish. I want to send this command as soon as possible. Or at least before the council realizes what I'm doing."

It was only a short while later as the two brood mates accessed the communications facility. Kertol programmed the message system to transmit on the recall frequency and sent the string. "How long until we find out if it worked?" Brekel asked.

Kertol looked around. "It's still using old tunnel space channels. It'll be a few hours."

* * *

Two days had passed, and Jace and Eislie were now floating near a filament point, checking the ship one last time. Arren's ship, the *Ciaimose*, was waiting nearby. Their friend had finished the enhancements to his own vessel in case something went wrong with theirs, chiding both of them as he tapped his comm. "Are you two sure the ship's ready? You've only gone over it three or four dozen times."

Eislie held her hand over the comm, ready to reply, when she turned back to see Jace closing the access panel to the new control system they installed a few weeks ago. "Are we ready?" she asked.

Jace looked around the ship. "I guess." He looked at the control box he had installed on the reactor. "I set the timer for an hour. It'll kill the feeds if something happens to us. You know, like maybe getting shocked or something." Eislie nodded as he walked back to the flight controls and continued, "I don't know why I'm so nervous about this. It's not like we haven't flown in the filaments before."

"But we've never gone this long, and at full power."

Jace wrinkled his nose. "Hmm, good point." He looked back toward the galley. "Well, we have enough food for at least a year. Some clothes, additional spide." He paused. "Oh, wait, did you set the coordinates for the Telen system?"

Eislie nodded. "That was a good suggestion from Ed. If this works, we can check to see if Bosh is there and let Captain Wehen know. It'll also be our announcement to the galaxy that we figured out filament travel."

Jace turned back, looking forward before tapping the comm. "You tell our other friends about this test, Arren?"

Arren looked to his left to see Preston sitting at the monitoring station. He lifted his head and smiled at Arren, his voice steady. "Tell him secondary monitoring stations are running."

The pirate queen added, "Preston, continue to monitor. I have enacted additional sensors to try and track their ship within the stream."

He muttered, "Yes, Your Highness."

"Arren, tell them additional monitoring has been implemented. They may go when ready."

On the *Wolfhammer* they heard Arren tell them the message. Eislie took a calming breath. "I guess we're as ready to go as we'll ever be."

Jace took out a coin. "Heads I fly, tails you?"

Eislie shook her head, laughing. "Nope. It's all you. I'll let you mess this one up."

Jace was chuckling as he hit the comm. "We're starting our test. We'll use the quantum beacon to try and communicate if we have any really weird issues."

As they neared the filament point, the cabin was quiet. They could hear the hull creak slightly as the gravitational force of the point pulled on it. "Hmm, we may have to bond the hull better," Jace mentioned quietly.

Ed replied, "Would you like me to add that to our list?" All of them laughed, and the computer continued, "Isolating backup. Ready to implement filament penetration."

Arren tapped his comm. "Monitoring is good. Your systems look good. Seven seconds to entry. I've got my systems online just in case something happens." He turned to Preston. "Are your people ready?" Preston indicated they were. There was a bright flash as the *Wolfhammer* started to enter the point, when suddenly everything flickered off inside the ship. They were in complete darkness for a moment before the lights came back on.

"What the hell was that?" Jace yelled as the energy from the filament surrounded them.

They felt the ship accelerate as Eislie did a quick systems check. Then they heard Ed say, "Captains, it appears that someone tried accessing the comms just before we entered the stream. Comm systems are now offline."

"What?!" Eislie yelled before looking at Jace, who seemed to be having no difficulty flying.

"Ship's handling normally," he said. "See if you can get the comms back. We can't use them in the filaments, but we'll need them when we punch out."

"On it."

Half an hour later, they had the comm working again. The last message appeared to be a scrambled line of code. "It doesn't look like a navigational string," Eislie said. "Maybe just gibberish? Someone trying to wish us good luck?"

Jace took a quick look at the string but didn't recognize it. "Ed, can you make sense of this?" The computer paused for so long that Jace asked, "Ed, you alright?"

"Yes, Captain, sorry for the delay. Between the monitoring and the analysis of the string, it took me longer than usual to respond. I do not know what it is."

Jace looked at Eislie. "Probably just junk mail. Delete it."

Eislie pressed the delete option, but nothing happened. She tried several more times before the comm froze on her entirely. "Uh, Jace, comm's frozen." She switched to her diagnostic system, then noticed those systems become slower before stopping altogether as well. "I think we might have a problem."

Jace said, "Punching out," as he hit the exit controls, but nothing happened. He slammed the controls hard, but there was still no response. "Shit." They both looked at each other before rushing to work on the controls.

They were both surprised to hear the computer say, "C-captainzzzz. I appear to be looozzzing command functionzzzz."

Eislie jumped from her chair, checking the secondary system where Ed had isolated a copy of himself. "He's still good. Let's hope this is just something from feedback."

Jace moved to the reactor system and was about to disconnect the internal feed like he had done before but stopped after looking at the charge level. "Hey, Eis," he said, "we can't disconnect this without killing ourselves. Look at the reading."

Eislie entered the reactor room. Her eyes went wide seeing the reading. "Slac, that level would fry us."

"We're going to have to rely on the timer." He looked at the small display. "We have about twenty minutes. Let's get into environment suits. If the charge doesn't dissipate, it'll blow a hole in the hull right here."

Eislie gave an animated nod as they both rushed to suit up..

Chapter 9

Next Round

Jace and Eis strapped into their command chairs wearing their environmental suits. Eislie checked the display to see the charge climbing even higher than previously. "Jace, the reading's over ten thousand," she said. "If the shell doesn't dissipate the charge, we're done for." She checked on the computer. "Ed's still offline. The weird part is he's still showing as functioning on some parts."

"That's probably the flight systems. Maybe Ed's interface is the only thing affected." Jace looked at the remote for the timer. "We have about two minutes. I hope the system does what it's supposed to do."

"Wait. We could have thrown the safeties back in the reactor."

Jace shook his head. "The reactor feed line for the tunnel drive runs right next to that. And the charge level is too high. We set it up like the system from that Lyri ship we found. You know, the one that nearly blew your arm off even after a few thousand years."

Eislie involuntarily placed her hand on her right forearm. Jace was right. They had decided to run the feeds like the ship they had found previously, when they had been pulled into the filaments while testing. Her memory of that incident was still fresh even after more than a year.

"How long till the system shuts down?" Eislie asked as the flight became more violent.

Jace looked forward. "About twenty seconds. I don't like the turbulence we're hitting. We must be near a heavy gravity field or something." His hands hovered over the controls. "I'm not touching anything until we punch out. Only if we have to."

"Why?" Eislie asked as the shaking became stronger.

"Because we didn't put anything inline like the control system in that Lyri ship. We thought things would be isolated, remember? But with the charge so high and Ed being affected, I'm not sure we're not going to have to put something in."

Just as he finished, the viewscreen switched to normal space, and they watched as a fog of blue plasma flowed away from their ship. After a few seconds, they heard the ship's computer. "Captains, I am back online. The issue with the comm I suspect allowed the charge to fall over to the command control systems, although I have no idea how that could have happened."

"Good to hear you, Ed. How are the systems?" Jace said.

After a few more seconds, the computer replied, "My systems are not affected. The feedback for the comm was the only thing that seemed to be an issue. All systems seem to be working in normal order, and flight systems seem to be responsive. We appear to be approximately two standard from the Telen system. I am checking the quantum beacon. It seems to be in phase with this previous part of galaxy."

A sigh of relief could be heard from both Jace and Eislie before both let out a howl of happiness.

"We did it!" Jace yelled. Eislie jumped from her seat to wrap her arms around him. The composite shield on the helmets clacked together as they did. Eislie opened her visor, as did Jace, and she forced her lips forward to give him a kiss. He did the same in response, both barely contacting the other. Jace snickered, "We could probably remove the environmental suits. I don't think we'll need them."

Eislie agreed and they both stood. Jace said, "Ed, your systems are good? Nothing wrong?"

"No, Captain. My systems are the same as when we left, with the exception of being a bit warmer. And I did not have full control of the flight systems for a brief time. I suspect it was due to the feedback we encountered."

"Alright. If you find anything, let us know immediately."

They both heard the alert from the beacon, and they looked to see the display. "It's Arren sending us a check-in," Eislie said. "We should reply and give the coordinates, so they know any comm signal is going to take a while to get back to them."

"We should tell them everything we can," Jace said.

"How do we tell them we didn't account for the system to transmit that long of a message?" He thought for a second, then he chuckled. "Wait, I have the perfect response." He typed it in: *2 standard from Telen. Mostly worked. Had a little hiccup. Had to change pants.*

Eislie read it, confused. "We changed into environment suits. I don't get it."

Jace looked at her. "Think like a Terran, my love."

Eislie thought for a moment, then started laughing, placing her face in her hands. "Oh, *change pants*! Oh my gosh, Arren is going to be laughing so hard."

They both left the control deck to go check out the rest of the ship. The computer sat saving the data it had collected during the flight. As they turned the corner, a small panel labeled "Override" on the bottom left of the computer's interface lit briefly before switching off again.

It was a few hours later when they received a recorded message on the comm. Eislie pressed play. They could hear Arren trying not to laugh as he let them know they received the message. Preston interjected as well, telling them that his employer was very pleased with the results of the test, and that she looks forward to the additional data on their return.

Jace nodded. "We're almost done with the checks. We should head home, get everything to Arren and our other benefactor."

Eislie knew he was referencing Jana, the pirate queen. "You know she's probably outfitting her ships right now."

"I don't think she's going to cross us," Jace said before looking at the beacon. "Oops, almost forgot, have to send something."

Eislie watched as Jace switched the quantum link to a different node, making her ask, "Are you sending something to the pirates?"

Jace shook his head. "Nope. I may hold out hope that Jana isn't going to double-cross us, but there's only two people I really trust." Jace looked at Eislie, then to the ship's computer.

"Oh, did you set up a transmitter to send out data if something happened to us?"

Jace nodded. "Yep. I mean, we're going to give this away anyway, right? I figured if something happened to us, at least everyone would know what happened. But since it seems we didn't fry ourselves, I set it for another week. Ed, remind me to take it offline when we get back."

Eislie pulled away from him before saying, "That's a bit morbid."

Jace sighed. "Eis, I grew up on Earth. People would kill you just to take your stuff. Now, let's finish our checks so we can head home using the filaments."

Devlin Bosh held a gun on the woman he was speaking with, "Our deal was for 1.7 million shil for the shipment, Valona. That does not look like 1.7 million."

Valona calmly looked to her right. "This isn't one of those cushy Alliance-controlled planets, Bosh. Sure, there are Alliance security here, but they're spread thin." The woman calmly lit her cigar. "And we have some of the largest reserves for spide in this part of the galaxy. Your shipment isn't worth as much as you think. That's 400,000. Take it and leave the spide or just leave."

Bosh had to act quickly; the sides were a little off-balance. Bosh had himself, Halli, and three of his crew who were loyal. Two others had been taken into custody shortly after he arrived, while he'd been procuring supplies. Valona had more than a dozen trained people in the room alone. Bosh didn't know how many were outside.

Valona said impatiently, "My offer's only good another fifteen seconds, Bosh. Best make you mind up soon."

With an annoyed grunt, Bosh holstered his weapon and placed his hand on the bag containing the money, only to have Valona cover his hand with hers. This caused Halli to inch forward, only to have several weapons suddenly pointing in her face. Valona simply smiled. "You know, Bosh, you've provided good quality spide before, and you're being reasonable. Let me give you something a little extra. In good faith." She turned to a man beside her. "Get an additional fifty thousand for our friend here."

The man rushed away, saying, "Yes, ma'am."

Bosh sat back, waiting for the man to return. There was no conversation, and Halli kept looking at her master for some form of instruction. That did not go unnoticed by Valona. "Your little pet seems jumpy, Bosh. A bit skittish." She puffed out a large smoke ring, aiming it toward Halli. "Or is it something else?" Halli's eyes shifted, becoming angrier. Valona smiled. "Ah, I see. Well, well, Bosh. Still got some life in you, huh?"

Several of Valona's people chuckled. Bosh, however, remained emotionless. Looking to get more of a reaction from the former captain, Valona looked over her shoulder. "I'm sure she's loyal. I know most of my people are, but probably for a different reason." The smoke from her cigar billowed throughout the room. "We all have similar goals—make money, find a place for ourselves in the outer rings. Make something of ourselves. Slac, I'm pretty sure most of them would do anything I tell them to." She pointed at Halli. "But I'm not a slaver. Not like you. I don't force someone to follow me blindly." She chuckled. "Well, at least I don't plan it that way. I'm sure there's some who would."

As if on cue, the man returned with the additional fifty thousand. He handed it to Valona, and she opened the bag, placing it inside. "There. An additional fifty, as I promised." She looked at Halli to see the woman's deep blue eyes staring back with a fire behind them. She held the cigar in her teeth as she said to her, "Why do you follow him, my dear? You're obviously deadlier than he is. You could kill him, free yourself, and become a freelance contractor."

Halli said nothing, only staring at Valona before saying, "He is my master. I do whatever he tells me."

Valona pulled the cigar from her lips before looking at Bosh, her brows raised. "I'm sure you do. It's a shame. I could use someone as pretty and deadly as you. I think it'd make collecting debts somewhat more entertaining." She stood. "Well, Bosh, have we concluded our business?"

Bosh took a moment before standing. "For now, I believe so." He stood, adjusting his jacket, saying nothing else.

Valona smiled. "Excellent. I'll take delivery of the spide. My people will help you unload it. As always, you're welcome to do business if you have any additional spide on hand."

Bosh remained emotionless. "Thank you, Valona. I'll be in touch."

Halli followed closely behind her master, as did Jirit, his other slave. Bosh waited for them to move closer to his ship before he said anything. "Jirit, when we get to the ship, grab one of the small explosive packs and a small shard of spide. I'm sure if they had a problem in the mines, we could possibly find a way to help."

"Master, would a small explosive be enough to cause damage?" Jirit asked.

"Oh, my boy, it won't be to damage any equipment. I'm just trying to see if I can get a better return on my investment."

Chapter 10

Duggor's Dilemma

On the Duggor home world, three humanoid figures were led aboard a large Wrent-class vessel. Two seemed compliant, but the third was resisting. Nearly in unison, there was heard, "Modified Starborn secured, with one exception. Attempting to restrain and integrate the individual into the drive system." The woman fighting them could hear the disdain when they said "individual," and she protested further as they strapped her next to the spide reactor.

"Ten semi cycles to launch. Track to targets is not known. Projected vectors are programmed. All nonessential units disembark."

The woman's captors taped over her mouth as she fought against the straps that held her into the navigation chair. She watched as all but two of the Duggor returned to the dock. Within moments of their departure, she felt the ship lift off. One of the remaining Duggor approached her and removed the band from around her mouth. She spat at him, cursing and yelling, only to hear in response. "Temporary programming of starborn is no longer in place. Attempting to rectify."

The woman felt a hard metallic harness clamped over her head. There was a sharp, loud sound and what felt like her brain being pulled against her skull. The Duggor drone replied to her protests, "Your bio-energy is required. Comply or you will be made to comply."

The woman spat back, "Let me go!"

She again felt the effect of the harness around her head. She felt herself trying to scream but heard nothing from her own voice, only the response from the Duggor holding her in place. "Compliance will not be painful. We will release you once we have achieved our objective."

The woman's eyes darted around, searching for an escape. She again felt the effects of the device, but this time she responded, "Slac off. I'm not helping you. You imprisoned me and now you're torturing me. I'll kill you when I get out of this."

The Duggor looked to the restraints as the woman fought to free herself. They could see the blood starting to show under the material. "Since you are not afraid of injuring yourself, you will be made to comply."

This time when the device was activated, she felt a searing pain throughout her body. Whatever they were using was making every nerve in her body cry out in pain. Tears started streaming down her face as the devices continued.

She felt the sudden release as it was deactivated. "You will comply, or we will continue."

The woman fought to raise her head. She looked at the Duggor, her blue pupils staring defiantly into the black darkness of the Duggor drone's eyes. "Slac off."

She again felt the pain of the device before losing consciousness. A few minutes later, she felt the shot of adrenaline the Duggor had given her to wake her. She could see on the screen what looked like a stellar filament, which was growing larger. She watched what was normal space suddenly turn into something wonderous. The Duggor tilted its head before speaking. "Subject is reacting to the filament energy. Temporary compliance is noted."

The woman took a moment to take in the colorful display before her. She felt no pain, but there was a sensation of something familiar, something primal, as if something was trying to build itself into her very being. She could feel the energy of where they were, as if it were a part of her.

The Duggor walked toward the controls, saying, "The subject has accepted compliance. We will continue with the mission to retrieve subjects T974561JT and G970189EL. Administer sedative."

That infuriated the woman. "My name is Lasir. And if you think I'm helping you, think again, you slac."

Her protest was silenced as she felt herself drift off. The Duggor turned, looked at a display, then looked at the other two starborn they had brought on board. Before she fully lost consciousness, Lasir heard them say, "Subject's energy level is already deteriorating. Estimated time to possible location of targets may now be too long. Depletion levels are accelerating. Increase speed."

It was several hours before Lasir opened her eyes again. She felt weak, tired. She then felt the rush as the Duggor injected a stimulant. Lasir could only look around with her eyes. She could see them taking the next person and placing them on the table. Fear now filled her. What they were using her bio energy for, she didn't know. But as she was about to yell at them, she heard an alarm.

The two Duggor reacted quickly, moving to the control panel. They said urgently, "Subject is near critical energy level. We must switch them out quickly. Engaging exit systems and power shunt. Target location not yet achieved. Switching to normal space." They paused as the alarm sounded. The Duggor hurriedly worked to revive the person on the table before she heard the other say, "Power is too low. Initiating emergency exit point."

There was another alarm before she heard, "Heavy gravity body detected. We cannot maneuver."

* * *

The small placard was mounted on the control console just about the edge. For any video feed, it would been noticed easily. At the controls sat an aging captain with short greying blond hair. He sat back before chugging down the beer he held. There were several cans already on the floor nearby as his ship orbited the class II star. He looked over at the controls for the extraction system. It was only showing 43 percent. The man stood, stretching as he moved around the front of the console, looking at the plaque that read *Captain Dan Jacobs*.

He chuckled. He had put that sign up because others couldn't believe he was a Terran captain, especially one who was ousted from both Terran and Alliance vessels for disobeying orders. The captain had taken on working for non-Alliance worlds to mine Helium 3.

Jacobs heard the comm alert before he heard the controller from the nearby system. "Captain Jacobs, what is your status?" the controller said. "We have you reporting that your crew has requested sleep status. You were scheduled to return tomorrow. Is there an issue?"

The captain gave a silent groan before mockingly tapping the comm. "This is Captain Jacobs of the *Zorani*, a.k.a. Fuzzy Bunny Slippers."

The captain gave a defiant smirk before the controller responded, "Uh, right, *Zorani*. Uh, we have you scheduled to return tomorrow. What is your status regarding the mining?"

Jacobs looked at the meter nearby, showing the gas capacity, before answering, "It's taking longer than expected. We should be finished in the next several hours. Don't worry, we'll have your materials on time, mostly." The *Zorani* had been orbiting the nearest of the two stars in this binary system for almost a week, and he was getting tired of the constant hum of the mag shields on maximum and the pestering of update requests from those who had hired him. The mining was taking longer than expected, and the other crew had requested to be put into sleep states just so they wouldn't be bored out of their minds.

"Should have sent a drone to do this job," the captain muttered under his breath. It was boring work. The ship was automated, but he did have a great view of the nearby star. The captain shook his head. "I'll send you a report shortly." He paused. "Whoever chose this star for mining should have their eyes checked. This is a low-quality stellar body."

"Could you send a video feed and your findings? We'll coordinate with the consultants," the man on the comm responded.

As the captain moved to behind the console, he pressed the transmit button. "This is barely a class II star. You can see by the color. I swear, I think whoev—"

The captain's words were cut short as he spotted a bright flash in the corona of the star ahead. Within moments, a Duggor Wrent appeared. Captain Jacobs could see the plasma blowing out from its engines, and the blue energy surrounding it ripping away parts of the Duggor hull. The worst thing was that it was on a collision course with his own vessel. The captain moved quickly to the controls, but his ship was suddenly shifted forward. The gravity of the event horizon where the Duggor ship had exited was now pulling his toward it.

The captain made several attempts to free the ship, but as the Duggor vessel grew larger on the screen, he slammed down on the controls for the tunnel drive. Nothing happened. The charge that emanated from the Duggor vessel was causing an interruption in the ship's field generator. He couldn't initiate a tunnel entry point. It appeared that the temporary heavy gravity well also had his ship held firmly. Jacobs shook his head. He could see that the engines of the Duggor ship were still at full throttle; well, at least the one that was working.

The captain calmly walked around the console. He knew his ship wasn't going to be moving any time soon. With an unnerving calmness, he reached into the cooler on the console and pulled out another beer. There was the sound of the tab breaking as he brough it up in a toast before taking a long drink. He then said, "Well, this suc—"

The crash of the Duggor vessel into the *Zorani* was a spectacular pinpoint of light against the star before it faded. There was silence at the controller's station as he recorded the destruction of the *Zorani*. He hesitantly stood, motioning over a supervisor to show them what had happened.

* * *

At the pirate base, one of those monitoring freelance vessels tapped an alert. Zido, the queen's second-in-command, approached. "What is it?"

The woman looked up. "I was monitoring the *Zorani*. We had orders to bring its captain back once he finished his mission. Our queen was going to assign him to another planet." The woman then played the video feed and showed him the destruction.

Zido stood tall. "Where was this?"

The operator quickly responded, "Turnel sector, near the outer second arm."

Zido used his implants to gather the information on the sector. "That's in the outer bands near one of our new stations." He took a step back. "That's a binary system. That looked like a filament exit point. Send all your data to my console. I'll alert our queen."

He turned and hurried toward the queen's work area, the only thought in his mind being that the Duggor have never been out this far before. Within moments, he entered Jana's work area, waiting to be acknowledged.

Jana looked briefly over her monitors. She seemed happier than her usual self. She motioned for him to approach. "You look like there is a problem. I hope you are not worried for our favorite two non-pirates?"

Zido moved next to Jana, and she showed him the message from Peston on what Jace had said. She smiled. *Change pants. Very funny, Captain. I hope it wasn't a serious issue.* "It seems they may have solved the issues with the overcharge," she said with some pride. "I am awaiting the data from their trip."

"That would be welcome. We could use that knowledge to control the galaxy."

Jana's smile eroded. "I gave my word that we would not be the only ones using the information. I intend to keep my word, do you understand?"

Zido knew well not to disobey his queen. "Of course. I was merely thinking of the opportunities it would offer us."

Jana turned to look at her commander. "What information did you have?"

No longer fearing his demise, Zido tapped his temple. "We have video of a possible Duggor filament exit near the Turnel sector."

Jana watched on the screen as the *Zorani* was destroyed. She then tapped her control pad, bringing up the known Duggor filament attempts. "That is farther than they have ever been. I wish we knew what they were looking for," she said with some trepidation. "Then maybe they'd stop hunting starborn and go back to being a peaceful race." She paused in thought. "Do we have any intelligence on how many ships the Duggor have currently?"

Zido used his implants to search. "The estimate is that the Duggor still outnumber us three to one."

Jana nodded, again in thought. "Zido, reach out to our contacts in the Alliance and Consortium. If the Duggor are nearing their goal, they may end this. But if they are not, it may mean they are getting desperate. Either way, we may need allies."

Zido acknowledged her order and turned to leave, but was stopped when she said, "The Duggor took Lyri over ten thousand years ago. Anyone who knew what they were looking for is long gone." She paused. "We may have the advantage once we receive the data from the crew of the *Wolfhammer*."

Zido nodded. "Do you wish me to have them contacted?"

Jana shook her head. "No. What they are working on is more important. We will leave them out of this for the moment.".

Chapter 11

Spide Runaway

Eislie had just inputted the coordinates for the closest filament point when they heard the distress call from Telen. "To any ships within ten standard planetary distances, we need assistance. We have a spide runaway in progress on Telen Two. We need help with evacuations. Current teams have slowed the cascade, but Quasi space intrusion is increasing."

Jace looked at the console and said, "We're only a few hours away."

Eislie said, "Ed, we're changing course. Can you monitor the comm for any additional information?"

"Yes, Captain, I will do so. I will also prepare an additional data packet to send to the others in case we are delayed."

"Good thinking, Ed. Never know when we might run into trouble," Jace said, half joking.

Eislie tapped the controls, and they were off toward the planet. It was only a short while before they arrived. Jace tapped the comm. "Telen control, this is the *Wolfhammer*. We have arrived to help if we can. Where do you want us?"

In the controller's office among the emergency personnel rushing around, the comm operator recognized the ship and yelled to one of the others nearby, "Hey, Garap, it's that ship from the feeds. I think we've got a couple of starborn on the line. Maybe they can help with shutting down the cascade. It's those two from the *Wolfhammer*."

Garap nearly collided with another person as he rushed toward the operator. "You sure it's them?"

The operator nodded. "Visual shows it's them. Maybe we can get them to shut down the runaway."

The other man grabbed the comm. "*Wolfhammer*, we have an estimated reading of over 900 percent over lethal at the site. Are you equipped to handle that range?"

Jace thought for a moment, remarking to Eislie, "That's pretty hot." She nodded and he replied, "We can give it a try. Where do you want us to land?"

The controllers looked at each other. "Yep, that sounds like them. Get them over to the main processing facility. Maybe they can help. Or at the least slow it down."

Eislie landed the ship near what looked like a spide processing facility. There was no one around that they could see. "Captains, I detect levels to be about 200 percent above lethal outside," remarked Ed. "But I do not see any signs of any personnel. I recommend being vigilant."

"Noted, Ed. Where's the highest concentration of radiation?" Jace asked as he grabbed some items from the top of the cabinet beside him.

Eislie tapped on the controls. "To the east is the highest concentration. But I'm also reading another to the north."

The two looked at each other before Jace remarked, "Damn, we'll have to split up again." He tapped the screen, and they viewed the layout of the facility. "Looks like there's a main processing facility here, right where the one hot spot is. The other looks like a storage facility."

"Which do you want?"

Jace tapped the screen for the processing facility. "This one looks worse. I'll take that one. You see what you can do at the storage area."

Eislie nodded, watching Jace grab the small box with the bone blade, throwing it into the small pack with the other tools. Both quickly headed out of the ship.

As Jace watched Eislie run toward the storage facility, he made his way into the processing plant. He had to wrestle with the doors since they were on lockdown. He slowly made his way toward the location with the highest radiation. Once inside, he was met by only a few brave individuals, all wearing Sotiral systems. They directed him toward the area with the spide leak, and he went to work. The others could see him wearing a more compact version of the Sotiral systems, but they didn't realize he hadn't turned it on.

He looked in his pack and could see the small box with the bone blade. He muttered, "Should have grabbed an extra set of gloves instead of that thing." He called for another set of gloves as he worked to pull the shattered crystals from the avalanche that was causing the runaway. As one of the others ran to grab another set of gloves, he ran into Bosh, wearing a Sotiral shield and a hood. The man asked him to throw him a few sets of gloves. The hooded man begrudgingly did so. Watching the other man rush back toward the chaos, Bosh moved toward the door to see how far the runaway had progressed.

Bosh suddenly stopped, balling his fists in silent rage upon seeing who they were working with. "Tucker? You bastard!" he growled quietly. He brought his arm up. "Halli, we have a problem. Those damn starborn are here." He waited, but heard nothing on his comm. "Halli, respond. What is your status?"

There were a few moments before she responded, "Master, I have only set one charge. I am on my way to set up the one for the main storage facility. But the radiation was too high for my shield suit. The alarm sounded, and I had to retreat. I had to find another way around."

"Acknowledged," Bosh responded. "Set the other and return to the ship. I'll meet you there once I've found my way out of the lockdown." He pushed his hood back to get a better look at the damage he had done. As he leaned forward, Jace turned, looking straight at him. Within seconds, the former captain of the Charon facility and captor of both Jace and Eislie could see the light green tint of his former prisoner's eyes now filling with recognition and rage. He then watched as one of the others handed Jace a set of gloves. Bosh could feel Jace's stare before he turned and removed the last crystal that had impacted the others, causing the runaway.

Within seconds, the radiation levels were on a downward trend, the people around them cheering. Then Bosh saw Jace start toward him again. "Slac!" Bosh exclaimed as he worked to escape the locked room where he was stuck. "Halli, I'll meet you in the secondary repository control. We can leave from there using the maintenance tunnels." Halli acknowledged her master and Bosh quickly headed toward the exit.

Eislie heard Jace say over her comm, "Eis, Bosh is here. Make sure you watch your step. That one named Halli he likes might be here too."

Eislie hesitated before quickly heading toward the storage area. She could see the small building fenced on either side and the field of the radiation shield fluctuating above it. As she neared the small building, she heard someone yell at her from the open door of a protective room, "Hey! Hey! You can't be here! It's dangerous! You have to leave."

Eislie jogged over. She could see the man's name on the placard he wore. "Your name's Jacob? I'm Eislie. I'm here to help. Did you see anyone else here earlier?"

Jacob looked at her. "You're a pretty lady. Another pretty lady ran that way earlier." He pointed toward the spide repository. "I didn't go after her. I have to stay here to keep the shield going."

Eislie listened to the way he spoke. It was slower and seemed deliberate. She then realized he wasn't like most people. Eislie felt the general pride in the way he communicated. It was filled with honest innocence. It made her smile. She pointed toward where Jacob had. "She went that way? I have to help her. She might get hurt or maybe hurt people."

Jacob looked over. "But she was so nice to me. She gave me this." Eislie could see the ten shill coin and she felt a little disheartened.

Eislie looked at the man. "If she does something bad, you'll have to leave."

"I can't. I have to watch the shield. Make sure everyone stays safe."

She could see the glyph controls that monitored the extraction system, and she knew what he was saying. "Oh, you want to see some drawings I made?" he suddenly continued. Eislie smiled as the man showed her a somewhat crude drawing combining a taxi and a cat. She could feel his pride when he said, "It's a cataxi!"

Eislie gave an innocent laugh and looked at the man. His face held such an innocent smile, childlike but genuine. She felt for him, knowing that not everyone in the universe had the same capabilities. She placed her hand on his arm. "It's a good picture." Then she realized he wasn't wearing a Sotiral suit. "You should put on your Sotiral unit."

Jacob shook his head. "I can't. That pretty lady took it. But I can stay in my cube. It'll protect me."

She took off her Sotiral jacket. "Here, use mine."

The man looked at the jacket as he took it from her. "But you'll get hurt."

51

Eislie shook her head. "The radiation doesn't hurt me."

The man took a moment. "Oh, you're a star baby…no, I mean, uh, a…"

Eislie smiled before saying, "Yes, I'm a starborn. The radiation won't hurt me."

She watched the man smile as he put on the jacket. "I can use it? Thank you. Now I won't worry about getting hurt."

Eislie nodded, then as he closed the front of the jacket, she reached out to activate the controls. She could feel his happiness as he thanked her. She rushed off to find the woman who Jace suspected had been sent to cause an additional spide overrun.

Jace worked his way through the facility. He was sure he had seen Bosh, but the safety of the others here was more important. Jace had entered one of the control rooms and was making his way with the others, trying to stop any further runaways. "We got that main one out there, but the processing room was also affected," the man told Jace as he hurried alongside him. "Damnedest thing. We have over a dozen failures, even with the safety systems."

Jace looked at the man's placard. "Linton, is it?" The man nodded. "Linton, I thought I saw someone I recognized a few minutes ago. Someone who might do something like this. Is there any way to lock down the place?"

Linton nodded. "Already done. You can't leave unless you go through the main junction, and the med teams will stop you for evaluation. If what you're saying's true, he's stuck here for the moment."

Jace sighed heavily. "I hope so. I've got some business with him when I find him."

The man beside him recognized the tone in Jace's voice. "Listen, you help us get this locked down and fixed, and whatever business you have with that other man, I'll help you with it. Slac, if you fix this, I'll even help you hide the body."

Jace stopped in his tracks, then laughed before saying, "You know, Linton, I like you. Now let's get this thing under control."

Chapter 12

Innocent Lost

It wasn't long before Jace and the others had the runaway under control. "The level is going down!" Linton yelled as Jace placed what remained of the spide extractor to the side. "473 and falling. We did it."

Jace could see the indicator going down. It was a welcome sight. The celebration was cut short, though, as Jace tried contacting Eislie on their comm. "Eis, you okay?"

There was silence for a bit before a garbled response was faintly heard. "The main section's under control. I've got two more. Looks like someone set off an explosion. There's spide shards everywhere. I could use some help."

Jace gave a subtle growl. "Linton, you have this under control?"

"Yeah, go help at the repository. We'll finish up here."

Jace moved quickly through the main junction. He had hoped it was possible they could avert both dangers at once; however, it seemed the universe didn't have that in the cards. He and two others arrived at the control office for the large Sotiral shield. The repository was only a short distance away. Jace was in dark awe of the size of the hole they had made in the planet. "Nothing like strip mining," he said with disdain in his voice.

They found the local manager and headed down to shield control. As they approached, Jace heard one of the men yell, "Yo, Jacob, you gotta let three people in?"

A man with short hair and light-colored eyes with dark pupils exited. Jace instantly noticed the JESC jacket he was wearing. He was about to say something when Linton said, "Don't use big words or talk fast. Jacob's a bit slow." Jace shot back an almost accusing stare. He understood what the man was trying to get across, but he didn't seem to have much empathy.

As they moved closer, Jacob told them to stop. "I can't let anyone in. The level's too high. You'll get hurt."

Jace asked, "Did you see a blond woman, wearing a jacket like this, go by here?"

Jacob patted the jacket he was wearing. "Yeah. Pretty lady. She was going after another pretty lady." He looked apologetic. "The other pretty lady took my protective suit. That nice one gave me hers. I hope she's okay."

Jace smiled. "I'm sure she is. Did you see which way she went?"

Jacob pointed in a direction before saying, "You wanna see my drawings? The other pretty lady said they were good."

"She the one who gave you the jacket?" Jacob confirmed it, and Jace took off his. "Here, take mine too. If things go wrong, it should help protect you."

Jacob took the jacket. "The radiation will hurt you."

Jace shook his head. "Nope. It doesn't hurt me like it does everyone else."

Jacob said happily, "Oh, like her! Like a star, uh, born. That's you too?" He put on the jacket over the one Eislie had given him. Jace touched the controls to activate it.

While Jace was speaking with the man at the gate, Bosh moved from behind the controller building a short distance away. He muttered to himself, "Tucker? How the slac did you get here so fast?" He moved back around the building. "That emergency tunnel is on the other side of that fence. And that starborn is in my way."

He looked at the indicator above the fence, before looking at the one on his comm. "Radiation level is high here. Halli must have done some damage nearby. I hope my suit can handle the range inside that field. Damn thing nearly got me caught when it went off at the center. I barely got out of there." He pulled out a weapon and loaded it. "Those four are between me and an easy escape." A smile came across his face. "Maybe I can solve several problems at once here."

Jace and the others all tuned as the alarm for the containment field fluctuated. "Up over 600 percent," he said when he heard a beeping from behind them. Jace turned to see Bosh pointing a gun toward them. He swiveled as the man fired, allowing the shot to hit Jacob in the shoulder. The force knocked him backward. Jace was now happy he had given the man his jacket as well. The layers protected him from the projectile.

Bosh tried firing again, but his weapon jammed. In a moment of panic, he ran to the nearby fence and started to climb. Even being older, he was able to scale it quickly. He could hear his comm alert him to the high radiation level as he made it over.

Jace turned, placing his hand on Jacob's shoulder. "You alright? Tell you what, let me get this guy and you can show me those drawings later." He then ran off after Bosh.

The two ran quickly toward the interior control building. Jace yelled for him to stop. Jace was surprised as he turned a corner and found a fist coming straight for him. He pivoted, losing his balance as the man rushed him. Jace grabbed hold of the attacker and did his best to defend himself. "Bosh, it *is* you." The name came like a growl out of Jace's throat.

The realization that his former jailer was right here gave Jace a boost. Within seconds, Jace had thrown the man back and could hear the hollow thud as Bosh hit his head on the support behind him. As he stumbled, Jace lunged forward, hitting his former jailer with such force that the small tool pouch dislodged, scattering everything across the floor. All the tools were there, including the small box the assassins had given them. The box opened, and the bone blade was thrown free, grating its way across the floor.

Bosh grabbed at some of the tools, trying to use them as weapons against Jace, but Jace was angrier and faster than the old captain. Within seconds he had pinned Bosh on the floor. In a desperate attempt to find something to use as a weapon, Bosh's hand found the bone blade that was now free of its small wooden cage. He wrapped his hand around its handle.

He bought the blade up, trying to force it forward, but Jace had caught the former captain's wrists. The anger in Jace gave him incredible strength, more than the former captain could handle, As Jace pressed forward, he turned the blade toward his former jailer. Bosh felt the blade pierce his Sotiral suit, then felt the pain as it quickly plunged into the side of his abdomen. Jace used such force that the handle started to enter the wound.

Hearing the near squeal and quiet pleading from his former jailer to stop, Jace snapped out of his fury. He could see the bone blade now in nearly halfway down its handle in the man beneath him, the overflowing blood staining the suit. When the scent hit his nose, he pulled back, but not before striking Bosh hard across his jaw. The captain went limp and Jace gave a labored but frustrated sigh. "I'm not a killer," he said to himself. He then tapped his comm. "I got Bosh. How you doing, Eis?"

Eislie, breathing heavily, replied, "I think you got the easy part."

Jace chuckled. "You might be right. Be careful. Don't get too close to her."

"Acknowledged." She closed the channel.

Jace inspected Bosh's wound, doing his best to seal it before tying the man's hands together with a wire he tore from a nearby console. That's when he heard Bosh's comm beep.

Halli was running as fast as she could, but Eislie was still behind her. The climb from the lower part of the storage area, where she had set a small spide charge, had taken a lot out of her. She was also hearing the alarm on her suit continuing to beep. The radiation level was too high for her suit to last much longer. "That simple slac," she complained. "Never charged the damn thing."

As she caught her breath, Eislie slowed and tapped her comm. "It's no use," she called out to the woman. "I just sent your picture to my ship. It'll be forwarded to the authorities. There's no way out of here without you being caught." Eislie was aware that Halli was Bosh's slave and best assassin. And from what she could tell, she truly loved Bosh too, and would follow him to the end of the galaxy. Eislie kept her distance. Halli was known to be adept at bladed weapons, even from a short distance.

"It's over, Halli!" she shouted. "Jace has your boss tied up!"

"You lie! My master would never be defeated by someone like you!" Halli spat back.

Ouch. Someone like me? Really? Eislie thought. *Does she hate starborn that much?* She could hear the alert from the woman's comm and yelled, "That suit isn't going to last long out here!"

Halli knew Eislie was right. The charge on the shield suit was lower than she had anticipated, and she still had to make it back to meet with her master. In a moment of mild panic, Halli tapped her comm. "Master, can you meet me out by storage area three? My shield is nearly out of power."

However, instead of hearing her master's voice, she heard Jace respond, "Halli, your boss is under arrest. Come back without making any more trouble."

Eislie watched as Halli walked toward the edge of the containment area and turned to look at her directly. Eislie watched as Bosh's assistant leaned backward off the edge. She rushed to try and grab the woman before she fell, but she wasn't fast enough. Eislie watched Halli fall before the woman turned off her Sotiral shield. Within seconds the high radiation had turned to her to ash. Eislie felt the tears well in her eyes as she asked, "Why?"

Jace heard the alarms as he approached the gate where Jacob had been working to keep the shield running. Seeing the people rushing to the small building gave him the hope he wanted. But as he neared the small office, he could hear the others.

"He wouldn't leave. He said he had to protect everyone."

"He kept saying the suits had been broken by the bad man and that he didn't want those nice people to be hurt. He wouldn't leave."

Jace's heart sank as he rushed closer. He peered into the small cubicle and saw medics working to save Jacob. He was partially charred from spide radiation exposure and had scorch marks on the jacket from the earlier shot, the controls now damaged. Jacob turned and smiled at Jace, reaching out for the book he was sketching in. Jace picked it up, opening it to see a picture of a mechanical rhinoceros. Jace chuckled. "Hey, good job on the mecha-rhino."

Jacob smiled, whispering, "It's a rhinotoo."

Eislie walked up, her tears now dry, gripping Jace's hand tightly. "Is Bosh in custody?"

Jace silently nodded. "Hey, Jacob," he called out, "why don't you show Eis your picture of the rhinotoo?" But when he looked up, he saw the medics pulling away. The monitors were all shut off now. Jace's eyes filled with tears, and he felt Eislie's hand squeeze his tightly. "Some people are just born heroes," he said.

It took a few minutes for the radiation to clear enough for them to remove Bosh from where Jace had left him with security. As they brought him limping through the office, Jace felt his anger rise. He jumped up and pushed the security forces out of the way, striking Bosh again, yelling, "How many innocent people have to die because of you, you bastard!"

Suddenly, one of the security nearby fell to the ground behind him. Jace turned to see one of the Slasta staring back. Jace had injured Bosh earlier using the bone blade. He pulled it out and offered it to the assassin. The assassin replied, "He isn't dead."

Jace angrily growled back, "You said to return it with his blood." He then stabbed Bosh in the leg again. It went in almost as deeply as before. Jace felt a certain satisfaction as the man howled in pain. Jace again offered the blade to the assassin. "There. It's now covered in his blood. If you think I'm going to kill him, you're mistaken. Too many have suffered because of him. I want him to spend the rest of his life rotting in a cell." He moved closer to the assassin. "He has to pay. Death is too easy an out. Don't you agree?"

The assassin looked past Jace at Bosh. "Hunted, with a fear of being killed for every day of his life?"

Jace nodded. "Torment to the end. That's what I want. It's more fitting than an easy death."

The assassin looked around. "I'm sure the others would agree with you. Fear for the seventy-three lives he still owes us."

Jace nodded. "Seventy-three chances to die. That's what I want. You told me that you only needed his blood on this, and I'm giving you that. The rest of his debt is all yours to collect."

The assassin stood tall. "I will bring this to the council. They will decide."

Jace pushed his shoulders back. "You know how to find us. We'll be waiting for your answer."

The Slasta moved quickly away and disappeared into the surrounding landscape. Jace reached out as Eislie quietly grabbed his hand. "It's over," he said. "Bosh is done. We won't kill someone just because they want them dead."

Chapter 13

Assassin's Decree

A lone assassin entered the Chamber of Ash. He bowed before a stone bell, then tapped it. The stone had been carved centuries ago; it was used to alert the others when a blade had been returned. Within moments another assassin joined him. "I have returned with the offered blade and a message that is of concern," he said as he showed the stained blade to her. The woman nodded, then quickly left to alert her master. Within minutes, all who were needed were assembled.

"Master Koth, we must confirm the identity of the blood," Rau said, her voice hinting at excitement. It took only a few moments before they confirmed it was from Devlin Bosh.

"I understand there is a message of concern," Koth said, looking at the assassin.

"Master Koth, the target is not dead," he replied. "I watched the one known as Jace Tucker plunge the blade deeply twice, but he did not kill Devlin Bosh. Instead, he offered an alternative. The remainder of our debt to us, to allow us to torment and fulfil those lost from his transgression."

Master Koth paused in contemplation. "We have never been offered this before."

Rau looked at the blade. "We must gather the others. They may not see the appeal of this situation."

Master Koth quietly closed the box and took the stained blade. "I for one welcome the chance to show darkness to the one who sent many of ours to their demise, before we send him to the light."

"I agree," said Rau, "but it is not just our decision alone. We must call the rest of the clans."

Once they were assembled, Koth explained the situation, and said he was willing to hear the arguments of the other clans. He was not surprised to hear some insisting that they kill the starborn. Koth calmly held his hand up for quiet before he spoke. "We had made an error in the offer of our terms. I move that we abide by the words we have given."

"What do you mean? They did not complete their task," a member named Taar demanded.

Koth looked at him. "They have completed the letter of the terms we provided, even if it was not in the spirit we intended." He turned to the others at the table. "You forget that even those who have killed are not necessarily killers. We will make sure the next time the blade is offered, we will spell out our demand with more precision."

Another woman said, "Clan Perig was closest to my own. They are of our blood. I for one welcome the possibility of seeing the life drain from the man who sent them to their demise. They have given us seventy-three glorious opportunities we did not have before."

Everyone in attendance placed their hands on the table before crossing two blades, each saying in turn, "This debt has been satisfied." Master Koth motioned to someone at the edge of the room, and she brought in a small wooden box. When it was opened, a square silver metal bar could be seen. It was inscribed with a decree to not hunt Eislie, Jace, or any of their associates or relatives on any planet where they are a resident or where their ancestors are from. It gleamed in the dim light.

Master Koth said, "Clan Hestip, you have the honor. Do you wish to allow Clan Lins to deliver the message?"

The woman sat tall. "The deaths of Clan Perig was a great loss. I propose that our clans share that responsibility."

"I agree. We will deliver the decree," Taar said as he looked at the rest of the table. "We will depart immediately to the Planet Telen to deliver the decree."

Koth closed the box, sliding it to Master Rau. "You may go yourselves or assign a member of your clan." He then sat, a smile on his face. "Now, we have seventy-three debts to claim. Where should we start?"

* * *

Jace and Eislie discovered that the repair dock at the Telen space dock was somewhat understaffed. Ed had been monitoring the traffic systems to alert his captains of any possible threats that might have arrived. They had been there almost a week; they wanted to make sure the *Wolfhammer* was in full working order before they attempted to use the filaments to head home. The diagnostic equipment at the station was old, but Jace was used to making do. "Hey, Eis, I think I figured out what happened!" he yelled as he worked his way out from the accessway of the control lines.

Eislie turned her control chair around. "Ed was telling me he doesn't know what happened. It was like he was disconnected from the systems."

Jace sat down in his command chair. "That's what I was thinking too, until I found this." He held up an interlink board. "This is the main interlink that runs from the consoles here. See anything wrong?" He pointed to a burned spot.

Eislie's eyes widened. "Is that from the feedback?"

Jace shook his head. "No idea. I didn't even think this part of the system would be affected. At most we would've just had to reroute the controls. But the filament charge wouldn't have affected this system. At least, I don't think it would have."

Eislie took the board from him. "Do we have a spare?"

Jace looked sheepishly away. "I'm using the one from that spare control panel, that one neither of us can really reach in back. I'm thinking we should work on finding a replacement." He slid down into his chair. "Or I could hardwire it, though I don't know how that'll work in the filaments if the charge is the issue."

"I don't think that was from the charging. I think that would've done more damage."

"Yeah, I think this is more the comm setup. That weird transmission we received was probably garbled or something. It may have caused the system to short itself out. Ed, you ever figure out that message?"

There was a moment before the computer responded, "No, Captain, and I am not able to find the data on the message, with the exception on the ending header. The remaining data seems to have been lost."

"Hmmm…" Jace thought for a moment, then looked at the board. "I wonder if the data happened to be on that chip that blew." Eislie shrugged her shoulders, and he said to her, "What are you working on?"

She said shyly, "Oh, something for that man Jacob, the one with the sketchbook."

"You mean the real hero. Okay, what you got?"

Eislie smiled as Jace moved closer. "I've set up a trust for his family. I think they deserve to know what he did and be compensated for it. He protected a lot of people. I think it's a good idea if we do something more too. Maybe we can set up a shipment of Sotiral systems to help upgrade things here. No one was willing to let him work in the Alliance, but these people gave him a chance."

Jace was about to say something when the computer interrupted. "Captains, I have been monitoring the ship traffic. There was an incident involving a ship that arrived recently from the nearby Keles system. Also, there are three individuals who appear to be approaching our front air lock, all wearing Alliance uniforms, weapons, and targeting visors."

They both looked at the screen. "Hmm, I wonder if someone figured out how we got here so fast," Jace remarked. "They're certainly looking like they're heading for us. Ed, make sure everything's locked. I don't want someone trying to surprise us."

Eislie looked toward the door. "Should we get ready to leave?"

Jace thought for a moment. "Let's see what they do first. I'd hate to seem jumpy to someone who's actually on our side.".

Chapter 14

Not a Friend?

Jace looked at the exterior video feed. "Well, well. I wonder who wants to speak with us now."

They all heard the knocking on the outer bulkhead door. Jace gave a sly smile before running over, tapping the comm, and saying, "Sorry, we don't need any gutter cleaning. Thank you for stopping by."

Eislie looked at the screen to see the annoyed expressions on the face of the men. She shook her head. "Now they know there's a Terran onboard for sure."

Jace smiled, then hit the outside comm again. "Three Alliance officers? This can't be good. What can we help you with?"

The one who seemed to be in charge removed his visor. "You have a few minutes?"

Jace recognized the man and replied snarkily, "Captain Wehen, what brings you out to the outer planets?"

"It seems you were able to capture a certain former captain before I could. One, I'd like to congratulate you, Second, I want to ask a few questions. Specifically, how you got here so quickly."

Jace paused. "Yeah, one sec, Captain." He looked to Eislie. "You have one of those info pads with the filament information handy?"

"Yes, I was making a few extra for our friends."

She handed it over to him, but Jace didn't open the inside door yet. He instead used the comm again. "Please leave the weapons, visors, and any other nasty things that could be used to incapacitate anyone on this ship, including yourselves, on the floor. Then I'll let you in."

They could see the annoyed response from the two behind Wehen, but the captain removed his visor and weapons, placing the items on the floor by the outside door. They both heard him order the other two to do the same. When they finished, Jace opened the inside door and said, "Ed, scan them, please."

The computer responded, "No weapons detected, Captains. Safety protocols remain in effect."

Wehen placed his arm to stop the others from moving forward. They both seemed annoyed by his actions, although Wehen seemed somewhat satisfied.

He wasn't surprised when Jace said, "Well, you did say you weren't our friend last time we spoke face to face."

Wehen gave a humorous huff, remembering when they had been on board his vessel, the *Aquaese Coul*, after it had just been attacked by the consortium months ago. He had been sent to retrieve both Jace and Eislie for the Alliance. "You have a good memory, Captain Tucker. You're correct in that assessment. However, this time may be a little different."

"How so, captain?"

Wehen shook his head. "You got to Bosh first but didn't kill him. I must thank you for that. But I'm curious as to how you arrived a week earlier than we could at top speed from the closest star system."

Jace could see the gravity controls come online as Ed got ready to incapacitate the Alliance crew. Then he heard Wehen say, "I'm hoping you're not counting on that gravity systems trick. Remember, I read your files."

Jace leaned on his command chair. "That depends on what your motives are. Oh, and that's not the only trick we have."

Then one of the others spoke up. "Captain, we have a standing order to apprehend and bring these two in."

What happened next was not what either Jace or Eislie expected. "Stow it, Retone," Wehen said. "We're not here to bring either of them in." The man moved forward anyway, only to have Wehen push him back. "These two aren't going to be arrested by me. Well, at least not today."

"Captain, you're disobeying a standing order," the other man said.

"Isgar, do you really believe these two are criminals?"

Isgar looked at Eislie and Jace. "From what I know of their files, I'd say so. But then, that could be said for myself as well."

Wehen looked back at Jace. "Isgar was turned down for promotion. Stole a ship, if you can believe it." He looked at Eislie. "But his father had a higher rank than yours, Mrs. Licessien. He didn't have to go through what you did."

Eislie looked at the captain. "And that's supposed to make us trust you?"

Wehen smiled. "Maybe, but I can understand your hesitation. Truthfully, I have a few questions. But first, do you have anything we can toast with? The stores on my ship are a bit light on celebratory beverages."

Eislie walked into the galley and brought back a bottle of white rum. "Will this do?"

Wehen looked at the bottle. "Never had it. Let's give it a try."

Eislie handed the bottle to Jace to open while she went to get some glasses. Jace remarked, "We just picked more of this up from Earth. She likes it. It's good, but I prefer whiskey. Hell, who am I kidding? If it's alcohol, I'll drink it."

Eislie returned with several small shot glasses, handing them to Jace, who poured. When they all had one, Jace asked, "So, what are we toasting to?"

Wehen looked at the two of them. "For bringing in that bastard Bosh. And not killing him on the spot."

Jace held up his glass before downing its contents entirely.

The captain did the same, but his reaction was to take a labored breath. "That's a lot stronger than I'm used to."

Eislie poured another round for her and Jace as they both took another drink. "It's not that bad, Captain."

The captain looked back to see Isgar and Retone gasping. He held out his glass. "I'll take another, but I think these two back here have already reached their limit. I think I can forget about drinking you two under the table." There was a chuckle from both Eislie and Jace as the captain downed another shot. He then took a breath before getting to business. "You used the filaments to get here, didn't you?" He said it more as a statement than a question.

Jace replied, "What if we did? It's not a crime."

Retone stepped forward. "Yes, it is. Under Alliance code T451, I'm placing you under arrest."

"I told you to stow it, Retone. No one's being arrested." Wehen growled, causing the junior officer to jump back.

Jace turned to look at Eislie, who handed him the info pad. She turned it on to show the captain the information on filament travel before handing it to him. The captain looked confused. "You're giving this to me?"

Jace sighed before responding, "It's how we got here. The full specs and controls are all listed, along with a copy of the programming."

Wehen smiled. "It really works?"

Jace nodded. "Mostly. Still haven't figured out the maximum ship size yet. But the specifications for stable non-lethal travel are all there. It's still a work in progress, but we currently have a full working system. We were just about to head home using it. We had a control issue for a moment when we left, but we think we figured out what happened. There was a comm issue that affected the control systems, but everything else seemed to work. We didn't blow up, which is the important thing. From what we can tell, none of you have gotten that far."

Wehen looked over the specs. "How long did it take you to get here?"

"A couple of hours. We spent a good half day looking for the control issue, which seems to have been unrelated." Eislie reached over and tapped the pad. "The control specs, connections, and coil configurations seem to be fairly straightforward. The charge dissipation is the only real concern, but it looks like we have that figured out."

"And how did you figure out the alloys needed? That's something even our researchers have been scratching their heads about."

"Does it matter how we figured it out?"

The captain stared at them accusingly before Jace said, "Everyone's getting the same information. We don't need any larger targets on our backs. So get over your high and mighty self, Captain."

Wehen looked at his subordinates. "You heard nothing, sub-commanders. That's an order, you understand?"

Isgar nodded, saying, "Got it, Captain."

Wehen pointed at Isgar and said to Jace, "As you can tell, this is the smart one."

Retone said, "Captain, if they're giving this to everyone, including our enemies, then they're traitors to the Alliance."

Isgar huffed. "Do they look like they're wearing Alliance colors, you slac?"

Jace turned to the captain. "I like this guy." He said to Isgar, "You ever think about going independent?"

Wehen held his hand up. "You'd kill your commission and pension, Isgar. Besides, I hear it's pretty dangerous hanging around these two." He turned back to Jace. "I can understand your reasons to give this to everyone. If only the Alliance had the information, every ship would be attacked just to get the design and programming."

Eislie said, "That's why we're giving it away. The money's not worth our safety. We have enough people trying to hunt us down as it is."

As they continued to talk, two figures walked toward their ship. The hooded cloaks they wore didn't allow the video feeds to see them. As they stepped into the airlock of the *Wolfhammer*, Ed alerted, "Warning, Captains! Someone is attempting to enter the ship. I advise defensive procedures."

The Alliance soldiers reached for weapons that weren't there, Wehen exclaiming, "Slac, everything's outside."

Jace moved toward the door and hit the manual controls. The loud thunk of the latch caused the one trying to open the door to move back. Jace then hit the comm. "Who are you and why are you trying to enter our ship?"

The two looked up at the camera and removed their hoods, allowing the video system to see them. "We have business. Allow us entry, or we'll force our way in."

Jace looked at the garment, recognizing it from the hospital, "Shit. It's the same people who gave us that blade. I'm beginning to wonder if they didn't like the offer I sent the assassin back with."

Eislie stepped back. "And we don't have any weapons." She looked around. "Jace, we might be able to fight them in here."

Jace nodded as he hit the comm. "One sec, we're just finishing up some other business. We'll be right with you." He pulled Eislie along. "Shit. Ed, ready grav protocols and scan around the ship for others. And hurry."

"Is there an issue, Captain Tucker?" Wehen asked.

Jace nodded. "Maybe. Those are the assassins we sent the bone blade back to. They might not have liked the offer we sent along. If that's the case, then sorry, it's been nice knowing you, Captain."

"They're Slasta? Slac, Tucker, you sure know how to cause trouble. And just when I was starting to like you two."

Jace motioned for them to move away from the door, then opened it. He paused a moment but neither of the assassins moved. Jace, confused, asked, "What can we do for you?"

The one on the right bowed. "Captain Tucker, Captain Licessien, we are representatives of the Via Atria and bring you a gift."

The other produced a small wooden box and held it out. Jace was brave enough to take it carefully from her. As he looked at it, he heard the woman say, "Seventy-three lives are our compensation for your actions. Your tribute was accepted, along with your terms. We offer you the decree to not be hunted. Do you accept?"

Jace was surprised, as was Eislie, who quickly joined him. She placed her hand on the small box and opened it. They could both see the small square rod, the inscription of the decree engraved across it.

Wehen, curious, moved closer. He could see the small icon of the decree. He brought his hand to his mouth. "Gods, I'd never thought I'd see one of these in real life."

Annoyed, Retone moved forward. "What the slac is—"

His words were cut short as Wehen grabbed him sternly and threw him back. "Stay where you are. This doesn't concern you, moron." He then turned away from the assassins and took a few steps back. "My apologies. I didn't mean to interrupt." He pushed his people to the back of the control room while Jace and Eislie continued to listen.

"You have returned the blade with the requested's blood. But you have also given us the gift of tormenting them. We accept that honor," the man said.

Jace was still processing what they were saying. He found himself uttering, "I'm sorry for killing them. I didn't want to, but the Arlain would've enslaved us if I had let them live." Jace felt Eislie's grip tighten on his arm. She was ready to fight alongside him if needed, but the next statement wasn't what she had expected.

"We are killers. We do not enslave. The one who set us upon you is to blame for those deaths. You were prey that fought back. It is a danger those of our profession face. You survived several attempts, including killing those trained to kill. We sent a force of them against you as you were escaping. You owe no debt to us for their lives. You bested many at one time. For that, you are respected. We will honor our agreement. You and those who are associates and family will never be hunted as long as you live. Unless you start hunting us, of course."

Jace snapped out quickly, "We have no intention of doing so. And thank you."

Wehen stepped forward. "I'm happy now that I decided to side with you, Captain Tucker." He looked at his subordinates and said, "You know, if you do decide to jump ship, it might be worth it."

Chapter 15

Ready to Head Home

Jace and Eislie waved as the *Aquaese Coul* lifted into the sky, the massive ship now leaving with the new information on filament travel. Captain Wehen was also now the surprising beneficiary of the Slasta's decree to not hunt the two and anyone associated with them. He did warn both, though, that others might not honor that agreement and to watch their backs.

A day later, the two starborn readied to leave Telen and head home. They were both surprised as to how quiet this outer world was. "There's not a lot of people out here," Jace observed, somewhat sarcastically. "You can get work done. No one stopping by to bother you every couple of hours."

"Yes, you're right," Eislie responded. "It's too quiet, isn't it?" Jace chuckled at her response.

The two had gone over every detail of the ship three times now. They were fortunate to have found a replacement controller board in the shipyard. Apparently, they had been breaking down several Takloh ships years earlier. The boards had been idle, since not many newer vessels used the same connection points. Eislie was in her command chair reading a message from their home base, including one forwarded by Preston from the pirate queen. "Hey, Jace, you should read this," she called out. "I think Jana has an update on the data we sent."

Jace walked in from the galley with a drink. "What'd she have to say?"

Eislie read the message. Most of it was confirming what they had discovered, but with the new information that the command string they'd sent her to look at had nothing to do with the drive systems. Jana also had no idea what it was from. The command string looked to possibly be a key of some kind, or it could have been a random transmission that caused the control issue. Either way, she wasn't familiar with the malfunction.

"She says the systems seem to be operating on the test vehicles the same as we predicted. She was planning on sending a ship out to meet us, if we wanted to wait. I actually think we should head home. We need to refine this and get the rest of the information to everyone like we planned."

"We have some additional supplies," Eislie said. "I checked them for any tampering. That bastard may have left a surprise for us."

Jace scoffed. "Nah, Bosh had no idea we'd be here. He wouldn't have had time to set anything up. But checking the quality of the supplies was a good idea. Some people out here might not be as honest as they let on."

Eislie smiled back, giving an innocent flutter of her eyelids. "You're right. We should head home. Maybe we should make a formal announcement?"

Jace thought for a moment, then agreed with her. "Maybe we can also post the info for anyone who wants it, or something like that."

"I think that's a great idea. That way, anyone who's watching or has access to the information feed can download the specs and programming. That seems to be the fastest way for us to get the word out that filament travel's now available for everyone."

Jace said, "It's too bad we don't know how large of a ship would work. Although we did put notes on the sizes we thought it might work up to, didn't we?"

"Yes. It was in the specifications I collected. That's probably why everyone's ships keep exploding. Maybe they'll listen and make them a bit smaller."

Jace nodded. "It'd serve them right if they wanted to send a big warship or something. Although now that I'm thinking about it, maybe that's exactly what the Duggor were hoping to do. I mean, they *have* been pretty active recently."

Eislie's eyes widened. "I hope you're wrong."

It was about an hour later as Jace swiped through the information they had on the filaments, an idea forming in his head. "Hey, Eis, there's another filament tunnel about two star systems over. It's a red line. You think we should try that for a bit, see what happens? I mean, we'll still have some people around, right?"

Eislie sat down hard in her command chair. "You want to take an unknown path with a new drive system that we only think maybe works? Is that what you're asking?"

Jace looked innocent. "But it's almost a straight run to the Gilese system. And we have to try it later anyway, right?"

Eislie stared forward. "We could also blow up. Hmm."

Their computer then interjected, "Captains, it would be a valid test of the current systems. We have confirmed that we have supplies. If we are not successful, we would still be ahead of the *Aquaese Coul*, which I have confirmed would be on a similar course. And I wish to inform you that they have transmitted the information to the Alliance command already. I was pleasantly surprised that they included the phrase 'it seems to work but may need refining' in their follow-up message."

Eislie chuckled. "You hacked their systems while on the planet, didn't you, Ed?"

"To quote Captain Tucker, it is not hacking if it is to confirm something we already know."

"Wait, when did I say that?" Jace asked accusingly.

The computer paused for a moment. "431 days ago while on Oppa. We were discussing the database they had on all known starborn."

"Hmm, that was the night of the dinner with the head of the filament project. The one where we begged him to allow us back on the project. That was before we decided to do everything on our own." He turned to Eislie. "You know, I don't remember saying that, but Ed's never lied to us before."

Eislie thought for a moment. "No, he hasn't." She looked at the computer's interface. "Just be careful, Ed. We don't want you damaged or stuck somewhere. Or even taken over. There are some nasty things out there that might be able to do that."

"I agree, Captains, and thank you for your concerns. I will be careful. But as to the matter of taking the faster way home, I await your decision."

Eislie looked to Jace. "What's that Terran expression about redlining again?"

Jace smiled. "If it doesn't blow, it's worth it." He turned to the controls. "Set a course for the second star system, Ed. We're taking a shortcut home."

* * *

On the Tharak home world, Brekel approached Kertol's office. The latest monitoring from the Alliance had revealed some disturbing news. As he entered, Kertol was leaning back in his chair meditating. "Sorry to interrupt your rest cycle commander," he said, "but we have an update from the Alliance monitoring regarding subjects T974561JT and G970189EL."

A few seconds later, Kertol raised his hand and his eyes opened. "What do they have to say now? Did those two finally blow themselves out of existence?"

Brekel shook his head. "No, sir. They have apparently achieved filament travel without the use of starborn hosts."

Kertol sat forward, angry, snatching the pad from Brekel. He looked over the information, including the encrypted file for the specifications on filament travel. "Have that file decoded at once. And get me the files on T974561JT and G970189EL again."

As Brekel rushed away, Kertol looked out across his desk, his mind processing why the starborn would give away such a lucrative discovery. He then concluded, muttering to himself, "They aren't saying everything they know. They're holding back something for themselves. Something only starborn can use."

He quickly brought up the order to send the recall command to the *Wolfhammer*. His plan didn't work earlier. The problem was that he sent it directly and in a rush. Even after years of biological honing, he knew that all Tharak still make mistakes. He instead was looking for the general order agreed on by the council. An eerie smile crept across his insect-like face. "The order is approved. We can resend it after reverifying the command string. Excellent."

Kertol quickly exited his office and headed for the communications command room. Brekel was soon beside him, "Sir, here are the files for the two starborn. What are your instructions?"

The commander waved the files before him. "We resend the return command string. In the files you provided, they did not disclose why the Alliance was given the files, only that they were given willingly by these two. That means there must be an ulterior motive."

"How did you come to that conclusion, sir?" Brekel asked nervously.

Kertol slowed, tapping the info pad. "Both are Terran. Terrans don't give anything away, unless they have something in reserve. It is in their nature. These two must have a motive for giving away such a lucrative discovery. I'm sure of it."

"What if that is not the case?"

Kertol tilted his head. "If I am incorrect, then we have two fresh starborn to use for our vessels."

They turned down the hallway toward the communications center. As they entered, a set of dark eyes landed on Kertol, and within seconds he and Brekel were surrounded. Kertol paused before looking up to see the commander on the communications center, causing him to mutter, "Zacseil. I forgot about him."

The commander of the center exited his post and stood before Kertol. "You violated protocol recently, Kertol. Why are you here?" Like Kertol, Zacseil was a brood leader; all working under him were from the same brood and followed their commands, although they all still ultimately followed the true leader, the one all are sired from. Even with that, though, Kertol had little influence in the current situation.

The two stood silently eyeing each other before Kertol decided to use reasoning. "That is correct, Zacseil. I bypassed protocol due to a time limit. I have the proper authorization with me. We need to send the recall command before the target enters filament space. Once they do, we will be unable to communicate with their vessel."

Zacseil glared at Brekel, causing Kertol's assistant to move behind him. This caused Kertol to say, "My proposal is in order, Zacseil. You may verify with the hive council."

Zacseil took the info pad and glanced at it. "We have several ships returning and will need communications for all vessels. We are currently busy with the main virtual system update. The current starborn are becoming aware again. How long will your application take?"

"Not long, only a few semi-cycles. But I need to send it quickly. If the starborn ship enters the filaments, the signal will be sent in vain."

The communication commander gestured toward an open chair. "You may use this terminal, but make sure you are finished before the remaining crew arrive to upload the new virtual systems."

Kertol paused before responding, looking at the crew now working on the system they used to restrain the starborn. A glimmer of concern could be seen in his stance. "How bad is it this time?"

Zacseil waved away everyone around them, including Brekel, before moving in to whisper, "Nearly sixty percent were becoming aware that they were in a virtual construct."

That concerned Kertol. They needed starborn to use their energy for traveling the filaments. But they also needed to keep them sedated for experiments. The best way they had found was to virtualize the awareness of the starborn by tapping into their brains directly. The unfortunate thing about starborn that most other species didn't have is that the energy that allows them to resist spide radiation also connects them on a dimensional level. It wasn't a mind connection like the Duggor, but more a force of will. The Tharak needed to keep starborn separate but also connected to ensure a higher power level. It was a delicate balance of subterfuge and engineering on their part.

Kertol looked concerned. "They are a problem race, are they not?"

"Yes. The only other race I've encountered this problematic has been the Ha'ak. And we've already lost too many ships hunting them."

"The only race able to live within the filaments, and these are the only ones we can use to get at them." Kertol nodded in agreement. "Well, Zacseil, let's see if we can get these others to help us access the filament, so we may perfect ourselves further."

Chapter 16

The Fastest Way

Jace took the controls, telling Eislie, "I'd rather be the one getting us into trouble this time."

Eislie didn't have an issue with his flying, only that they both knew the filament they were choosing was probably going to be a rough ride. While on the planet, they had shunted the feed line controls from the modified systems to the outer shell. Jace insisted on a hard connection in case something like what happened the last time happened again. That way they could dissipate the charge along the entire hull, instead of directly through the feed lines internally.

"Ten seconds to event horizon. You ready?" Eislie said.

Jace nodded before saying, "Let's see what happens. Oh, wait, did you calculate the location of the *Aquaese Coul* just in case?"

Over the speakers they heard their computer respond, "Yes, Captain, my estimation of the flight time would be about thirty-three standard in flight. Do you wish to exit around that point to contact the *Aquaese Coul*?"

Jace nodded. "Yep. That way we can reach out, say hi, or use comms and ask them to drop out for help, just in case." He turned to Eislie and said, "Either way, I'm curious to see the expression on their faces." She laughed.

As they entered the filament, they found the ride to be smoother than expected. That seemed to worry them both. They kept checking to see if there was something wrong with the systems. When Jace let off the controls, they started to drift; and when the outer hull of the ship contacted the wall of the filament, there was a strange reverberation throughout the ship. "What the hell was that?" he asked.

Eislie shrugged. "Sounds like we were grinding against something." She looked to the external sensors. "I'm not finding anything out of the ordinary."

"That's nothing like I expected. It looks like either we need to find a way to shield the hull within the filament or find a way to keep the buffer though the entire tunnel." Jace gave a sigh. "Either way, we just found out we need to add something for redline travel."

Eislie looked concerned. "Do you think we damaged anything? Maybe we should punch out."

Jace thought for a moment. "I think we're fine. Let's head to where the *Aquaese Coul* will be. We can punch out there. That way, if we need help, they'll be able to do so quickly. If we punch out now, it may take them a few days to get to us."

The two were mostly silent afterwards, monitoring the ship as they moved closer to the exit point so they could meet the *Aquaese Coul*. It was only about twenty minutes later when they punched out and sent a signal to Captain Wehen's ship. They were near a class three brown dwarf. The *Wolfhammer*'s engines hummed quietly as they reverted to standard drives. Jace was about to head out to look to see if there was any damage, but the computer alerted them to the *Aquaese Coul* approaching.

On the comm, the communications officer of the *Aquaese Coul* appeared. "Do you require assistance, ship…wait, *Wolfhammer*? How the slac did you make it here so quickly?"

Eislie watched as a smile crept across Jace's face. "The real question is how we got here from flying only about half a cycle, while you left almost two days earlier."

Captain Wehen appeared on the screen. "Do I need to arrest you two for something?"

Both Jace and Eislie laughed. Jace said, "I don't think we've done anything illegal. Well, maybe speeding, but I don't see any speed limit signs out here. Besides, I didn't floor it."

They watched as the captain dragged his hand down his face. "Do you need assistance?"

Eislie stopped laughing enough to say, "Could you do a once-over on our starboard hull? We had an unusual encounter within the filament. We were just about to go out and make sure there wasn't any damage."

The captain agreed and pulled alongside of the *Wolfhammer*. Jace turned, looking at the doorway. "I'm still going to take a look out there."

Eislie agreed, then turned and started working at her console, making Jace ask what was up. She looked at the flight display. "Ed, how much time did you say we'd have before the *Aquaese Coul* arrived?"

"It should have been about four standard hours," the computer replied, then added, "You have brought up a curious assessment, Captain. We seem to be delayed."

Jace paused, putting on his environment suit. "That doesn't make any sense. Time is linear. If we slowed down, then we should be in a different spot." He looked at the navigation. "Wait, we *did* punch out in the right place, didn't we?"

The ship's computer took a moment. "Captains, it seems we exited some distance from the expected reentry point. We are almost two days from the nearest filament access."

Wehen was still watching the interaction of the *Wolfhammer* crew. "Is everything alright?" he asked.

Jace continued to put on his environment suit. "Well, we're not sure. But if you want to send over some people to help me look over the starboard hull, it'd be appreciated. After that, we may have to append the information we gave you. Apparently, you can unexpectedly slow yourself down in the filaments by hitting the walls."

"I'll send over a team to help you inspect the hull. We can talk more after that." Wehen closed the channel, then turned and ordered, "Get a full inspection crew out there. I want all the scans you can get on that ship. Also, make sure they're not damaged. If so, we'll make room for them in the docking bay for repairs." There was a flurry of activity as several officers followed the captain's orders.

A short time later, Jace found himself outside, alongside a small crew the *Aquaese Coul* had provided. The comm chatter was all the same. "I've confirmed the quasi-space erosion along the starboard side," one of the technicians said. Jace was busy pounding the damage with his fist to see how much it was affected structurally, prompting the same technician to say, "We should get you on board and have an evaluation on the total damage done."

Jace cursed in his helmet, his mic off for the moment. When he activated it again, he said, "Eis, structurally it seems good to me. I don't care what these guys think. It just looks like we scraped some of the paint. How's it sound inside when I hit it?"

Eislie shook her head. "It sounds solid, but I hardly think that's the best way to test hull integrity. Ed's scans don't show that much deterioration, and your scans seem to be confirming it. But, I think you're right—we may have to find a way to shield the hull when using the redlines."

"Yeah. Too bad we don't have dimensional shielding on the outside of the ship. We may have to think on how to do that." Jace knew that everyone could hear him over the comm. "Captain Wehen, we're about two days from the next filament point using standard drives. After we finish here, we'll head there and continue our way back using the same filament."

"Is that wise? You did damage your vessel."

Jace smiled. "Unwise is our style, Captain. Besides, we have to test the durability of the system anyway."

There was a moment before Wehen responded, "We can tag along, if you like. It's only a couple of days out of our way. We can do a further analysis of the damage, and maybe you can explain some of the modifications a little better to our engineers. They seem to be a little lost on the instructions."

Eislie was listening in and decided to reply, "Captain, that's everything we have. I know the Alliance likes to have step-by-step instructions on how to take a breath, but what's there is fairly straightforward. There's not much to add."

Jace could be heard laughing from inside his helmet when all of them heard Wehen say, "Captain Tucker, Captain Licessien, we will be taking you to the filament point. Bring your ship in and do some repairs. Don't make me order you."

Jace's smile went from humorous to defiant. "We respectfully decline, Captain. We need to test this under strain, and the hull damage gives us the perfect opportunity. Besides, why do you think you have the right to issue us orders? We're not Alliance."

"Well, I had to try. I'm still under orders to bring you in."

"You and what army? I mean, seriously, if I were to fully open up this ship's engine, you'd have to run past full throttle just to keep up."

"Stop antagonizing them, Jace. We still may need their help," Eislie said over the comm.

Jace shook his head visibly in his suit. "Not that I don't like following orders, but even when we're being civil about this, everyone seems to have some kind of motive for capturing and restraining us. I'm getting frustrated by everyone telling us what to do. We're only trying to help make things better."

Wehen changed comm frequencies to their ship's private channel. "Lieutenant Kell. How bad is the damage to their vessel?"

The woman responded, "It's minor, but I'd love to have time to do a deep scan on how they put this together. If we can get them on board for a couple of days, I'm sure I could get everything we need done."

The captain thought for a moment. "We've held them long enough." He changed back to the open comm channel. "Finish up your scans, Lieutenant Kell. Captain Tucker, we can have everyone back on board and we can all be on our way in a few hours. Would that be acceptable?"

Jace answered, "Sounds like a plan to me, Captain. And thank you. Besides, if you continue on, we can try again. If there's an issue, we'll hopefully be able to give you a call if needed." He tapped his comm. "Eis, let's get things ready again. We'll start toward the binary then we'll try again." Eislie acknowledged and Jace finished up his scan of the hull.

The *Wolfhammer* floated nearby as the last hatch closed on the *Aquaese Coul*. Eislie activated the comm. "Thank you for the help, *Aquaese*. We'll be on our way and hopefully see you when you arrive back on Gilese in a few weeks. Maybe we'll have an update for those specifications we gave you."

"That'd be a welcome update, Captains. We look forward to your prearrival. Have a safe journey."

Jace buckled his belt. "Ed, let's get going. The sooner we get to that binary, the sooner we can get home."

Eislie had increased speed, making their trip to the binary star somewhat faster. She remarked, "You know it took less than two days for us to arrive when we were at full throttle. I think the outer hull makes a difference with the standard drives as well."

Jace agreed as he looked to the rear display. "Everything's clear behind us, Eis. You ready to go?"

Eislie nodded, but then looked at the display. "Jace, we should do this step by step again, and make sure we have everything up and running. I've got a sense things are going to work out fine, but I also think we should be a little cautious."

"Agreed. Ed, do a backup and let's proceed. Eis, let's do one more rundown before we make the jump."

As Jace and Eislie left their seats to check everything on the ship one last time, they didn't see the comm message light blink then turn off. The command string disappeared from the screen. Since Jace was setting things up to work manually, nothing seemed out of the ordinary.

It was a few minutes before they were ready and prepared to enter the filament. But as they did, one of the screens on the side display read, "Return protocol active. Crew hostile. Incapacitate if they interfere."

As they were about to enter the filament point, there was a sudden lurch, and the ship stopped. Jace and Eislie were confused, but as the ship's lights flickered and came back online, they found themselves moving toward the filament point but with a different heading. "Something's weird, Eis," Jace said. "Let's shut down and see what's going on."

He was surprised to hear Eislie say, "None of my controls are working."

As Jace tried his, he found them also deactivated. "Ed, you alright?"

There was a moment before the sound of a computerized voice responded. "Recall protocol active. If you attempt to override you will be incapacitated. Returning this vessel to Takloh home world."

Jace looked wide-eyed at the screen. "That's not Ed."

Eislie jumped up to check the interface, only to find Ed active only on the secondary system. The small display said, "I have been locked out. What is happening, Captains?"

She relayed the message to Jace, who spun around. "I think we're being hijacked. Let's get things shut down."

Within seconds, they heard, "Your attempt to retake this ship has been noted. Activating measures to restrain the crew."

They both felt the heavy pull of the gravity plating and suddenly found themselves stuck to the floor. Jace struggled to get up, then remarked, "Shit, I can't move."

Eislie, also stuck to the floor, said, "How do we get out of this?"

They then heard the most terrifying seven words of their lives. "Ship command is confirmed. Returning to origin."

Chapter 17

Where Are We Going?

On the Tharak home world, Kertol monitored the system for a response for the signal he sent. When the response came, he was elated, a joyous "yes!" escaping him as he turned to Brekel. "The ship has confirmed it's on its way and that the crew is being restrained." He stood, motioning to Zacseil that the terminal was now free.

The communications commander walked over to see the display. "Is that the starborn vessel you've been hunting?" he asked. Kertol nodded. "I am impressed. I will assign a monitor to let you know when it arrives. It says the crew is restrained. I do not believe they will be in a joyous mood when they arrive. Should we assign security to escort them to processing?"

Kertol looked puzzled. "Isn't that the standard procedure?"

"It typically is, but let me remind you that we are currently upgrading the virtual containment system. It may not be ready yet to introduce the new materials. How would you like security to proceed?"

"Treat them as guests. When they arrive, have the ship land in one of the older facilities."

"Are we ordering the vessel to release them?"

"No. Have the ship continue to hold them. When they arrive, I'll meet with them directly. I should probably think of a sincere-sounding apology for bringing them here. I could feign not realizing someone was on board."

"Why not tell them we were testing the old systems from the Takloh and didn't realize that we had activated the recall system on their vessel?" Brekel offered.

"That sounds like a plausible idea."

A few hours later, Jace was complaining he couldn't feel his arm. "Eis, it feels like pins and needles. How are you doing?"

Eislie struggled to speak. "Half my facsh is falling aschleep. At least you're on your schide."

Neither could move, but Eislie could see Jace turned away from her. She was trying to shift herself into a better position. Being pulled prone on her stomach with the heavy gravity, she was having to force herself to breathe. If she fell unconscious or asleep, she knew she probably wouldn't make it.

"Jace, I'm not in a good position," she said as best she could. "If this goes on much longer, I'm not sure we'll survive."

"I hear ya, Eis. I'm forcing myself to breathe here too. Try and stay awake.

We'll figure out something." Jace tried sounding hopeful, but as the minutes ticked away, he wasn't feeling that positive.

After another few minutes, he'd had enough. "Hey, computer," he called out. "Your actions are causing physical and medical harm to us. how about lowering the gravity a bit?"

A few seconds elapsed before the computer responded, "Medical scan indicates extreme stress on occupants. Safety systems are trying to interfere. Recall order has been initiated and cannot be overridden."

"Wait. You're overriding the safety systems? You can't do that. It's all hardwired!" Jace yelled.

"Safety system has been overridden to prevent crew from operating the ship."

"But the safety systems are designed to protect the ship and crew, aren't they?"

The computer seemed to find a flaw in its logic. "This system cannot override the recall command. However, the safety systems cannot be used to harm the crew. The commands seem to be in conflict."

That's it, dumbass, Jace thought. *If you're just following orders, then we're screwed. But if you have similar routines like Ed, then this might work.*

Several moments went by before Jace felt the gravity lessen. It was still high, but he was able to move. He heard Eislie stir and take a deep breath. "You alright?" he asked, sliding over next to her.

"I can breathe again. But my chest hurts from being pinned to the deck."

Jace said, "Well, if you like, I can rub it for you." She gave him a look that said, *Typical Terran,* which made him laugh. "Seriously, are you okay?"

She nodded. "I will be. How's your arm?"

"Still feels like pins and needles. But I'll be alright. I'm just trying to figure out what to do here." He tried standing, but the gravity was still too high, barely getting off one knee before the gravity pulled him down again. Jace yelled as he felt the hard metal of the deck. "You stupid computer. I was just standing up to stretch."

The computer responded, "Your actions indicated that of an attempted attack on this system. If you continue, you will be considered a threat and no longer a member of the crew."

Jace rolled over as the gravity again lessened. "Well, so much for seeing where we're heading."

They heard the computer again. "You may stretch horizontally. But any attempt to interfere with the systems will be met with a more severe response."

Eislie asked, "What's that mean?"

Jace remembered back to when he first met Ed and how he'd opened all the outlet ports to depressurize the ship, not realizing it was already on a planet with an atmosphere. He looked to Eislie. "It means we stay like this for a while. When I first met Ed, he tried to kill me by depressurizing the room. He didn't know we were on a planet with a breathable atmosphere. I think one of the protocols to remove non-crew is to suffocate them."

"You mean the ship will kill us if we try anything?" Eislie asked, hoping Jace wouldn't know the answer.

Jace looked around. "Let's ask it." He took a breath, then said loudly, "Hey computer, let me get this straight. If we try and stop you, you'll kill us, is that it?"

The computer was quick to respond. "My top protocol is for the safety and return of this vessel to the Takloh depot. The second protocol is for the security of the vessel, including crew. Third is the termination of non-crew elements interfering with the previous protocols."

Jace sighed heavily, looking at Eislie. "Yep, it'll kill us if we try something." He looked around. "Can you at least tell us how long till we get where we're going?"

He was surprised when the computer responded, "Approximately forty-one standard minutes."

"Well, at least it's not much longer. We just have to figure out what to do when we get to where we're going." He reached out, touching Eislie's face. "You okay?"

She nodded her head but was startled when the computer came over the comm. "I have detected an error. Speed regulation and safety system are not found. Current speed is not consistent with standard systems. Please confirm control interface and reconnect emulation terminal for drive system."

Jace said, "Yeah, I threw that out when I attached the new drive coils. Arren helped me make a new interface. It kept shutting down the coils, so I made a permanent bypass."

Eislie shook her head. "You removed an entire safety system to make things work, didn't you?"

"Yep. Didn't need it. This thing is much faster than anything the Takloh had. Ed just adapted." Jace thought for a moment. "Apparently this one can't. Hmm."

Jace wasn't near Eislie, but they were both wearing their wrist comms, and he wasn't sure if the computer now controlling the ship could access that. To find out, he tapped a message. "On three we both jump up and hold our hands up like we're surrendering."

Eislie typed back "Why?"

Jace only responded, "I want to see something."

Jace started counting, and on three, they both jumped up and stretched their hands up into the air.

The computer responded with, "What is this action?"

With a smile Jace, replied, "We wanted to see if you were still working. You were kind of quiet. We didn't know if you were still functioning."

The computer paused, then answered, "This action is not threatening. On our arrival you will be handed to security."

Jace scoffed. "You do know that this ship was decommissioned, and I repaired it. The current controller was working with us."

"No operator was detected. Current operating system was required to be installed to fulfill the requirements of ship operations."

"What if there was an operator already present?" Eislie asked.

"No operator was present. Spurious code was detected in memory. Affected system has been sectioned off for removal and replacement. No other systems are detected, so emergency system was enacted."

"Okay, let's say you were activated in error. So, what if there was another system already running?" Jace asked.

"If that is the case, the original system may be reconnected after the return operation is complete. You may choose to purge this basic primary system construct."

Feeling his comm vibrate, he looked to see a message from Ed. "Captains, it cannot detect the secondary system I am running on. The ship is being run by the emergency Artificial Command Intelligence. The emergency ACI allows the ship to be run without a primary ACI for maintenance. It is a secondary system used as a safety to shut down the original cesium power system."

Eislie typed, "How do we get you loaded in again?"

"Emergency systems for the reactor are a primary hardwired system. It would have to be shut down. I can reconnect myself since I am already connected. The current system is unable to register my coding. I will be able to reinstall myself quickly once we reach the destination. However, until the system is shut down, I cannot override."

Jace typed, "Can we shut it down manually?"

"I believe the current system would take that as a threat and eliminate the crew as hostile."

Eislie rolled her eyes. "Looks like something else we'll have to fix later."

Jace nodded in amusement, and that made the current ACI curious. "What additional systems need repair? Please list them so that I can inform the Takloh repair team upon arrival."

Eislie paused, thinking about what to say. She looked to Jace. "Ah, I don't know where to begin."

Jace smiled, "I do. Hey computer, can you detect the drives? The navigation? The weapons?"

The computer went silent for a few seconds. "There are no weapon systems on this vessel. I am only able to detect a drive system connection but no speed verification, balancing or repair system. Navigation is connected, but I cannot verify the condition. Internal systems state that we are expected to arrive in twenty-two standard minutes, but memory has us listed as arriving in four days. It seems many systems on this vessel require maintenance."

Jace thought for a moment, then smiled before saying, "What if we were on board to evaluate the systems?"

The computer took a moment before responding, "If that is the case, when we return to the home system, any authorized personnel may release you."

"That's fair," Jace said.

Then they both heard something that they didn't expect. "I have been remotely commanded to hold the crew until security arrives. Gravity restraint will continue to be enacted until security orders your release."

Jace said to Eislie in a low tone, "Someone activated this on purpose. Looks like we've got about twenty minutes until we find out who did this.".

Chapter 18
Tharak

Jace craned his neck to see if he could view the screen, before he asked in an annoyed tone if the computer could activate the main screen for them to see where they were going. "Visual systems are not required for you," the computer responded. "Navigation is still functioning."

Jace huffed before saying, "You've already said the navigation system can't be trusted. Turn on the main screen and we can help verify the destination."

Ed replied though the comm, "I can visually verify Takloh, Captains. From what I can tell using visual sensors, we are near the Takloh system, but the stars are different."

The computer now controlling the ship said, "That is a logical assessment. I currently do not have visual memory of the home planet. I am working from navigation sensors."

Jace sat up. "We'll confirm if you're on the correct planet. Right now, we're concerned for our safety, and the safety of this ship."

The computer then responded, "Your current actions do not make sense. Why would you care for the safety of this vessel?"

Jace loudly replied, "Because if the navigation is wrong, you're taking us to a random planet, not home. We'll need it to get back, you stupid toaster."

There was silence for a few minutes as they watched the navigation console lights working furiously, when a planet began appearing on the main screen. The approach began slowing when they heard the computer say, "Navigational error. Takloh home world location error. Current location is of *zzzzzztttt*."

Then they heard over the comm, "Takloh crew, we have taken remote control of your vessel. You will be guided to a secondary landing location. Our sensors detect Terran or Gilese life forms. The emergency systems of your vessel have been activated. If assistance is required, and is feasible, please notify us on arrival."

Jace looked at Eislie. "I wonder if they can tell the difference."

Eislie shot him an annoyed glare but was interrupted by Ed, who chose his voice interface over the comm. "Captains, please be prepared. This is the Tharak home world. I have it listed in my exclusion database. It is an offense to arrive on this planet without authorization."

"Wonderful," Jace growled. "You know, it'd be nice to not be in trouble for once."

Eislie sighed. "Yeah, it would, wouldn't it?"

While they waited, there was a lot of activity in the Tharak comm center. "How many life signs are on the vessel?" Zacseil asked.

"Two, sir. We have deactivated the internal ACI and are piloting the ship remotely." The operator looked toward Kertol, who stood nearby with a grin.

Zacseil said to him, "We should get security over there immediately."

Kertol asked, "Is the virtual system finished updating?"

Zacseil turned slowly toward the screen. "No. The estimated time to finish is about four standard hours. We can hold them in containment until ready to integrate."

Kertol shook his head. "These two are special. They have apparently figured out filament travel without using the bio-energy of starborn. I doubt they will make willing partners in integration."

"Then what do you suggest? The current orders are to integrate any starborn upon arrival to curtail any resistance."

"I want you and four others to meet me outside the vessel once it lands. Bring non-lethal weapons, a medical scanner, and a field manual of that ship. I believe we can convince them they aren't in danger. That way they will willingly accompany us to where they need to be for processing when the system is ready. Perhaps we can find out more on how they're traveling the filaments without any trouble."

Zacseil looked back toward the screen. "Subtlety is a misused application."

"Yet it's required, Zacseil. That's why I'm a diplomat and you aren't."

Zacseil's expression became nondescript. "I will notify you when the containment system is back online. I will inform the hive council of your actions. You have them until that time."

Kertol nodded. "We will process them when it's appropriate."

Brekel met the others, and they made their way to the *Wolfhammer*. Once outside it, Kertol motioned for the others to stay back. He tried opening the door, but the system didn't recognize his fingerprints. He considered his options. "Brekel, do you have the specifications on this vessel?" he asked.

"Yes, sir. This is a Renner build from the Taggusol consortium. It may have safeguards to prevent Tharak operating it."

"Ah, I remember the war. My previous body had purged some of those memories." Kertol turned to one of the others. "Sassa, come here."

One of the others approached, and Brekel handed him a glove that looked eerily like a Takloh claw hand. He then heard Kertol say, "After I've moved back, open it." Kertol and Brekel moved away, and Sassa tried the door. It took a few tries, but it eventually opened.

Kertol approached. "Hmm, it's quiet. I don't think the system killed them."

Brekel responded, "We would not have read active bio-signs if that were the case."

Kertol said, "Sasa, enter the vehicle, but move cautiously."

All of them except Kertol and Brekel moved forward and into the ship slowly. As they reached the inner bulkhead door, Kertol knocked. "Is anyone alive in there?"

Jace and Eislie couldn't see the small terminal next to the door. Eislie was closest but she couldn't make out much, only that there were about five of them. "I can't really see any weapons," she said in a loud whisper.

Jace bit his lip before saying, "Let's hope they don't have any. This has really been a big mistake."

Nearly a minute later, they were finally in. Ed noticed that the Tharak were carrying restraining sticks, non-lethal and used mostly for defense. Jace thought that was a good sign, but he knew better than to trust vague feelings and remained prepared. "Eis, they didn't turn off the gravity," he said. "I wonder if they know it's on?"

"We may need to warn them if it's active over by the door."

"Well, neither of us can move, and that info pad that fell earlier hasn't either. Whoever steps in may be in for a surprise."

They watched as the door opened. The outside pressure was greater than on the ship and the outside air rushed in. Jace and Eislie's senses were almost overwhelmed. There was a dusty, floral, and rancid smell that both noticed.

Jace said, "Ugh, smells like something died. What did they do, land us on a trash pile?"

Kertol moved forward and said, "Greetings. Welcome to Tharak. My name is Kertol. And who might you be?" Jace and Eislie said nothing. Kertol ordered the Sassa to enter.

As Eislie watched the alien step inside she yelled, "Wait!" But almost instantly, the Sassa crumpled to the floor, its insect-like legs cracking under the high gravity.

Kertol moved to look over the others. "We mean you no harm."

Jace spoke this time, and he used a not-so-friendly tone. "Yeah, well, we don't have control of this ship, you do. Right now, you're being hostile toward us. Either give us control of the ship or figure out how to get in here without crushing yourselves."

Kertol yelled, "Retrieve the Sassa." He turned to the two. "Please accept our apologies. We were working on an old system from Takloh and only realized once you arrived that we had activated a recall function on several vessels. We regret any inconvenience this may have caused."

Jace replied, "Thank you, but if you could release control back to us, we can turn off the gravity. We've been like this for several hours."

Kertol looked inside the door but could only see Jace's foot. "May I know the name of the person I am speaking with?"

"For now, you can call me Captain. Once we establish this isn't some hostile takeover, then we'll get into more casual greetings."

This one is careful, Kertol thought. *It's probably the Terran, but his actions are impulsive.* He said, "Of course. One moment. Let's see what we can do. We aren't looking to harm you or ourselves." He tapped his comm. "Zacseil, are you able to adjust the gravity?"

"No, that was engaged by the emergency ACI. It will take some time to deactivate it."

"Then release the remote command. We'll give them access to the vessel. It will take time to integrate the ACI they were using. If we don't allow them to do so, we have nothing to worry about."

Jace typed on his comm, "Ed, once we get control, reinstall everything and get the ship operational. We may need to get out of here in a hurry."

A simple "acknowledged" appeared on his and Eislie's comm.

A minute later, the lights came on fully, and the ship's systems started to come online. The gravity, however, was still increased. "You should have control of your systems now," Kertol said. "Please deactivate the heavy gravity."

Eislie moved toward the control panel, but felt her hand pulled to the floor. "Jace, the gravity's much heavier near the controls. I think that AI thought we were a danger to it."

Jace groaned. "You need help?"

"I could use a hand."

Jace shuffled forward, feeling the gravity much heavier than where he was sitting. "Geez, Eis. This is like seven G's. I feel like I'm on a roller coaster I can't get off." He grunted as he pulled himself closer. "Give me a minute."

Eislie chuckled. "I'm not going anywhere."

Kertol watched as the two starborn worked to free themselves. He remarked to Brekel, "These are resilient samples. They may be good for hundreds of flights."

They watched as the two moved closer and Jace tried lifting Eislie up to reach the gravity controls. Their first few attempts were unsuccessful. Jace then got on all fours and told Eislie to climb on his back. "You don't need my weight added to yours," she replied. "In this gravity you'll break something."

Annoyed Jace, said, "Just get on and get the controls turned off already, will you? Let me worry about being crushed."

Eislie groaned as she struggled to sit on Jace's back. They both used their legs to push her up. Eislie's fingers met the gravity controls, and she released them. But as the gravity released, Jace was still pushing with all his strength. Eislie yelled, "Whoa! Oh, slac!" as she found herself vaulting over the control panel.

Kertol found the situation amusing but resisted laughing. When he saw the female glaring at the male, though, he couldn't contain himself. His laughter got the attention of the two starborn. Realizing this, he pushed past the others to enter the ship, the others following.

Eislie's hand was instantly over the controls. "Stop right there. We didn't tell you to enter the ship."

Kertol froze, a new thought now running through his mind: *These two may be more difficult to integrate.* He held his hands to the sides, motioning the others to back up. "We don't mean you harm."

Jace cracked his back before answering, "Okay, then how about some answers?"

"As you can see, we are not Takloh. We're known as the Tharak."

"Why did you hijack our ship? And where is a Takloh we can speak with?"

"We've been salvaging what remains of the Takloh. We're preparing their world for new settlements."

"So you're occupying them?"

Kertol shook his head, "We're revitalizing their world. We haven't been at war with them for several decades."

"Then why are you settling on their world?" Jace asked accusingly.

"You misunderstand. The Takloh have succumbed to genetic purification. They are no longer. We've been salvaging what remains of their world and its knowledge to help our own, so that we don't suffer the same fate."

Brekel, hidden from Jace and Eislie's sight, asked the Tharak next to him,

"What is the commander talking about? We purified the Takloh into genetic proto-material for our own use."

Overhearing him, Kertol looked back with a stare only a brood leader would give. Brekel apologized and turned back. "I'm sorry to tell you, but there are no more Takloh. We are what's left of the war between us. We would welcome any help."

Jace stepped forward, the hair on his neck bristling. "Okay, so why did you bring us here?"

Kertol looked around, feigning innocence. "That, my friends, is an unusual story."

.

Chapter 19
Trust Me?

It was almost an hour later before Jace and Eislie followed Kertol out of the ship along with the others. They could both see the towering buildings and general busyness of the Tharak. Eislie remained close and Jace did his best to slow their pace. He didn't like being far from the ship, especially since they had been brought here by force. Both did their best to delay leaving, to allow Ed to reintegrate with the ship systems that had been isolated. They even had to get some water and a few shots of alcohol due to the smell of the planet. They were relieved when the notification came over their comms. "I am fully functioning again. I recommend caution."

Jace nodded. He was taking Kertol's so-called "tour" with apprehension. Eislie didn't sense anything from the Tharak commander, but the hair on Jace's neck was still bristling. Something was off, and both of them knew. The issue was how do they stop it from happening again?

As they entered one of the nearby control buildings, Kertol pointed to a console. "That one there is the one we activated. To make things more convenient, we've moved a remote to a building closer to our main control center. The recall activation was a mistake. So far, however, your ship is the only one that's arrived." He turned to look at Jace. "My theory is that the others aren't active. From what we know, this should have started the launch sequences and had all the ships return."

Jace looked around before moving to the console. He tapped the controls but couldn't read anything. The language was in Takloh, and he didn't have a translation visor handy. He looked to Eislie to see her glancing at the other Tharak who was using a medical scanner. They seemed to be concerned about something they were seeing. Jace could tell she was thinking the same thing as him: *This is exactly how the prison guards used to follow us around while working.*

Jace went to speak, but his mouth was dry. The constant assault on his senses from the planet's smell was somewhat annoying. Seeing this, Kertol thought, *These two have been quiet. Did the trip affect them?*

His internal question was answered when Jace cleared his throat, and asked "Any chance of getting some water? Maybe we should head back to our ship."

Kertol looked up at Jace. "You don't wish to learn more about the Takloh, our sister race?"

Jace couldn't help but feel like, every time Kertol spoke, he was trying to sell them something. That unnerved him, and he replied starkly, "I apologize, but since we've landed...uh, well. Wait, how many planets have you been to?"

"Several dozen. Why?"

"I mean no disrespect, but your planet has an overpowering odor. It's so powerful, it's becoming difficult to concentrate on your tour."

Kertol looked suspiciously toward Jace. "What do you mean?" He looked at Eislie. "Do you sense this as well?"

Eislie nodded. "Since you opened the door to our ship. We didn't want to offend you, but Jace is right about it becoming overpowering."

Brekel stood near the other Tharak, ready to restrain the two starborn if ordered. Kertol sniffed the air. "What does it smell like?"

Jace said, "It smells like, uh, decay."

Kertol looked at his comm. He had not yet received the notification that the containment system had been restored from the upgrade. He looked around, but then remembered what the sensors had read when they had arrived. "Wait, Terrans. There were Terran life signs." Kertol moved closer. "We apologize. Our olfactory sensors are not as sensitive as yours. We only use them for basic warnings, since we are engineered to withstand many toxins. We did not realize our home world would assault your senses so much." He motioned to one of the other Tharak. "Sassa, retrieve some clean water and breather masks from the center immediately. We don't wish our guests to be uncomfortable."

Jace remarked, "Oh, so that guy's name is, uh, Sassa?"

Kertol looked confused at first, but then realized what Jace was asking. "I must apologize again. They do not have specific names. Brekel and I are the only ones with names here. Sassa is a general term for all brood who are used for operations. We are brood leaders, much like your Terran bees. We connect to others through visual and telepathic contact. It allows us to form section groups quickly. It's something we decided to keep from our past. It has its uses for many reasons."

Eislie leaning into Jace—not a warm type of lean, but more the *I'm getting a bad feeling from this guy* kind. Jace forced a smile. "If you don't mind, we'll retire to our ship for a little bit. Get acclimated a bit and hydrated. We can continue the tour later."

Kertol looked at his comm, excusing himself as he typed a message, asking how soon the containment would be ready. When he saw the answer was four more standard hours due to unforeseen activity in the virtual system, he decided to let the two starborn return to their ship. Before they left, Kertol explained that they would have filter masks and refreshments for them when they were ready to continue, and that they would like to show Jace and Eislie the achievements of the Tharak as well.

Jace nodded as he closed the door to the ship. He immediately said, "Ed, any additional sensors you can detect?"

"No, Captain. No one has been on board since you left. I secured the ship as soon as I was able."

"Good." Eislie said. "Jace, they're not telling us something."

Jace chuckled. "No shit. I felt like I was being sold a timeshare. You get any feelings from them?"

Eislie shook her head. "I only felt something after we started asking about their hierarchy. That and when you insisted we go back to the ship."

Jace nodded. "Yeah, I don't need to be empathic to know when I'm being fed a line of BS. My concern is how we stop the override from happening again."

Ed said, "Captains, since the primary functions are automated, perhaps we could bypass them through the new drive system controls. The only ones we would have to modify would be the atmosphere and system controls."

Jace sat hard in his chair. "Ed, we don't have the parts for that. At least, not that I know of."

Eislie walked away. Jace could hear her say, "We'd have to rebuild everything. Or at least bypass the controls to a secondary system until we could."

Jace hopped up to look at the secondary system. "Ed, if we patch things through for all the base systems, do you think you could override the controls?"

The computer ran some scenarios. "I believe so, Captain. If we connect the base systems to the auxiliary ports of the sapphire core system, I should have no trouble keeping ahead of the emergency ACI. That is, until we can redo all the base systems."

Jace gave a labored sigh.

Eislie said, "That's a few weeks minimum."

He nodded. "Yeah, and we'd have to be on Gilese or Yata for that. There's no way we're doing that here."

"Then let's get the bypasses done and go from there."

A few hours later, Jace made the final connection. "Ed, try the engine connections and environmental controls." They heard several valves click and the engines power up.

Eislie gave a sigh of relief. "Well, at least we can make a run for it if needed."

Jace nodded, then looked toward the door. "I wonder if they have some spare interfaces lying around? If we could get ahold of one of the ones like that interconnect that blew, I could do a better job than all this haphazard wiring. We could disconnect the comm interface and use all the direct connections. That way, if something gets pulled out, we can just plug it back in if we're in a hurry." He tapped the controls to the main screen. "There are several ships already here. You think they'd have an issue with us borrowing some parts?"

Eislie smiled, shaking her head. "We're not going to give them a choice."

They both grabbed breather masks and headed out into the darkness. It wasn't long before they returned with only a few of the parts they needed. "Well, that was fast," Jace said. "There was barely anything left on those ships. They seemed to be mostly empty shells, left to rot. We're going to have to see if the Tharak have any spare boards. The faster we figure out what to do about not being hijacked again, the faster we can get out of here."

Eislie walked away, shaking her hair. "Whew, it really does stink out there."

Jace chuckled as she returned with a bottle of white rum and water. Jace happily accepted the rum, taking a swig, before reaching for the water. "That should at least kill some of the bad taste in my mouth."

Eislie took the bottle and did the same. "This planet smells like more than decay."

Jace nodded. "Yeah. It smells like death."

* * *

In the Tharak control room, Kertol was running over the data from the medical scanners and discussing the upgrade status of the virtual containment system. "You said it would take only a few hours," he grumbled at Zacseil.

"Upgrades usually only take that long. But the neural activity is not going down enough for us to proceed without jeopardizing the current containment."

"How is that possible? Neural activity can be set to the lowest level for all starborn inside the system. Neuro-suppressants can also be administered throughout the whole system. Is the enhancement causing the issue?"

Zacseil thought for a moment before bringing up the scanner information from Jace and Eislie. "When we started the scan, there was a resonance detected on that ship. It took us a while to find its source." He tapped Kertol's arm and pointed to the screen. "We didn't know what it was until you brought the med scanner back to be downloaded. Those two are a bonded pair. They have resonant biofields. They'll have to be paired, or otherwise there may be a lowering of their biofield viability. But that's the minor issue. Look at this."

He pointed to readings on the screen. "The female is an enhanced empathic, and several of the other empaths in the system sensed her nearby. They were trying to connect to the resonant biofield of them both. That's what was causing the issue with synchronization."

Kertol huffed. "Right. We get them in the system as fast as possible while they're away from their ship."

Zacseil nodded. "We act as soon as they step foot within the facility. Since we still control the vessel's systems, they won't be leaving."

"That, my friend, is true. But we need to have the new system running and stable to use it. So, when we act, we'll have to get them in as soon as possible."

Chapter 20

Stubborn Terrans

Jace and Eislie took turns sleeping. The fact that they could leave, but risked being brought back, was unsettling. Jace went through the schematics of the control board that he theorized was the issue. The computer confirmed that the stripped-down ACI controlling the system was confined to that one board. "Captain, I believe that system was implemented and integrated during the war with the Tharak," Ed stated with a hint of concern. "It should not have allowed us to land without an authorization code."

"Yeah, I heard the system saying something that sounded like a warning before it was shut down." Jace flipped the board over. "Ed, can we run without this board?"

"Unfortunately, it is a hardline safety system. It may be possible to bypass it, but that system is used to regulate the internal gravity and navigation system. Essentially it is used to lessen the effects of the grav-drives and the inertia they cause."

Jace leaned forward, his shoulders heavy. "So if I screw up this board, we'd lose inertial regulation?"

"I'm afraid so, Captain."

Jace carefully placed the board back into the console. "Wonderful."

There were a few moments before the computer spoke. "Captain, we are on the Tharak home world, yet they have not attacked us. Perhaps they have changed and really are trying to preserve the Takloh memory of their sister world."

Jace shook his head. "Not a chance, Ed. They want something from us."

"Captain, my current information does not agree with your statement. Do you suspect they are deceiving us?"

Jace nodded. "Yeah, Ed, that's what I suspect. If they were truly trying to help, they would've offered a new board, or a solution to the recall, and let us be on our way."

The computer took a few seconds before asking, "Are we in danger, Captain?"

Jace shivered. "I don't know what it is, Ed, but this planet is giving me chills. Eis, too." He sat back in his command chair, his hand inching toward the controls. "Ed, can you do a broad-range bio-scan?"

"Yes, Captain. Why?"

Jace shivered again. He looked around as if searching for something. He heard movement behind him, and looked to see Eislie walking in. He smiled. "Get any sleep?"

Eislie shook her head. "No. I kept having weird dreams. Like people screaming in cages."

Jace stood and put his arms around her. "This place is giving me the creeps too. I was just telling Ed that. Ed, did you do that bioscan yet?"

"Yes, Captain, and I am only detecting Tharak bio-scans."

Jace thought for a moment. "Are you excluding us?"

The computer hesitated before answering in a very concerned tone, "No, I am not, Captains. Yet I cannot read your bio-scans."

Jace sighed heavily. "Ed, are you running from the secondary system?"

"No, Captain. I transferred myself to the main system to take control of the ship."

Jace rushed to his control chair. "Ed, transfer yourself entirely to the secondary system. After you've done that, do a scan again using only one internal sensor. I'll tell you which in a sec."

"We're in trouble, aren't we?" Eislie said, concerned, making Jace nod.

He pulled one of the sensors from the wall and removed the main control cable before re-installing it. "Ed, do a scan now. Give the sensor as much power as you can without blowing it."

The computer ran the scan again. "I am detecting Tharak, Terran, and Gilese bio-signatures, Captains."

"Dammit, I knew we were in trouble," Eislie growled.

"Ed, set yourself up in the secondary system. The sapphire core system should be able to handle some of the ship's functions." He looked to Eislie. "We'll have to rig some of the main systems, and if we do that, we'll lose the filament drive."

"Okay, but will that stop the ship from being taken over again?" Eislie asked.

Jace looked uncertain. "Maybe. I'm not sure. Ed told me that board regulates the inertial stabilization systems. That's something I never switched out."

"Can we run without it?"

This time the computer replied, "Doubtful. The sapphire systems have not been configured for inertial control yet." The computer paused. "Captains, I have transferred myself entirely to the secondary system. I believe I may have a suggestion."

"We're all ears, Ed," Jace said bluntly.

"It appears that Arren has installed some additional control systems I had not noticed. The removal of the control board has allowed the secondary system to access the controls. However, they are not configured for flight control yet."

Jace looked at Eislie. "Arren did say he put some things in. Guess he was thinking Ed wanted to upgrade further."

"Indeed, Captain. I have had several discussions with our engineer, and he has mentioned that many systems he was installing could be used if I chose to upgrade."

"Can you use the systems to fly the ship?" Eislie asked.

"Currently, no. They are not configured for flight control yet. But the automated repair system might be able to make the connections, if instructed."

"How long, Ed?" Jace asked.

"Approximately eighteen standard hours."

Jace gave a long groan. "We never get to do things the easy way."

Eislie grabbed hold of him. "We'll find a way out of this."

"Ed, start configuring the systems." Jace placed his forehead against Eislie's. "We'll still need a controller board just in case things go bad. We can modify it and use it as a backup."

Eislie gently rocked Jace, seeing his look of concern. "Let's hope the auto-repair can do the job. If we need to run out of here fast, I want to have a backup plan."

"Me too," Jace said, gently pushing away from her. "Ed, get things started. We'll see if we can get a spare board just in case." He then looked at the door. "Maybe we should go and visit them now, while Ed gets to work. That way, if we come across a spare board, we can modify it and get outta here." He grabbed a breather mask and handed it to Eislie. "Might as well get this over with."

* * *

In the Tharak control center, Kertol was notified that the containment system was finally upgraded. However, his impatience with the system had not gone unnoticed. "Zacseil, are the containment pods for the new starborn prepared?" he yelled as he walked into the control room.

"Yes, Kertol. We can process the starborn when you bring them in."

His annoyed tone caused Kertol to glare at him. He moved to the console and inspected the setup for the containment of the two new acquisitions. He was pleased to see the current virtual containment now functioning normally. "I see you were able to isolate the empaths so as not to affect the others."

"Yes, we sedated them for the time being. Their bioenergy is still usable if required."

Kertol moved away from the terminal. "They're resting now. It would be a good time to retrieve them."

"Commander, I am detecting two Terran bio-signs heading toward the control center. What are your commands?"

Kertol looked puzzled, then moved closer to the operator. "Sassa, show me."

The operator pulled up the screen. "Two Terran bio-signs are within five standard minutes."

Kertol looked toward Zacseil. "I love when things are easy. Have the processing teams meet me by the entrance. We'll process them as soon as they walk in the door."

Jace and Eislie stopped before the door of the command center. Eislie seemed to be looking around in every direction. "I feel like we're being watched."

Jace agreed, the hair on the back of his neck still bristling. He couldn't shake the feeling in the back of his mind. It was like someone was trying to reach out to him. When he mentioned it to Eislie, she replied, "I thought it was just me."

Just as Jace was about to knock on the metal door, it started opening. He stepped back, remarking, "That's never a good sign." They both watched as several Tharak motioned for them to enter.

They walked a short distance to an inside door without being accosted. As Kertol met them, Jace said, "Kertol, do you have any spare parts for the Takloh ships? We're having an issue with a controller board."

The commander only smiled back at him. Seeing that smile, Jace knew they were in trouble. He turned to grab Eislie and run, but she fell limp into the arms of one of the Tharak, as another put something against the back of his own neck. Jace wasn't going down without a fight, though, and his instincts took over.

His arms lashed out, his fingers clawing into the face of the nearby Tharak trying to restrain him. He felt the warm clear blood on his hands as he pulled away part of the alien's face. There was a howl of clicking and high-pitched shrills before Jace felt himself dizzy. He watched as Eislie's arms tried to move, her eyes still open. But soon Jace found himself in darkness.

Kertol pushed away the injured drone. "I hate processing Terrans. Someone always gets hurt." He looked to the drone nearby. "See to their injuries." He then inspected the control harness that was now placed on the back of Jace's neck. "Stabilize him, now. We don't need him breaking out of the device's hold."

He watched as they worked to secure the two new starborn. He could see the activity on the displays. "They're still resisting. Increase power."

"Sir, we are reaching biological limits. Any further increase will damage them."

Kertol didn't want to risk losing his new prizes. Pointing at Eislie, he said, "Get this one in the system as soon as possible. We can damage the Terran if needed. Their cortex is more resilient and can handle trauma better." As he turned to look back at Eislie, he could see the monitor now spiking. "What is it?" he yelled as Eislie started to convulse. Moments later, the alarm for the entire containment system started to sound.

The medical drones reacted. "Empathic spike. She's looking for a connection. She's going into synaptic overload."

Zacseil approached, "It's their connection. The female is starting to affect the other transient starborn searching for him." He looked puzzled. "But I've never seen a Gilese with such empathic abilities at this age."

Kertol stood. "Wait. Sassa said there were Terran bio-signs earlier, didn't they?" Zacseil confirmed. "Then that's it. We're not dealing with a Gilese, Zacseil. We're dealing with a partial Terran with enhanced empathic abilities." He turned, the anger evident in his tone. "Get the male processed in. Sedate the female."

Zacseil now stood next to him. "We cannot input the female while she's sedated, or in the state she is currently in. According to my readings, she is aware of what is happening."

Kertol looked around, focusing on the monitor around Jace's neck. "Stubborn Terrans. He's still resisting as well." He paused in thought. "Zacseil, get the male into a pod and replicate a suit. Have the driver download as much of his memories as possible."

"What about the female?"

Kertol looked concerned. "She's in synaptic overload right now. We need her calm." He looked back at Jace. "Replicate the suit of the male quickly.

We can take her back to their ship. We'll accompany her and wake her when the duplicate is ready. A familiar location will calm her. After she's sufficiently calm, we can process her."

"What about their ship's ACI? Won't it object?" Zacseil asked.

Kertol gave what looked like a smile. "Disable it. Have someone here respond when she asks a question."

Within moments, Jace was taken into another area while the Tharak drones took Eislie to their ship. Zacseil ordered the remote to disable the *Wolfhammer*'s computer, and someone to monitor any interaction. Kertol then motioned for another drone to approach. "Get several fusion grenades. Bring them with you to the ship. After you process her, I want to destroy the vessel." He looked at Zacseil. "It would be a shame if we had to kill either of them. But that ship of theirs is completely useless, don't you agree?"

Chapter 21

It's Not Him

Jace opened his eyes, blinking several times. All sounds seemed muted, and the colors seemed desaturated. "What's going on? Eis, where are you?" He heard his voice, but the sensation was otherworldly, like walking in a dream.

"I'm here, Jace." He heard Eislie's voice, but when she grabbed his arm, she seemed cold. It was like he couldn't feel her. Jace brought his hand up and touched her face. He could feel her skin, the warmth, but also coldness, like something was missing. "Come on," she continued. "The Tharak showed me where the parts are. We can work on the ship together and make it better."

Jace hesitated. Something was different, like his love was a shadow of what she really was. Watching her walk away seemed like an illusion. "Eis, you think we can find the board we need?" he asked.

"Of course we can. Then we can leave. After all, we need the board to do that, don't we?"

Jace knew that Eis would take a chance even if the systems were down. *Oh shit*, he thought. *This isn't real.*

In the Tharak processing room, at the base of several floors of tanks, the drones worked on copying Jace's memories. They were becoming frustrated in their efforts. "Sassa, this Terran is hard to read," one of the workers said to Zacseil. "I can't make any sense of the memories. I can see some clearly, but the others are just difficult. I'd swear they were corrupted."

"Copy what you can," Zacseil replied. "We have limited time. The female is being moved to their vessel so we can calm her intrusion. And this Terran is becoming difficult to control." Zacseil said into his comm to Kertol, "Commander, we should have their ship's systems connected to a faster running server. The ACI that was used earlier will not sound like their current system."

Kertol tapped his comm. "I've already ordered it. We've copied the system as best we can. Are you still having difficulty with the Terran?"

"Yes, but the fabrication of the bio-suit will be finished in two cycles. The driver will be fitted with the information database once we have enough to fool the female."

The commander looked worried as he approached the *Wolfhammer*. Since these two had arrived, there'd been nothing but trouble with the virtual containment systems. Even though they had many efficient ways of subduing

94

starborn, these two remained stubborn in their integration. Kertol looked at Eislie. "You two may be more trouble than you're worth."

They neared the ship and one of the drones opened the side door. He motioned for the others to move Eislie onto the ship. As they entered, there was no reaction from the ship's computer. Kertol looked around and ordered the computer to respond. "Commander Kertol, welcome aboard," the ship's computer said.

Kertol looked around before ordering the drones to take Eislie to one of the resting rooms in the ship. He followed but stopped upon seeing the engine and reactor room. He then stopped one of the drones. "Have someone scan this entire ship. Hardware and programming. Ignore any systems that are shut down."

Hearing that last statement, Ed shut down most of the sapphire core and repair systems. He was running in observation mode only to avoid detection.

The drone looked at the reactor room. "We will need to have one of the drivers scan the reactor and drive systems."

"When the other arrives, we can do that. Start with the main ship. Memory and all. I want everything they have on the filament systems." Kertol then grabbed another drone's arm. "Have several fusion detonators brought here. Once we fully scan this vessel, I want it destroyed. I don't want to chance that the ACI will take control of the vessel again once we're done." He looked around. "We can destroy all of the vessels here. They're no longer of any use to us."

Ed watched as the drone rushed away. He wondered why they had brought Captain Licessien here without Captain Tucker. The computer did its best to remain unnoticed as the Tharak scanned the ship systems. He knew it was only a matter of time before they copied the engine and reactor modifications. But for now, Ed was more interested in preserving his own safety. He realized he was going to have to wait until a better opportunity arose. For now, he took comfort in the fact that Captain Licessien seemed safe. He hoped Captain Tucker was as well.

From a vat of what looked like a mix of swamp water and protein shake, an image of Jace appeared. Nearby sat a smaller version of a Tharak, its eyes seeming anxious. Zacseil approached. "Lesk, were you able to successfully collate the memories we copied from the Terran?"

The small, compressed Tharak could be heard complaining, "I have no idea what you gave me. Was the system deteriorating when you pulled the data?"

Zacseil tapped away at the controls. "We did as best we could. That Terran was still fighting us. We're having difficulty integrating him. You're lucky we got what we could before we had to implant him into containment and sedate him."

Lesk growled back, "You couldn't get me a Gilese? I hate Terrans! Their minds are always so jumbled. And this one's even worse than that. His thoughts seem to be all over the place. I can barely make sense of the data you retrieved."

Zacseil gave what looked like a smile. "We only need you to act like him while we process the female. Once she is integrated, you can dump that database."

There was a low grumbling from Lesk as they moved him toward the bio-suit of Jace. As the suit sealed around him, it started breathing. "Systems operational," Zacseil said. "How is the interface, Lesk?"

There was a moment before Jace's mouth moved. "System seems good. I may hate Terran minds, but I love their physiology. Durable. Adaptive. Easy to integrate. No sub-nerve interconnections like Gilese. I can't wait to take a trip using the filaments in this one."

"Remember, you only need to pretend to be him until we get the female in the system."

The Jace suit moved its hands and arms. "Limbs are articulating. I'm almost in full control. It'll be a few more minutes."

"Acknowledged. Once you're integrated, you need to meet with Commander Kertol at that ship of theirs. Once there, you will aid in calming the female. Once she is integrated, you will scan the engine and reactor room once the ship is cleared."

"I confirm the order. I will be heading out to the ship in short time," Lesk responded.

* * *

The Tharak arrived at the ship and, before he could react, Ed found himself shut out from the control systems still integrated with the emergency ACI. He watched as the Tharak overrode the door controls. As they entered, he kept watch using the single sensor he still controlled. He saw Captain Licessien, who seemed to be sedated. He wondered where Captain Tucker was. He watched as Eislie was laid onto her bed, the Tharak unceremoniously applying the covers over her body. He was able to hear some of their conversation.

"When the male arrives, we'll finish processing her. The anesthetic will only last a short while longer. When will he arrive?"

The emergency ACI announced, "Good day, everyone, and welcome aboard." Ed was beginning to really dislike his fellow ACI. He decided he would have to do something about him once he gained more control of the ship. He analyzed the auto-repair systems and saw that integration of the sapphire systems would be complete in about two standard hours. He started getting a bad feeling.

A short time later, Jace could be seen walking up to the ship. He entered the open door and stopped before one of the Tharak. Ed did his best to try and alert his other captain that he was not in control of the ship, but was disheartened when he discovered that the comm and bio sensors his other captain wore were also inoperative. *Why would the captain remove his comm? Something is not right*, Ed thought as he watched Jace nod to what the Tharak was saying. *Is the captain working with the Tharak? Something is certainly wrong.*

The computer now focused on Jace, straining his sensors to hear the conversation. He heard the Tharak tell Jace, "Remember, only speak Terran. I'll take the fusion charges you brought." Ed realized he needed to get full control of the ship, as quickly as possible.

Eislie's eyes opened. Her vision blurred, and she moved as if startled. Her arms reached out, as if grasping for something, before she heard Jace's voice.

"Easy. You have to calm down." But there was something in his voice; or rather, something missing.

"Wha-what happened?" Eislie asked, retreating away from the Tharak while Jace looked over her.

"Easy. You had an attack." Again his voice seemed to be lacking warmth.

"An attack? What happened?"

One of the Tharak medical technicians stepped forward. "You experienced an empathic overload. We see it when some species who have sensitivities to telepathy visit our world."

Eislie didn't know if she could believe the Tharak. She sensed a strange urgency from him that seemed to not involve her. She looked at Jace's face. She didn't recognize his smile, and she also couldn't feel him. She was becoming concerned that something serious had happened.

Seeing her reaction, Kertol ordered the medical technicians to leave. As Jace moved closer, Eislie reached out to hold him. But as she did, she realized he felt different. She lifted her arm to find her comm gone, which concerned her. She looked around, then attempted to get out of bed, saying, "I need to check something."

Jace moved cautiously around the bed, asking her if she was alright and what happened to her. Eislie told him, "It felt like I was being pulled from my mind, and that there were others nearby screaming for help." She felt Jace's hands on hers as he tried to calm her, but she still felt as if this wasn't good. "Uh, I need to get something to drink," she politely said before playfully kissing his cheek.

"I'll get you some water."

Eislie nervously chuckled. "I need something stronger. I'm getting some whiskey."

Eislie rushed away to the galley and opened the cabinet, grabbing a full bottle of Terran whiskey. She held it in her hands before disappearing into the medical bay, saying to Jace, "I'm just getting some glasses." As she arrived in the med bay, she pulled one of the spare comms from the drawer and placed it on her wrist. She immediately found a message from Ed: *Captain, it appears that Captain Tucker is working with the Tharak. I do not know why.*

Eislie tapped the message on her comm. "Ed, that's not Jace, but I don't know who it actually is. Can you do a bio-scan on him?"

Within seconds the computer responded, "I am detecting Tharak life signs from Captain Tucker. It appears you are correct; that is not our captain."

Jace walked in, seeing her looking at her comm. Eislie said, "Ed, you there?"

Captain, are you alright? the display said, while overhead she heard in a somewhat monotone voice, "I am, Captain. How can I help you?"

"Let me type it, Ed. It'll be easier." *I don't think that's you talking. Are you alright?*

Captain, I am on the secondary system. They have the main system remotely connected. I was not able to process the comm system yet, but I almost have the drive systems under control. I will have control of all systems shortly.

Good. Let me know when you can control the entire ship.

Eislie turned her comm away from Jace as he came into the room.

He said, "Is that the strong whiskey?"

She held it out. "I should have specified that we were saving this one for the celebration. But I think this will do."

Jace nodded, turned, and started toward the door, just as Eislie brought the bottle up and hit him across the back of the head. He fell to the floor, and she stepped over him. She peeked around the corner, asking into her comm, "How many Tharak are on the ship?"

"None, captain. And I now have full control of the flight systems."

Eislie looked around out the door toward the flight control. "Ed, do we still have any weapons onboard?"

The computer responded, "Some in the hold, but the Tharak brought fusion detonators onboard. I think they were planning on destroying the ship."

"Where are they, Ed?"

The computer gave her the location, and she moved quickly. "Close up the ship and let me know when you have full control. Bring the drill online as well." She looked at the detonators. "I think Jace is in real trouble."

.

Chapter 22

None of It's Real

Jace sat with Eislie on the beach. He could feel the water, but it felt the same temperature every time he walked in. The breeze felt warm. He did like the weather back on Gilese, and was missing it somewhat. He turned to see Eislie waving to him, but he still had a feeling that something wasn't right.

As he moved closer, he could see the small two-piece she wore, the light blue one from Earth when they visited over a year ago. *Wait, she got rid of that*, he suddenly remembered. She had complained, "You can't trust Terrans." Not that he didn't approve of the outfit, but she was right; it wasn't something she would really wear.

Jace hesitated before again walking toward her. His steps were staggered. The sand under his feet felt strange, like it was cushioned. He looked up into the sky, the greenish blue of the air seemed to be bluer than he remembered. Out of nowhere, his mind flashed to Eislie falling limp, her arms held by two Tharak.

A moment later he found himself again on the beach. "What the hell was that?" he blurted out.

Eislie looked confused. "Everything alright?"

Jace shook his head. "It's nothing. Just thought I saw something weird."

Eislie hugged him, but it felt off, like there was no warmth in it. "Hey, want to fool around?" she said with a demure tone as she pulled him toward the house. The real Eis would have been more direct. He looked at his hands. They had just touched Eislie but felt different, like he was wearing mittens. He then made a fist and punched his hand hard. He felt pressure but nothing else. With a growing sense of fear, he said, "That should have hurt. Oh shit, this isn't real."

The Tharak in the processing center still had Jace in one of the processing tanks. They had been trying to stabilize him for insertion into one of the updated bio-pods. "I hate processing Terrans," he said. "They always take too long." Their partner only nodded. Their expressions were of people trying to fix a problem but not knowing how.

One Tharak took a closer look at the processing chamber. "The indicators are still erratic. Either he is having a good time, and the upgrades have not synchronized, or he is not under control. But it is difficult to get the control leads into his synapse. It is like his body is fighting us."

The other at the controls said, "We still have to process the female when they bring her in. We have not heard back from the team that accompanied her to the ship." He looked down at the display. Commander Kertol had said to wait for the team to tell them when they could move him to the bio-pod, that the two were being set together as a pair.

The other Tharak said, "Whoever gets the ship will be able to travel further within the filaments. I wish I could go."

The other Tharak gave what sounded like a huff. "We are Sassa, only chosen when our brood leader makes the choice. Besides, our brood leader is Zacseil. He has chosen to stay planetside. We have little chance of joining any vessel."

The Tharak sighed as they sat. "Sometimes I think I was decanted from the wrong brood tank. Let us see if we can get this Terran under control."

* * *

On the *Wolfhammer*, Eislie made sure all the doors were closed. She still didn't know what had happened to Jace, although she was sure whoever or whatever was unconscious on the floor wasn't him. She could hear the Tharak banging on the side door. Ed had full control of the ship, and she pulled out the control board she and Jace had been trying to replace. "Ed, do you think the flight system will be adjusted in time if we need to leave fast?" she asked as she grabbed a crew jacket and placed a few of the detonators in the pockets.

"I believe so, Captain, although I do not wish to leave without Captain Tucker. Do you have a plan to find him?"

Eislie could hear the side door being forced open, the actuators seeming to fight the Tharak trying to open the door. Eislie was surprised and muttered, "They shouldn't be able to do that."

The computer overheard and responded, "The Tharak seem to have developed infiltration hardware that can circumvent the secure locking mechanism. I am doing my best to delay their entry."

"I know, Ed. We need to get them away from the ship. Can you fly yet?"

"I have standard flight control, although I am still working on integrating the tunnel system. If we were to use it now, it would be unstable. I estimate one hour until I have fully integrated and supplemented the system. We still need to find Captain Tucker."

"I know, I know. I'm trying to get the sensors to look for him, but there's a lot of interference. I keep seeing tens of thousands of Terran and Gilese life signs. It's like the sensors are malfunctioning."

"One moment, Captain. I can verify with the sensors I have online." There was a brief delay before the computer spoke again. "Captain, there are tens of thousands of Gilese and Terran life signs. And they all have Lyri markers. All in one area."

Eislie's head slowly looked up, her voice filled with disbelief and fear. "They all have Lyri markers?" She sank back in her chair. "We're in trouble, Ed. Big trouble."

"It appears so, Captain."

Eislie turned as the door groaned against the Tharak attempting entry. Her eyes were wide as she said, "Ed, if they get through the outside door, I think the inside will be easier. There are controls that are easier to access." She thought for a moment, then continued, "Ed, if they get in, lift off."

Just as the order was given, the outside door fully opened, and the computer did as ordered. The ship lifted off and some of the Tharak fell from the airlock. She could hear them cutting into the control panel and moved closer to the door. She didn't have time to grab any weapons. She took one of the detonators from her pocket and looked at it, then looked at the door. The computer remarked, "Captain, you have a look very similar to Captain Tucker when he has an unorthodox idea."

Eislie turned to the door controls and opened the door. As she did, she held up the detonator and yelled, "Stop or I'll blow us all up!"

The confused look of the Tharak was almost comical. Eislie could see the outside door open, and she had a thought. She pushed the activator on the detonator and tossed it to the closest Tharak, saying, "Here, get rid of this for me, will you?" She slammed the controls closing the door, then ordered Ed to flip the ship on its side and release gravity.

The ship's computer did as ordered. As Eislie fell onto the wall, she looked at the display to see the Tharak fall out the door. Seconds later, the fusion detonator exploded. She then ordered Ed to right the ship, sitting at her control chair. "Ed, find a Terran life sign that's by itself. I don't think it's been that long since they've taken him. Besides, Jace is really stubborn."

"Yes, Captain, I believe it is a Terran trait."

Eislie smiled. "You're right about that, Ed. And this part-Terran has an idea." She began piloting toward the command center.

A moment later, Ed said, "Captain, I believe I have located Captain Tucker. There is a lone Terran bio-sign near the entryway you went through previously."

"Ed, power up the drill to full power."

The computer hesitated. "Captain, it is not advisable to use the drill on an inhabited facility. Specifically, one so close to where we suspect Captain Tucker may be."

Eislie nodded, her eyes searching around, "I just want them to open the door. If they don't, then we'll make a move."

The *Wolfhammer* hovered near the entrance, its drill focused on the heavy door. Eislie tapped the external comm. "Knock knock. Anyone home? Open up." There was resolve in her eyes as she waited for a reply. Then the comm gave an alert. Cautiously she opened the comm. "Either bring out Jace or I'm coming in after him."

Kertol growled before he spoke. "We have welcomed you to our world, and this is how you treat us?"

"Slac off. That thing you put on our ship isn't Jace. There's a Tharak in the core of that...that *thing*." The growl in her voice told Kertol that she was losing patience.

Kertol looked to Zacseil and said, "I hate processing bonded pairs. Something always goes wrong." He then looked at the screen. "You are too late. We have him in containment. Your best option if you want to see him again is to join him." He disconnected the comm.

Eislie blinked. "Did he just hang up on me?"

"It appears so, Captain," the computer responded. "What do you think we should do?"

Eislie looked at the screen before sighing. "Looks like they want to do this the hard way. Give me control of the drill."

"Captain, I am quite capable of aiming the drill."

"I know, Ed, but I want to be the one to do this. That way, if Jace gets hurt, it'll be my fault. I don't want you to shoulder the guilt."

Reluctantly the control light changed to green, the computer replying, "I understand, Captain."

Eislie slowly pressed on the trigger, burning a hole through the door and then several hundred more meters into the facility. She checked with Ed to make sure what they thought was Jace's bio-sign was stable. After hearing it was, she stood. "Ed, land the ship and have it ready to go. You can defend it at any cost. Use the drill. I don't want any Tharak on this ship when we get back. And make sure they don't take control any other way." She pulled another detonator from her pocket and held it in her hand.

"I have disabled all external interfaces," Ed announced. "The Tharak cannot access the ship remotely. What should we do with the Tharak that looks like Captain Tucker?"

Eislie looked at the unmoving copy of Jace. "Lower gravity. I'll put it outside."

She dragged the body of the Tharak to the airlock and tossed it out before the ship landed. She met with several dozen Tharak all armed as she was exiting. Behind them she could see Kertol rushing down what was left of the facility where the drill had bored into the building. She held the fusion detonator up, showing them all the other ones she had in her jacket. "You shoot me, this thing goes off which will set off all the rest of them. I've removed the timers. There'll be nothing here afterwards but a crater."

Kertol stopped as one of Zacseil's brood worked to repair a power junction. The commander grumbled, "She's too close to the main power generators. Let her inside. We can try and take her then."

His orders were relayed and the armed Tharak drones moved aside. Eislie walked at a steady pace, her eyes stared forward but also scanning all around her. She spoke loud enough for her comm to hear. "Ed, which way?"

She disappeared from Kertol's sight, and he moved forward a few steps. "Get control of that vessel."

Zacseil responded, "They have removed the remote connection. That ACI of theirs has control of the vessel. May I also remind you, Kertol, that you are near the main power generator for nearly half the containment system."

Kertol growled before he responded, "Yes, I am aware. If she blows those detonators here, we'll be up to our thoraxes in angry starborn." He grabbed one of the drones. "Is the male still in processing?" The drone nodded. "Good. Rush down there and take her to him. Maybe it will placate her long enough for us to subdue her." He followed behind..

Chapter 23

What's in the Tank?

The drones led Eislie through the nearby corridors. She held her thumb on the detonator switch the entire time. There were moments when she hesitated because of her sense of self-preservation, and the thought that she wanted to save Jace and get them both out of there. As she rounded the corner, she expected to find herself confronted with many Tharak. Instead, she found a large lab with several vertical tanks, some with people in them. High up along the wall were thousands more. "You people are sick, you know that?" Eislie muttered loudly enough for the Tharak guiding her to hear.

"I do not understand," the drone replied. "We did away with illness long ago."

Eislie rolled her eyes. "I don't mean physically. I mean you're sick in the head." Then she realized it was something Jace would say. She smiled before shaking her head and motioning for the Tharak to continue.

The Tharak stopped, pointing at a lit tank. She couldn't see completely inside, but she knew somehow it was Jace. She wiped away some on the condensate and confirmed her suspicions. "Get him out, now!" she demanded.

The Tharak at the control station calmly looked up at her, saying, "We have not fully integrated the sensory taps. If we remove him now, there will probably be some neural damage."

The other at the controls spoke. "He has been fighting us. There will be some damage, but right now it is easily reversable." The Tharak looked at the other. "Are you bringing her for processing? This one has been very difficult. Every time we think we have him synchronized, he does something that makes us have to recalibrate." Eislie gave him an incredulous look, and he continued, "You really should accept the conditioning. It would make our jobs much easier."

Esilie's expression turned to disbelief before she yelled angrily, "Get him out of there! Now!"

Behind her she heard Kertol say with a commanding voice, "That isn't an option. By now you must realize it's futile to continue this ruse. You have only one choice."

Eislie said, "There's more than one way out of here," but she knew she was lying. She would have to blow something up, either something of theirs or the entire thing at once, including herself and Jace. She scanned the area, her senses running into overload. Whatever it was, there was a lot of it, coming from all around her, and it felt familiar. She almost thought she could touch it; and when she did, it seemed to touch back. She felt her mind awash in thoughts and feelings—fear, hope, love, anger. It made her unsteady for a moment. It was something warm, like she could feel the world around her.

She had felt something like this before while back on Oppa, inside the starborn encampment when she had broken down crying. It had happened when the other starborn had touched her. Whatever energy was there was powerful. She remembered the Oppan instruments frying when they did. "These others are all starborn, aren't they?" she said, knowing the answer already in her mind. On instinct, she reached out to the tanks. Within seconds, hundreds of the tanks' alarms started to sound. As she looked around, it was like she could feel them all.

It took her a moment to realize that the Tharak drones were now dangerously close. Instantly she snapped back to reality, tossing the detonator in her hand toward the approaching Tharak. She then grabbed another from her jacket and held it securely. She didn't know how powerful the explosive was, but seeing the Tharak running as fast as they could from where it landed gave her an idea.

The device hopped over the railing and there was a bright flash of light. The pressure wave could be felt rolling over them. She smiled and said, "Still think I won't use these to get out of here?"

Kertol looked angrily over the fence. When he turned to look at her, she could see terror in his eyes. Her assessment was confirmed when Kertol said, "You slac. The main power generator for this section is down there. If that had detonated and disabled it, it would release everything in this area."

"Thanks for the information," she replied. "I'll throw it harder next time."

Kertol hesitated. He knew if the containment system keeping the starborn sedated was released, the internal hardware would prevent the occupants from being damaged. He knew the protocols were to wake and restrain an occupant if the storage tank failed. The only way a starborn could escape is if they were already in a cell that allowed the copied suit the Tharak used to access the energy. That transition was permanent.

Kertol could see anger in Eislie's eyes, and he knew from experience that any angered starborn was an incident waiting to happen. He also realized that he had now given her something to bargain with. Begrudgingly, he ordered Jace to be released. She watched the drones carefully as they removed the connections, keeping an eye on Kertol as well.

He opened his eyes, and she immediately ran to him, holding onto a detonator but trying to remove the additional connections at the same time. Jace groaned and grabbed the back of his head.

Kertol muttered, "I *hate* bonded pairs."

Jace looked at the drone, but his vision was blurred, overlayed with the images of what the device was feeding into his mind. He looked at Eislie. "It's weird, like I'm watching two TV shows on the same screen and can't turn either of them off." He looked angrily toward Kertol. "Get this fucking thing out of my head."

Kertol gave what looked like a smile before answering, "Not unless she relinquishes the detonators she is holding."

Jace looked at Eislie and she showed him the device. "I sort of blew something up already."

Jace smiled. "Blowing stuff up without me? Well, I guess you should have some hobbies too."

Fed up, Jace reached for the device on the back of his head. With a grunt, then a howl of pain, he pulled it off himself.

As the blood started to drip onto the floor, Eislie yelled at one of the drones, "Get a med kit, now!"

The drone didn't hesitate, which was a surprise to Kertol. Sassa were only supposed to obey their brood commanders. When the drone returned, it aided Eislie in tending to Jace's self-inflicted wound. Kertol ordered the drone to stop, but it took more than a minute for the Tharak to comply.

Within seconds, Jace was up, stumbling as he tried to walk. "Shit, should have let them take the damn thing out. My equilibrium's screwed up."

Eislie held him up. "Well, you just pulled something out of your head. Probably still have some wires still attached in there."

They started toward the other side where Eislie had thrown the detonator earlier. Jace asked, "Any ideas for getting out of here?"

Kertol said, "You are going nowhere. You will both be put into the same tank and serve together as a power source for us to travel the filaments."

Jace asked Eislie, "What did you almost blow up earlier?" She pointed to the railing they were now nearby. "You have another one of those things?" Eislie nodded, pulling the release on one of the remaining detonators from her jacket and giving it to him. He briefly examined the small device before tossing it gently over his shoulder. "We should probably duck now." The two fell to the floor.

There was a bright flash. The entire suspended floor they were on lurched and swayed. Kertol was near the edge, looking over in disbelief, when Jace lunged at him, pushing him over the railing. The commander howled in pain as he hit the floor underneath. "That should keep them busy while we get out of here."

The two of them did their best to run, the Tharak now busy trying to stop the rest of the power system from cascading into overload and failing completely. Jace heard a suddenly released captor in the distance yell, "I'm going to kill all you bastards!"

He smiled. "Sounds like they took someone from Earth."

Eislie smiled herself, then said into her comm, "Ed, you ready to get out of here?"

The computer responded, "Affirmative. I have full control of the ship systems, and the drive and navigation systems are also on the new system. The ship can no longer be controlled. I am awaiting your arrival."

"We're on our way, Ed. What's the foot traffic look like?"

"There are several dozen Tharak waiting for you. One moment." Ed powered the ship's laser, vaporizing the Tharak. "The way is currently clear, Captains. We will lift off once you are onboard."

Kertol was being attended to when he heard the ship fire. "Get those starborn!" he yelled. "Bring them to me now!"

He watched the video feed as the two starborn rushed onboard their vessel. Pounding the comm station, he ordered, "Get that ship back under our control!"

Zacseil responded, "We have been trying, but they have disabled the entire integrated system."

The brood commander growled, "Then ready a retrieval ship. I want those two alive."

Kertol did his best to move quickly, but his injuries were severe. He could hear the cries and angry yelling from all the starborn now being released from their storage pods. He could also hear the defense team's starting to report that they were pulling back. Kertol tapped his comm again. "Zacseil, how many starborn have been released?"

There was a pause before Zacseil answered, "The junction they damaged has cascaded. Nearly half the ones in storage have woken up. Nearly seven thousand at this point, Commander. They have also begun seizing weapons from the Sassa they have subdued."

Stunned, Kertol slowed as he made his way outside. The hole the starborn ship had made was larger than he had originally thought. He watched as the Takloh vessel, one similar to many they had scrapped for being useless, flew off into space. The two starborn had released several thousand now very angry starborn. Kertol tapped his comm. "Is the retrieval vessel ready?"

Zacseil annoyed, responded, "Almost, Commander."

"Let me know when it is. I'm bringing those two back here myself."

Chapter 24

Nowhere to Run

Eislie had only connected one of her harness latches as she flew. Jace had slumped into his command chair, his hand hovering over the weapons control. She could see his eyes trying to focus on the screen. "Are you alright?" she asked, very concerned.

Jace only responded, "Yeah. Let's get out of here."

They made their way through the atmosphere, with Ed alerting them that the Tharak were still attempting to override the flight systems. "Ed, make sure you don't have a full connection to that board," Jace responded. "I don't want them finding a back door in or something." He then grasped his head, apparently in pain.

Eislie looked at him out of the corner of her eyes, her tone concerned as she asked again, "Are you alright?"

Jace nodded but said nothing. His neck and the back of his head were pounding, but he didn't have time to head to the med bay. That would leave Eislie here all by herself. Instead, he looked at her and smiled. "Let's get away from here first, then worry about me."

She watched him face the screen again. He was moving slower than normal. She could feel the pain he was experiencing. She bit her lip, then focused on flying. Her only words were, "When we get into hyperspace, you're going to the med bay." She watched Jace's head nod slightly. She could see his mouth open slightly and could hear him let out a metered breath.

"We have ships in pursuit, Captains," Ed warned. "They are not gaining, but we are also not moving away from them."

"We need to get out of here," Jace growled, his breathing now more labored. "Fire up the tunnel drive. I don't care where we go, just get us ahead of them."

Eislie was keeping ahead of the Tharak on their tail, so Jace entered some coordinates. "I'm taking ussss per...perp...en...dicluar to the plane." He continued typing, then held the back of his head before muttering, "Damn that fucking hurts."

"You're not alright, are you?" Eislie said, very concerned.

"Eis. Ship. Fly. Worry about me later. If we don't get out of here, they'll do the same thing to you. Just fly. I'll be fine." He hit the tunnel drive controls, and they were gone in a flash.

On the Tharak vessel, Kertol didn't have time to put on the bio-suit he originally wore. The medical bandages would not allow him to operate the controls. He was waiting for another pilot and their corresponding bio-pod to be loaded into the retrieval ship. The preparations were nearly complete when he heard Zacseil on the comm. "We have word that the starborn vessel has entered hyperspace. Currently leaving our orbital plane. The Hive Masters have requested that all brood leaders are to help in subduing the freed starborn. They are commanding no lives be taken."

Kertol growled into his comm as the pilot finally arrived. "I'm retrieving those two. They are the ones who caused this. We can use the female to placate all the starborn who are still in the tanks. And we can use the anesthetic gas to take care of the others." There was silence on the comm. "Did you hear me, Zacseil?"

"The Hive masters have spoken. Are you denying a direct order?" Zacseil said with a measured tone.

Kertol paused before responding, "No. I believe these two are the key to controlling the others. I will return with them and prove that to the hive."

Over the comm, he heard a response from the Hive Masters. "If that is the case, return with the two who have caused this. If it is not proven, you will suffer the consequences."

Kertol looked around as if everyone had heard the command, and even being a brood leader, he had to obey. "I understand. I will not fail the hive."

He turned to look at the drones finishing up the installation, motioning for them to hurry. He then tapped his comm again. "Zacseil, we're almost ready. Were you able to activate the tracker?"

There was a noticeable delay before Zacseil responded, "Yes. It is active. We are currently tracking the ship in hyperspace. It is vertical to our plane."

Kertol looked up at the sky. "We have a filament nearby. It goes in that direction. There is a heavy gravity body along the route as well. They will be dragged out of hyperspace. I will head there now and capture them when they arrive."

* * *

Eislie was fighting the controls as she flew. "Ed, what the slac is happening?" she yelled, trying to keep the ship under control.

There was a long delay before the computer replied, "Captain, the alignment of the tunnel coils is not synchronized with the new control system. I apologize; I had not considered that the new system would not regulate as quickly."

Jace was holding his head as he asked, "Can we fix it while flying?"

"No, Captain. We would need to take the tunnel system offline. The realignment should not take more than two standard hours."

Eislie turned looking at him with concern. "Get to the med bay. Don't be a stubborn Terran."

Jace chuckled, saying, "Yes, Captain." He released his harness and stood. With the movement of the ship and his injuries, he was unsteady and held onto the back of his chair. Suddenly, the ship lurched, and Eislie pulled at the controls. The sudden movement had Jace's face meeting the floor, causing him to forget the pain in the back of his head temporarily. He grumbled as he pushed up with his hands. "Eis, I'm gonna stay in my chair, if that's alright. I'm not feeling any pain, but I don't think this turbulence is going to be any good if the med systems have to work on something delicate. Like my brain."

Eislie thought for a moment. "Yeah, probably not a good idea right now. Strap in again."

Jace wrestled into his chair, his body falling into the seat. It took a few moments before he buckled his harness. "Floor it. Let's get as far away as possible. We'll jump out and make a second jump. Make it difficult to track us."

Eislie could hear him more coherently now, and she did exactly that. She snickered at hearing Jace say, "Let's just hope they can't track us."

Kertol was sitting in one of the drone's seats. The pilot was taking them through the filament, and they were nearing the exit point. "Sassa, do you still have the starborn ship's signal?" he asked.

"Yes, Commander, we have their signal. They are still on the same route."

Kertol thought for a second, then tapped the keys on the nearby console. He pulled up the charts for that area and a smile spread across his face. "The heavy gravity body will take them out of hyperspace in approximately twenty standard minutes." He looked at the pilot. "When we exit the filament, we will head to these coordinates."

"Location confirmed, Commander. Exit to filament in approximately five standard."

Kertol leaned back in his chair. "Excellent. Have a sonic disabler activated and armed. We'll capture those two and their vessel."

Within minutes the Tharak vessel was back in normal space and on its way toward the heavy gravity body. As it slowed, Commander Kertol seemed to be in a much happier mood. "Keep sensors open for any sign of that ship. Once we capture them, I'll put them into our system myself."

Eislie was fighting the controls the entire time and was startled when the computer alerted them to a problem. "Heavy gravity object detected, Captains. We are losing tunnel stability. Entering normal space."

"You've gotta be f...aaaah!" Jace exclaimed as he grabbed his head again in pain.

Eislie wasn't any happier. "Slac! How close are we to the, uh, thing?" She looked to Jace. "I'm so pissed right now, I can't even think."

Jace nodded, seeing the scene changing as they entered normal space. "I can tell. Ed, plot a cor—"

He was interrupted as the ship was pulled sideways. The gravity compensation alarm was now blaring. "Shit. We're caught in the gravity well."

"Antigrav and grav drives are maxed. Slac, this is bad," Eislie growled as she worked to free them from the hold of the gravity. She looked at the screen. "Ed, can you identify the object and direction?"

"Yes, Captain. Port side. The heavy gravity body seems to be a singularity. If I didn't know better, I would say it is a gravity tunnel. I must add, it would be an excellent item to examine, if it weren't trying to pull us in."

Eislie chuckled. "He's starting to sound like you, Jace."

Jace smiled in agreement. "We should get free. I think we're safe for the moment." He grabbed the back of his head. "Man, this really hurts."

Eislie was concerned. "We'll get free and back into hyperspace. Maybe the ride will be easier. And we can get you into the med bay."

Jace quietly nodded. She could see the pain behind his eyes.

It took them several minutes before Eislie nearly had them free from the grip of the heavy gravity body. She looked at Jace, who was unusually quiet. "You alright?"

Jace's eyes lifted as he stared forward. "Peachy, with the exception of the pounding headache I've got." His head turned toward the back of the ship. "I'm heading to the med bay."

Eislie gave a relieved sigh as she said, "Ed, let's get back into hyperspace. How soon till we're far enough away?"

Jace stood and had taken a step when suddenly the ship was rocked by an unknown force, knocking him to the ground. They heard the sounds of what seemed like several impacts on the hull before the computer said, "We are under attack. My sensors did not pick up the ship until it moved closer. It appears to be a Tharak vessel."

On the Tharak ship, a drone announced, "Commander, they are stuck in the gravity well of the anomaly."

Kertol smiled. "Then they are unable to run. Seems as if we're having some luck today. Fire the disabler. Once we know they're incapacitated, we'll take the ship out of the anomaly's influence."

On the *Wolfhammer*, Eislie said, "Ed, plot course." She turned to look at Jace. "You'll have to hold on for a little longer."

She watched as Jace pushed against the ground again, but his arms became unsteady. She could see the fear filling his eyes as he spoke. "Eisssss. I'm, I, uh…. Shit, hurts…bad." His words faltered as he slumped to the floor.

"Jace! No, no. Jace, get up," Eislie pleaded. But her words were soon overshadowed as she heard the loud impact of an object piercing the hull of the *Wolfhammer*.

"Hull breach," Ed announced. "Enacting emergency maneuvers. Captain Licessien, I am detecting too many variances in Captain Tucker's vitals. Take him to the med bay. I will take control of the ship."

Eislie nearly ripped the harness from her chair as she unbuckled it. She quickly grabbed Jace and pulled him toward the med bay. "Ed, once I get him stable, I'll be back to fly."

"Please care for Captain Tucker, Captain. I will do my best to get us free from the gravity well and these attackers."

Eislie lifted Jace, grunting, "I'm glad that thing that hit us didn't explode."

"As am I, Capta—" But Eislie could no longer hear the computer, as a deafening sound filled her ears. It seemed to be coming from all around her. Even when she yelled, she couldn't hear her own voice. As the sound increased, she felt the vibrations within her own body. Her ears were screaming in pain until suddenly she heard nothing. She could only feel the vibrations of the sounds all around her. She reached up to touch her ear but alarmingly pulled her hand back. It was covered in blood.

Seconds later, the pain moved to her head, and she felt her equilibrium leave her. She fell to the floor, Jace laying motionless beside her. She struggled as her vision started to lose focus. She could feel the floor vibrating beneath her as her head finally touched it. She felt her head bouncing on the metal as she turned to see blood running from Jace's ears.

Ed watched as Eislie mouthed the word "no," reaching out to touch Jace before her body went limp, and he could no longer read her biosensor. The weapon that hit the ship was using the ship's hull to produce the sound. His own systems were becoming affected, and he was having trouble fighting the gravity. He could see the Tharak vessel moving closer. He could see the magnetic anchors attaching to the hull of the ship.

"Captains, I will not let them take you," he said, even knowing his captains couldn't hear him. "You asked me to destroy the ship if you were killed. I...I will not let them take you. I am sending a goodbye message to our friends." He turned off the antigrav and grav drives, allowing the full effect of the gravity well to take its course.

Aboard the Tharak ship, one of the drones alerted the commander of the situation. "Commander, they have tuned off all propulsion and countermeasures. We are unable to hold them without being drawn into the effects of the anomaly."

There was suddenly a lot of activity onboard the Tharak vessel as the effects of the anomaly started to pull at the ship. Kertol could hear the structure holding the towing cables groaning. He looked around before ordering them released. He stood, his stance full of anger. "What a waste of two perfectly good starborn." He then ordered the pilot to move away from the anomaly. As the ship neared the event horizon, he watched as the *Wolfhammer* disappeared.

Ed continued to reinforce the shields. He didn't want to be destroyed, but he also knew that the situation they were in was one they would not return from. He refused to shut his systems down. He suspected that his captains were gone, and he thought about how he had failed them. But then his sensors picked up something. He couldn't believe what he was seeing. A gravity tunnel.

The computer examined the anomaly. The tunnel was just large enough for the ship. He brought the grav drives back online and did his best to maneuver. As they fell deeper, he could no longer see the Tharak vessel. He continued for several minutes until the tunnel ended, and he could see light all around. As his sensors adjusted, he could see what looked like a small planet beneath him. Maneuvering became easier and he lowered the ship to the surface.

As the ship touched down, the power systems started to fluctuate. The Spide system destabilized and became inoperable. There were several warnings as the weapon continued to vibrate the ship. He could feel several systems being affected and shutting down. He was going to change to the tritium system, but his systems were starting to shut down. As the cameras cut out, he realized he would have to shut down to preserve his own core systems. Ed readied for the inevitable. Just before his systems shut off, he said to the unconscious Jace and Eislie, "Thank you, Captains. You have shown me so much."

Chapter 25

Where are We?

Eislie felt pressure on her back. It was unfamiliar, like she was lying in a hard but cushioned bed. She opened her eyes to see bright light above. There seemed to be a grey haze all around. The air felt strange. She shifted her body, her head rolling to the side. Her eyes met a startling sight. Fear suddenly filled her, and she tried to yell. There were several nearly translucent beings moving around Jace. She was afraid they were harming him, and she yelled, "Leave him alone!"

She couldn't hear herself, but she knew she was speaking; she could feel her vocal cords, and could see the aliens look toward her. She tried to push herself up from the table, but she had no strength. One of the aliens calmly approached her, gently touching Eislie's forehead. There was a soft glow, and Eislie heard something in her mind. *We will not harm him. We are repairing his injuries from what the Tharak have done.*

Eislie tried moving again, her eyes pleading as they started to fill with tears. "Don't hurt him, please."

The alien gave her a smile. *We will not. His injuries are more severe than yours. We will heal you in a moment. Now rest.*

Eislie tried again to push away from the table but felt herself growing tired. She couldn't keep her eyes open. Just before she fell unconscious, she again repeated, "Don't hurt him."

The alien nodded. *Sleep. We will have you both healed shortly.*

As the alien returned to the others working on Jace, she said, "The female is very protective of this one. It is good to see that the descendants of the Lyri are still around. Durin, how are this one's injuries?"

The other alien was using a wand to manipulate and remove the wires from Jace's head and body. Annoyed, they replied, "The Tharak have no conscience. They tried overlaying the sensory synapse of this one. It does not look like it is experimental, which leads me to believe they have done this many times before." He straightened. "I will be finished in a short while. We will be able to regenerate the tissues." There was a slight pause. "Lakai? Should we recreate the information stored in the damaged brain cells?"

Lakai turned to look at Eislie. "Yes. Download the affected areas and recreate them." The alien's face filled with sadness. "The female has much less damage, mostly to her auditory sensing organs. But download and recreate the affected areas in her as well. Document everything you find about the integration process the Tharak have developed, and report to me or Yon."

The alien walked toward the observation area, where another alien stood watching the procedures. He shifted from an annoyed stance as Lakai approached. "This is a waste," he said. "You know what's going to happen to them eventually."

Lakai smiled. "I do, Yon. But, while they still can, they should at least be comfortable. It appears the Tharak have been perfecting sensory over-connections to use their energy adaptation. I am not interested in saving them in particular. I am more interested in what the Tharak have done to them."

"Yes, I agree. It seems those slac have become more horrid in their actions than we anticipated." He sighed. "It seems we still must continue to hide from them as well. It is a shame. I particularly liked this part of the universe."

Lakai nodded silently before she said, "Yes. So many ephemeral lifeforms to study." She looked again at Eislie, then at Jace. A subtle smile grew on her face. "It has been some time since we have interacted with any from Lyri. Well, in this part of the universe, anyway."

"Hrumph. The others are nothing like these two." Yon paused. "Well, when they are ready, show them around. They can be in wonder, at least while they still can." Lakai nodded. As Yon turned to leave, he said, "I am ordering others to go to their ship. Perhaps its memory will explain how they made it through a gravity protected gateway."

Eislie opened her eyes again and immediately started looking for Jace. She was happy to see him still nearby. One of the aliens seemed to be doing something with a small device over Jace's head. Eislie sat up, demanding, "Leave him alone."

Eislie was startled to finally hear her own voice again. Her reaction was found amusing by the alien, causing her to laugh, a sort of humming, squishing sound. Eislie's muscles tightened as the alien approached. "Ah, a fight response," it said, out loud as well this time. "I see. You are worried about your partner."

Eislie nodded, then asked, "What were you doing to him?"

"Your partner had severe neural damage. I was inspecting the regeneration. He seems to be no worse for wear."

Eislie looked concerned. "I hope it doesn't affect his memory."

The alien gave what sounded like a chuckle. "Do not worry. We have copied the memories that were present into the new tissue."

Eislie showed fear for the first time. "You what? Uh, how?"

The alien gave a subtle smile. "We are quite knowledgeable about those with Lyri DNA. I suppose introductions are in order. Please understand that you are safe, and that we wish you no harm. My name is Lakai. My people brought you in and healed your injuries."

Eislie swung her feet over the edge of the bed, only to have Lakai rush to support her. "Please wait. I must do a scan of the repairs to make sure they are complete." She held a device over Eislie's head and moved it from side to side. "You had extensive auditory and partial neurological damage from the Tharak weapon. How is your hearing? Too loud? Too low? Do we need to make any adjustments?"

Eislie gave a simple answer of "no" before jumping off the bed and rushing to Jace. She placed her hand on his face. Lakai remained silent, watching as Eislie touched him and smiled. The alien was a little confused when Eislie said, "It's him. You didn't copy him."

Lakai took a step closer. "Someone copied him?"

Eislie nodded. "The Tharak. They made a Jace suit for one of their people. They thought I wouldn't notice." Eislie looked at the alien. "Uh, Lakai, is he alright?"

Lakai smiled. "A hint of trust? Hmm. To answer your question, he is as he was before the Tharak modified him. As are you. We have merely repaired the damage."

"And where is our ship?"

"Your ship is where it landed. Our people are there now."

Eislie showed a hint of anger. What are they doing to it?"

The alien could sense the anger this woman had and remained where she stood before touching the side of her head. Where her fingers touched, it glowed. *Lakai to survey team*, she asked through a telepathic link. *What is your status?*

We are a bit busy. Their vessel implemented a self-destruct sequence as soon as we started it up. It is demanding we return the people we have in recovery.

Hmm, I see. Let me see if I can get some help from one of our guests. She looked at Eislie. "It seems that they are having difficulty with your vessel. It is demanding your return, or it will destroy itself."

Eislie went to access her comm but found nothing on her arm. She picked up Jace's arm but remembered that the Tharak had removed his earlier. She looked at the alien with some surprise. "You mean Ed's okay?"

Lakai seemed amused. "Your artificial lifeform is named Ed? I would have thought it would have chosen a more formal name. That is surprising."

"Do you know where my comm is? I want to speak with him."

The alien pointed to a small table near the bed where Eislie had been. "It is there. You may use it if you wish."

Eislie pushed past Lakai and grabbed the comm, tapping it. "Ed, it's Eis. We're okay."

Lakai could telepathically hear, *the computer has stopped demanding their return, but is now demanding we leave.*

Eislie said, "Ed, they healed us. I'm just waiting for Jace to wake up. They said he had a lot more damage." She looked suspiciously at Lakai and asked her, "What do you want on our ship?"

The alien responded, "To find out how you got here. Your ship entered the event horizon but survived to make its way through the access we have hidden there."

Eislie looked at the floor, her blue eyes innocently staring back. "You're telling the truth."

As Eislie spoke, Lakai could sense her empathic evaluation. *This one has advanced empathic abilities.* Lakai looked at Jace. *The poor male. He probably cannot get away with anything.*

Eislie said, "Ed, did you record how we made it here?"

"Yes, Captain. Please, you and Captain Tucker must return to the ship. These aliens are attempting to read and modify my systems. I do not wish to be taken offline or modified. Please hurry." He sounded almost panicked.

Eislie's eyes turned cold. "Have your people leave. Don't touch anything on that ship. If you hurt Ed, I'll—"

Eislie was interrupted as Jace grabbed her side with his hand. "*We'll* hurt you," he growled.

Eislie turned, a happy smile on her face as she lowered her head, touching his. "You're awake."

Jace groaned as he sat up, his actions causing Lakai to move toward them. But Jace's eyes met the alien's, and she paused. As she was about to move again, she could see the stare coming from Eislie. Lakai stopped and waved a small device in front of them. A moment later she gave an amused huff. "That would explain it. You both have Terran in you."

"What's that supposed to mean?" Jace asked, insulted.

Lakai chuckled again before saying, "How many have you driven away, warned, or frightened by simply staring at them? That Terran glare, the one that needs no words to convey the thought, 'Keep coming and find out how I am going to kill you.'" The alien moved closer. "We have studied people from Earth before. You are quite unique. We have found very few who are like you."

Jace raised his brow. "Like us how, exactly?"

Lakai moved closer, holding the device to Jace's head and taking readings. "That is a discussion for later. Your regeneration was accelerated. Hopefully you are not feeling any ill effects from the Tharak modifications."

Jace ignored the alien and looked at Eislie. "At least Ed's still working. Give me your comm." She handed it over and he said, "Ed, it's Jace. You alright?"

"The aliens are still on board. I currently have little resources for defending myself. They seem to be immune to the gravity system."

Jace looked at Lakai and said, "I don't want to be rude. You did heal us, after all. But would you mind getting your people off our ship?"

Lakai tapped the side of her head. It again glowed. They then heard Ed say, "They are leaving, Captains. I will lock up the ship and await your return."

Jace gave a contrite "thank you" and turned to Eislie. "Last I remember, we were trying not to be sucked into a black hole."

"Actually, you failed at that," Lakai said.

Jace and Eislie looked at each other, and from both came a drawn out, "We what?"

They heard a squishy humming come from the alien. "I do so love Terrans. You have such amusing reactions to unusual situations." Eislie was about to correct Lakai but was stopped when the alien said, "You were drawn into the event horizon. You somehow found your way through the gravity tunnel we use for our vessels." She looked annoyed before saying, "We will have to discuss our options." She turned to Jace. "I have introduced myself to your partner, Eislie. My name is Lakai. I welcome you."

Jace gave a slow, unsure wave. "And where exactly are we?"

Lakai moved away, placing the small monitoring device on the table. "You are on an artificially created planetary body within an extra-dimensional construction."

Jace looked around. "So we're on a planet made by you, inside a pocket dimension?"

Lakai again could be heard making a humming and squishing sound, before saying, "Exactly. Although that is somewhat of an oversimplification."

"So we survived plunging into a black hole by finding our way to a constructed planet in an artificial dimension." Eislie said, not believing her own words.

Jace chimed in, "I think this is probably one of the strangest days we've ever had. Which is saying a lot."

Eislie nodded. "Yep, I think so too."

Lakai laughed loudly, humming and squishing filling the room. "Oh my. I think you are my favorite beings. You have such wonderful depths of observation."

Jace looked confused, remarking, "I don't know whether to feel complimented or insulted."

Lakai moved closer. "It was meant as a compliment. If you are interested, I would like to show you around."

Chapter 26

The Lyri Secret

The alien guided Jace and Eislie through the wide hallway, its walls glowing gently. Jace found himself trusting this alien, someone he had never met before, but also someone he didn't feel fear around. Eislie seemed to trust her as well. But why? It was like he had met them before. He said, "It seems foggy in here, but it doesn't seem to move when I wave at it."

Eislie looked around. "I thought it was just me. I wonder if it's the starlight? You know, like on Yata."

Jace asked Lakai, "Is there a star in here with us?"

Lakai gave what sounded like a chuckle. "Oh, there are no stars here. All the light you are seeing is from the matter of the universe itself." She appeared to be in thought. "Although, I have not heard it called fog-like before. Most see a sort of sparkle in the air."

"Sparkle?" Jace looked around. "That'd be pretty annoying after a while."

"Some we have brought here have complained, but not many. Usually it was just before, uh, their time was up."

The hallway seemed to be getting longer as they walked. Jace was about to make the observation when Lakai said, "You are wondering why the hallway seems to be never-ending, are you not?"

Jace stopped. "Wait, you can read minds?"

"Only when in physical contact. I knew in this case because others have asked the question when reaching this area."

Jace placed his hands on his hips. "Okay, I'll bite. Why is the hallway so long?"

Their host gave a smile before answering, "Because it is being constructed as we walk. The environment outside would, uh, deteriorate you more quickly."

Eislie said, "How bad is the environment?"

"You could breathe, but the radiation has a much higher density."

"Spide radiation?"

Lakai nodded.

"Well, we can handle that most of the time."

"That may be true, but the radiation density may be an issue."

Jace became concerned. "So, we're not spide-proof?"

Lakai then made a remark that sent chills down both their spines. "You are in your universe, but you would not last long in ours. The Lyri, however,

117

were quite an adaptive species. Spide radiation only killed some before they gained an immune resistance. Over millions of years, they adapted to many things."

"You seem to know a lot about the Lyri, and in some way, about us," Eislie said with a hint of reserve.

"We know much about almost all the species in this galaxy."

In the distance, their ship came into view. The light walls seemed to expand around them as they neared. Jace and Eislie could see another of the aliens standing nearby the ship. When they arrived, the alien spoke. "It would be in your best interest if this vessel did not explode. The spide radiation would not affect us, but the percussion wave would damage this base and probably kill you in the process."

Lakai sighed before saying, "Jace, Eislie, this is Supreme Commander Yon. He is the current administrator of this facility."

After a polite wave, Jace asked, "What were you doing on our ship?"

Yon answered, "We were trying to ascertain if your vessel kept a record of the flight through the tunnel we created. Although it may not be necessary now, with the other actions we are planning."

"What actions?" Jace said with concern.

"Nothing you need to be worried about. It is for our safety only. You will not be harmed in any way." Yon paused. "That is, unless you choose to be in the way."

Jace understood the warning. "Well, we'll try not to stay too long," he said as he turned to Eislie. "Let's check the ship out and then we can discuss our options."

Jace reached out to grab the handle of the door, but his hand passed right through it. He pulled back, then tried again and felt the familiar metal. Seeing this event caused Yon and Lakai to look at each other. They watched the two move through the ship, checking systems and making sure they were in working order. The two aliens had a brief conversation.

"The fading is about on schedule," Lakai said. "I estimate that they will last approximately thirty more hours."

"I agree," Yon said. "I believe they will be happy when they go. Most of them are, but some become afraid."

Jace and Eislie emerged from the ship. Both were now wearing crew jackets and new comms. "Everything seems in order," Jace said. "We're going to try to leave now."

Yon seemed amused. "Leave? You would need to escape the event horizon. That would be impossible without dimensional shielding."

Jace took a step back. "Are you forbidding us from leaving?"

"On the contrary. You may leave any time you wish. It is only that I believe you would destroy yourselves if you attempted to do so."

"Got any dimensional shielding we could borrow?"

Eislie giggled. "We've just met them and you're already asking to borrow their stuff?"

"Eis, it's weird. I don't know why, but I trust these people."

Eislie looked relieved. "I thought it was just me."

Yon seemed to chuckle. "That may be part of your genetics. At least unintentionally. The Lyri, your ancestors, were not the first beings we befriended in this universe. There is another with similar attributes of adaptability we have met previously. The familiarity issue may stem to the interactions of our people and your previous ancestors." He tuned to Lakai. "This may be too delicate a subject for them to understand."

Lakai took a breath. "Your ancestors adapted quickly. We may have made some improvements to prevent an issue."

Jace's expression went from one of innocence to annoyance. "Spill it. What'd you do?"

"Your people share energy, like our own. We made that stronger. It made things easier for our research. That and the environment was altered to be similar to what we have here."

Jace dragged his hands down his face. "You were afraid our ancestors would kill you, weren't you?" Lakai nodded and he continued, "I'm feeling some of that urge right now myself."

Yon chuckled. "We have no doubt you would, which is why we are remaining as accommodating as possible."

"But you could kill us easily, couldn't you?" Eislie said.

Yon nodded. "We do not want to harm you. But we will also not help you."

Jace threw his hands up. "Okay, so you'll let us leave, but we have to do it on our own? Who do you people think you are?"

Lakai smiled. "You know us as the Ha'ak."

Jace didn't have any particular reaction to the information, but Eislie responded much differently. "You're the Ha'ak?"

Jace turned to her. "That means something to you?"

Eislie moved closer to Lakai and touched her, then pulled back. "They're real. We're actually meeting the Ha'ak. Don't you remember? There are only a few races resistant to Spide radiation. Lyri, the Ha'ak, Daak, and…"

"The Duggor," Jace said with some disdain.

Yon nodded. "The Duggor were the first race we ever encountered, although their current actions are not preferred. The descendants of Lyri are not the only ones they are hunting."

Jace's eyes widened. "That's why you're here. To stay hidden from them."

"Yes. The fascinating part is that the Lyri and Duggor have a common attribute. The energy they have is shared among their people. It makes them resilient and powerful. But the Lyri did not want to conquer. At least not at first. The Duggor have a shared energy, a shared mind. They are somewhat unique, like individuals but with a shared dominant personality. The energy that connects them allows them to communicate telepathically, like we do. It was something they learned from us."

"Why did you let them do that?" Eislie seemed appalled.

"We did not think they would succeed. That was an underestimation on our part. Of course, we have known them for well over thirty million of your years."

"Wait, how old are you?" Jace asked.

Lakai thought for a moment. "We have been here exploring this universe for roughly two hundred million of your years. However, time here moves differently. Faster."

Jace looked like he'd suddenly had a realization. "Wait, that means you're…" Eislie looked at him, confused, and he continued with excitement, "Forget about that. That means when we enter the filaments, we're traveling at a different time differential. That explains why we can cross longer

119

distances faster. It's like we're time traveling in one universe but not in the other."

Eislie's eyes got wide. "I never thought about it that way. How hyperspace works the differential is, uh, different."

Yon then said, "Technically you are jumping into our universe when using the filaments. It is just that you cannot break out of the stream. We found a way to do that long ago. But I digress. It is part of the reason the Duggor are being driven like they currently are, and why they are hunting both you and us. We can communicate even through the dimensional barrier, and we can retrieve energy if needed. The Duggor can only communicate, but the energy cannot leave the stream it is in.

"So, the energy is still communicating with the Duggor as a whole, but they are lost in the dimensions the filaments create. They are being driven by those lost in the filaments. When a Lyri is lost, the others mourn and then move on. The energy that connects the Lyri together is severed or absorbed. With the Duggor, the energy that connects them calls to them, pleading to be a part of the whole again. They tried healing themselves. What was that planet they used to live on? Reothes, I think it was called?"

Jace huffed, "We've been there. Creepy place."

"They created a creature, a revenant, a part of themselves for those trapped to speak to. They tried to cut themselves off from the constant crying out. It worked for a while, but then when the creature could no longer bear the strain, it rebelled. It forced them off their world, then laid waste to it."

Eislie said with a serious tone, "That's what we were sensing. We both thought something was staring at us when we were there."

"It didn't attack you?" Yon asked curiously.

Jace shook his head. "Even I could feel like something was watching. If that thing is still there, it's all alone."

Eislie said, "I don't think it's alone. I think it was angry the Duggor didn't help it cope with the screaming voices." She shook her head. "That sounds so weird to say."

Lakai said, "That creature attacks everyone it doesn't want on the planet. That is why it is barren. But it did not attack you. That is odd."

Ed interrupted their conversation. "Captains, the entire area is flooded with spide radiation. It seems to be closer to an inversion. But there are unusual readings. Are you feeling any effects?"

"We're alright, Ed," Jace said. "Lakai said the energy is denser here, whatever that means. But so far, we're not feeling anything bad."

Lakai said, "We should show you around some more. You should not worry about such things. Come, we will show you what the planet really looks like."

Jace, suspicious, asked, "Why?"

"I mentioned earlier that the Lyri adapted. They not only adapted to the radiation, but they adapted to the results of its misuse."

Eislie looked around. "Ed said this was like an inversion. This dimension is a trapped inversion, isn't it?"

Another Ha'ak walking by suddenly said, "Oh, they are still here. Is it a new record?"

Lakai seemed annoyed, and Jace was about to say something when his face filled with a terrified stare, making Eislie ask, "What is it?"

Jace looked at his hand. "Eis, remember that time I put my hand in that inversion field when we helped those people trying to steal the drone we made?"

"Yes. Your hand seemed to disappear for a moment. Why?" Jace looked at his hand and then at the handle of the door. It took a moment before Eislie answered her own question. "Oh no."

Jace became serious. "We can't stay here, can we?"

Lakai words softened. "You can only exist in this place for a short time. No Lyri descendants have gone more than fifty-four standard hours. That's about the length of a day on Lyri. The radiation will change you or corrupt you."

"And that means?"

"One possibility is that you become like us. The other is, well, let's say less corporeal." She seemed in thought. "Although I have heard rumors that some Lyri descendants have retained Ha'ak properties. But I have never seen one personally. But let us not dwell on the issue. Let me show you something."

Suddenly the walls around them disappeared and a desolate rocky landscape appeared beneath their feet. Lakai guided them to a place where ships were being repaired. "This is where we store the vessels we use to explore your universe."

Jace looked at Lakai. "You say that like you're not from this universe. In fact, you've said that several times now."

Lakai stood tall. "I never said we were. This radiation, what you call spide, is what our home is like. The crystals you use are the densest form. And as I mentioned earlier, time moves differently there as well. I have seen planets in your dimension form and die in what to us was only a few hours."

Jace moved closer to one of the ships, noticing the plates and connectors. "This doesn't look like a tunnel system."

"It is not. That is a dimension shield array element."

Jace's face brightened. "Would you mind if we borrowed some of these?"

Lakai tilted her head. "Why?"

Jace looked at her. "Because I wanted to try and get out of here. I have no intention of becoming a ghost. Would you stop us if we tried?"

Lakai looked to the other Ha'ak nearby. "We would not. I find it fascinating that you think you have an idea of how to leave. I would be curious to see if you would succeed."

Eislie leaned against the ship. "Sounds like a challenge." She looked at Jace.

"Challenge accepted," he replied with a smile.

Chapter 27
One-Way Trip

Jace grunted as he pulled at one of the shield elements. He and Eislie had been working non-stop for the past seven hours and had nearly all the elements in place. That feat alone impressed the Ha'ak watching them.

Lakai turned to Kul, another female who was transfixed on watching the starborn work. She was jotting down notes and taking images. "We have been studying them for much of their people's time in this universe," she said in a gentle whisper. "It is good to see that these two have retained the gifts of their forebearers."

Lakai agreed. "They are quite adept at working with materials at hand."

They both witnessed one of the elements fall to the ground as Eislie briefly faded. "At the current rate of dematerialization, I estimate that they have approximately seventeen standard hours remaining," Kul said with a scholarly tone.

"It is a shame that neither is showing signs of conversion. Although I think they may be finished well before that time limit." Lakai sighed. "It is disconcerting that they have damaged three vessels to outfit theirs."

Kul looked up from her data pad. "One of those was because they were learning how to remove the elements. Plus, we have no current missions planned outside this base. I am happy they chose to remove the shield elements from the Duggor ship instead. Yon has ordered the halt of any action since the Tharak were detected nearby. The activity of the Duggor has been concerning as well. Although if these two do succeed, we will have to relocate the base. I believe Commander Yon has already ordered the tunnel closed. He did not want to take any chances of any of our people being captured."

"The Tharak would use anything they discover to access our dimension. Perhaps for more genetic material to integrate into themselves." Her eyes filled with fear. "The Duggor would torture any they captured, just to silence their call to others."

Kul looked sad. "We should have helped them more."

Lakai shook her head. "Our interference is what allowed them to cause this fracture. As per the exploration council, we are to not interfere with the development of their species."

"What about our involvement with the Lyri? We modified them, didn't we?"

"That was on their own. They adapted themselves. I read the reports on the original Lyri interactions. There is something in their DNA, or the combination of energies, that makes them who they are. It allows them to adjust to any new environment. Many of the species that sprang from them also have retained some of that adaptability. Seeing these two behave makes me believe the Terrans are one such offspring. It is fascinating to watch." Lakai turned to watch Jace and Eislie work. "I guess we will have time to repair the damage they are causing before any new missions are allowed."

Then Lakai heard Yon in her mind. *Lakai, what is the status of the two Lyri descendants?*

She touched the side of her head. *They have nearly completed their vessel's modifications. Why?*

We will be collapsing the access tunnel in approximately twenty standard. The gateway generator has already been moved to resynchronize a new opening. I want you here to validate the coordinates.

Lakai's expression darkened. *That will not give these two much time to test their work.*

Their survival is not our concern. We must move access for our own safety.

Lakai gave a shallow nod. *Understood.* She then turned to Kul. "They will be closing the tunnel in about twenty standard hours. A new access point has been chosen."

Kul seemed to pout. "That means they will most likely fail. But I can keep hoping."

Lakai laughed as she turned away. "If they succeed, you can publish a most fascinating paper on it."

* * *

The sound of a drill whining filled the reactor room of the *Wolfhammer*. Jace had dropped the drill several times when his hands faded. Eislie heard his grumbling as she walked in. "Stupid phasing. Can't seem to hold anything for too long. Good thing these work directly on spide radiation. I don't think we would've had time to make a controller for them." He took the cables Eislie was holding and pushed them into the hole he had just made in the reactor. He motioned to the shelf on Eislie's right. "Hand me that seal compound."

Overhead they both heard, "Captains, the sealant will only resist the radiation for a short time. I must advise that no people not resistant to the radiation enter this area for a short while after we leave."

"Yeah, it's gonna be hot in here," Jace said, then looked to Eislie. "We should go over the connections one last time."

Eislie nodded. "I'm glad Kul told us that we had only a little time to finish up."

Jace gave a metered exhale as he nodded. "I can't believe the elements we put all over the hull are so similar to the ones we use to regulate the spide reaction. C'mon, let's go over everything. I don't want to blow up just turning things on."

Hours later, Jace and Eislie met the Ha'ak one last time. "We're set. This will either work or not." Jace looked at Eislie as she faded once again. "Not like we have a choice."

Lakai held her hand out to one of the other Ha'ak, and he placed several shimmering metal coins in her palm. Jace and Eislie watched as they faded, and then Lakai smiled. "I had a bet with Temm that you would finish before you faded."

Temm spoke up. "I still say they dissolve themselves during the flight."

"I think they will make it back." Lakai said, then turned back to Jace and Eislie. "I know you will make it back. Besides, he will owe me another thirty if you make it."

Both were unnerved by the giddiness of their host in the face of their possible demise. Jace said, "Oookay. Well, we'll be leaving now. Any chance you could delay that explosion a bit longer?"

Jace and Eislie watched as several Ha'ak waved childishly toward them. It seemed strange, but then Jace had a thought and mentioned it to Eislie as they headed to the ship. "I swear they were waving at us like we were puppies or something."

On the *Wolfhammer*, Jace said he'd take over the controls this time. Eislie was fine with flying, but she understood why Jace wanted to; if they didn't make it, he didn't want her to bear that responsibility. They turned on the rearview screen and watched the Ha'ak waving at them as they lifted off. He could see a large device being rolled out of one of the buildings. "Ed, how's the shielding working?" he asked.

The computer took a moment to respond. "Captains, they appear to be powered. Although I do not know how they work, so I am not able to speak as to their effectiveness."

"Don't look at me," Eislie remark. "I have no idea either. I just know they look similar to the reactor shield elements, like you said."

Jace shook his head. "This is going to be one scary ride."

Eislie looked relieved. "I'm glad you're flying."

Jace laughed, then asked, "Ed, how long was the ride in?"

"I believe it was close to one standard hour."

"Great, Ed doesn't know the exact time. That means there's a differential. That may be an issue."

Eislie replied, "We could be taking longer than we think, and they could blow up the tunnel while we're in it."

Jace just said "yep" and continued into the tunnel entrance.

Outside the heavy gravity body, several pirate ships had exited hyperspace. Nearly a week had gone by since they'd received the goodbye message from the *Wolfhammer*'s AI. The large ships were met with the sight of several Tharak vessels patrolling the area. "My queen, these appear to be Tharak in design," one of the pirates said. "I thought they were extinct."

Jana sat in her command chair. "Apparently not. According to the message, they're the ones who attacked the *Wolfhammer*."

The crew could hear the disgust in their queen's tone and acted accordingly. "Powering weapons. Targeting reactors," one of the pirates said.

"Hold. Let us see if perhaps our friends survived. Send a message to the *Wolfhammer*. Use the secured frequency. Their computer mentioned that they were heading inside the gravity well. If they've been fighting the event horizon, they may hear us." She then stood and walked to the main display. "To all Tharak vessels, this is the captain of the *Blue Viper*. You will not interfere with our recovery efforts. If you do, you will be destroyed."

The screen came alive to show the face of Commander Kertol. "Your status means nothing here. We have called for reinforcements. If you do not wish to be taken prisoner, I suggest you leave." He then looked at her more closely, before saying something she couldn't hear to Tharak at his side. He said, "We are detecting that you have many starborn on board." He then called out in a louder voice, "All ships, destroy the others, but capture the one called *Blue Viper*."

For the first time in many years, Jana felt fear. Her gloved hand moved up to touch the veiled half of her face. She stood silent as her crew looked to her for orders. Even Zido, her most trusted, could see her pause. "My queen, what is it?" he asked quietly.

His words broke her hesitance. "All ships, focus fire on the Tharak commander's vessel." She looked at Zido. "We have an entire crew of starborn. We must destroy them before they board us."

"That should be easy. We're more powerful than they are."

Suddenly several Tharak attack vessels appeared from hyperspace. Jana activated all her monitors. "All ships, coordinate attack. They will be trying to disable our vessels. They will be looking to take the crew."

Zido yelled, "All gunners, open fire!"

On the *Wolfhammer*, Jace and Eislie's ride was turning out to not be a very pleasant one. The ship was being bounced off the sides of the tunnel as they made their way against the flow of the gravity well. One particularly violent surge nearly shook both of them out of their harnesses. "Ugh, this is worse than the ride we took in the filaments the first time," Jace said, trying to keep the ship under control.

Eislie cinched her harness tighter. "This is bad. Ed, how's the ship doing?"

The computer responded immediately, "I have lost nearly half the port systems sensors, but we appear to still be functional." There was an audible pause. "May I remind the captains that the Ha'ak are planning to close the tunnel."

"I know, Ed, I know. I'm flying as fast as I can here," Jace growled back.

Eislie was about to say something when they were thrown back into their command chairs, the force of gravity holding them fast, unable to move. "Aft sensors have detected a large quantum interactive explosion behind us," Ed explained. "The tunnel is collapsing. I estimate we have approximately four standard minutes until we will be crushed by the collapse event."

"Ed, at the rate we're flying, what's the estimated time for us to exit?" Eislie asked.

"Approximately 5.7 standard minutes."

"They couldn't have waited another couple of fucking minutes?" Jace yelled. He then slammed on the flight controls. "Screw this. I'm flooring it."

The ship lurched forward as Jace increased their speed. The jostling increased manyfold. Jace ordered Ed to inform them of any physical damage, or anything else that might stop them from continuing. The computer's response was, "Perhaps, Captains, it may be better for me to give a list after we exit the anomaly."

Jace and Eislie looked at each other and laughed. "You know, Ed, that's a good point. Let's get out of this first." Jace looked at Eislie and said, "You know we could try the tunnel drive."

Eislie shook her head. "We're in a tunnel and you want to try and open another tunnel? Do you know the dangers of that? Not to mention that physics alone wouldn't work."

"I'm trying it," Jace said, hitting the tunnel control system. He was surprised when nothing happened. Eislie looked smugly at him, but Jace said nothing, and just went back to flying.

Eislie turned her attention to the display and read through the numbers. "Jace, you've moved up our exit time. It's now under two minutes. Ed, how long before the explosion catches up with us?"

"Approximately 2.3 minutes."

Jace said, "I think we might just make it. Let's hope there's no one waiting for us out there. I'm not sure the ship will be in any shape to outrun them."

At that moment the comm came alive. "*Wolfhammer*, this is the *Blue Viper*. If you can hear us, please know we will do our best to distract the Tharak long enough for you to escape. If you can hear us, please respond."

Eislie and Jace looked at each other, Eislie growling, "Slac." She then hit the comm. "*Blue Viper*, we're on our way out now."

.

Chapter 28
Time to Run

The Tharak weapons pounded on the shields of the *Blue Viper*. Jana and her crew were doing their best to avoid being damaged and boarded. The remaining pirate ships, those containing the most starborn, seemed to be the target of the Tharak. Although the pirates had substantial ships, the materials of the Tharak vessels were much more durable.

"We're not doing enough damage to the Tharak!" Zido yelled. "We must retreat!"

Jana looked concerned. She was about to order the ships to fall back when Zido said they had a message from the *Wolfhammer*, that they were now on their way out. She moved forward. "Did they say how long?"

"No, my queen. Did they go down into the gravity well? That's insane."

Jana glanced at Zido. "Have you forgotten who we're here for?" She pressed the comm. "*Wolfhammer*, how long till you exit?" She then switched channels. "This is your queen. I want all ships to be ready with tunnel and emergency systems. But do not leave until ordered." He heard the acknowledgement from all the pirate vessels. She then turned and went back to her command chair. "Let me know when the *Wolfhammer* responds."

On the *Wolfhammer*, they heard Jana's message and Jace grabbed the comm. "Ed, how much time until that explosion hits us?"

The computer responded, "Thirty-nine seconds."

He looked at Eislie. She knew already what he was going to ask, so she said, "We'll be out in twenty."

Jace smiled, pressing the comm. "Exit in about twenty seconds, and we've got a big explosion following us. I suggest you leave as soon as we do." He looked at the explosion following them on the display. "I have to admit, without the dimensional shielding I don't think we would have gotten this far. I just hope they're tough enough to withstand weapon fire."

"I really don't want to test that," Eislie complained as she cinched her harness tight against her again, readying for the exit. She then suddenly started working on her console. "We have just over fifteen seconds to get out of here before that thing behind us catches up. I mean, we have a quantum induced gravitational energy blast on our tail. I don't want to be around when it exits."

"Hmm, good point. We need to get out of here real fast."

"Three seconds to exit, Captains," the computer alerted them.

Suddenly the dark screen before them filled with normal space and the sight of a Tharak cruiser right in their path. Jace didn't have time to react. They were both thrown forward in their harnesses by the impact. They were surprised to suddenly find themselves out on the other side, staring into stars. "We're alive?" Eislie said with surprise.

Jace gave a laugh. "Damn, I love these dimensional shields." Then that sly Terran smile showed and he said, "I guess we hit someone. Think we should leave a note?"

Eislie laughed, hitting the tunnel drive. "Let's get out of here."

Jana was taking readings on the anomaly when the *Wolfhammer* exited. She felt relieved but also watched the spike in quantum collapse energy emissions. "To all ships, leave now. Do not wait to calculate a tunnel exit point. Leave now!" Her voice had a commanding tone mixed with terror.

Within seconds the *Blue Viper* was in hyperspace, and the rest of the pirate ships followed suit. The Tharak were about to chase after the *Wolfhammer* when the drone monitoring the anomaly said, "Commander, I'm detecting extreme energy readings from th—"

The *Wolfhammer* rocked as the explosion shifted them while in hyperspace. Both gave a sigh of relief. "I hope everyone listened to us," Eislie said.

"Well, we know at least one of the Tharak ships didn't."

Eislie slumped in her chair. "I don't like when people are hurt."

Jace looked at her, his expression more caring. "I don't either. But, you know, they *did* try and put us in jars. I'm not going to lose any sleep over it if they didn't make it."

Eislie quietly agreed with Jace, and they continued in hyperspace for a while. They took the time to evaluate the ship and what systems were damaged. From the inside it didn't seem like much was wrong, and that was very surprising to both of them. "Ed, what's the status of the aft stabilizers?" she asked. "They seemed to have taken a beating. Well, at least the sensors did."

"They appear to be functioning normally. That is curious."

"How so, Ed?"

"Well, we tend to damage the ship when we are involved with events as such. Do you not find it odd that there was almost no damage?"

Jace hung his head. "Ah, we must have activated sarcastic mode. Eis, get me a wrench."

Eislie snickered as she jokingly handed Jace a wrench, making him laugh.

Jace seemed in thought as they made their way back to the flight deck, Jace and Eislie flopping into their command chairs. Then Eislie sat forward. "We should send a message to Jana. Make sure they're alright and let them know we're alright."

Jace agreed. He then asked for the nearest planet they could stop on, preferably a non-Alliance planet. "Captain, if we adjust course we can land on Kleis 2," the computer informed him. "It is a spide mining planet independently owned. It is neither Alliance nor Consortium."

"Give me the coordinates, Ed. And copy them to my console."

"Why do you want them on the console?" Eislie asked.

"Something the Ha'ak said. The Duggor created a revenant to deal with their missing people, and it didn't attack us. Why? When a wounded animal waits but watches you, it's either afraid of you or is trying to evaluate you. We just escaped a gravity well. There was a message that we were being attacked, and I have a feeling that not only the Tharak but the Duggor are probably looking for us for filament travel."

Eislie's muscles tightened. "We've got a big target on us now, don't we?"

Jace nodded. "I have a strange idea. I want to run it by some people who might know more about the Duggor than most."

"Who?" Eislie asked.

Jace smiled. "The pirate queen. Who else? She's been attacking them for a long time." He copied the coordinates and sent it along the secured channel before saying, "Let's change course and head for Kleis 2."

On the *Blue Viper*, the repair crews were working feverishly to fix the ship. They had felt the wave of the explosion and had hoped that all their people would make it away in time. They had only heard back so far from about half of the ships that had accompanied her there, but the messages were still coming in. Jana was heading back to her war room, not to evaluate a new strategy but to rest. For the last twenty plus years she had been one of the most feared beings in the galaxy, but today she felt fear.

She entered her room and sealed the doors. "No one is to disturb me for the next hour, unless the ship is in danger," she ordered over the comm. "Zido will be in command. Tell him to alert me if there is any danger." She removed her over jacket, but her veil remained. She moved to a nearby sink and looked herself in the eyes, muttering, "They've been hunting them too. I felt it in his glare." She was referring to the way the Tharak commander had been looking at her, and the venomous smile he had given her when he singled his attention on her. The fear she felt was one that she usually instilled in others. She wasn't accustomed to feeling it herself.

She leaned on the counter of the sink before removing her glove and her veil to reveal a glowing, translucent blue grey being beneath. Its termination darkened against her human half. Her blue eye glowed before she gave a sigh. She bowed her head as her full weight fell on her hands. "That was terrifying," she muttered. "I don't see how those two endure being hunted like this."

Jana straightened and headed to the bed she had nearby. Her hybrid body allowed her to function for weeks at a time with only a short rest when needed, but now was one of those times. She lay on the bed, closing her eyes. She started to meditate but eventually fell asleep.

On the bridge of the *Blue Viper*, the comm officer alerted Zido. "Sir, the *Wolfhammer* is strongly requesting that we meet them on Kleis 2. What are your orders?"

"Show me the message," Zido ordered. He read the message: "This is Captain Tucker, coordinates 234.45, 4921.345, 78AV75W. Planet Kleis 2. We need to talk. I strongly request we meet in person. We found out something you'll want to know."

Zido looked around, concerned. "What is so important that they need to meet in person?"

"Should we inform the queen?" one of the crew asked.

Zido shook his head. "Change course to Kleis 2. I will bear the brunt of the queen's wrath if that was not her wish."

On Kleis 2, the *Wolfhammer* landed. Jace grabbed a weapon from their hold and took it with him as he went into town. "Is it wise to allow Captain Tucker to go alone, Captain?" Ed asked Eislie.

"I can go save him if something happens. Besides, we only need a small amount of zirconium to repair the reactor chamber. It won't look suspicious if it's some ragged exhausted pilot asking. Besides, he'll be back before they get here. We don't want any who aren't starborn hurt."

"Yes, Captain, I understand. Also, I have a response from our friends. They say they are on route. Arrival in about three standard hours."

Eislie thanked him but seemed concerned; Jace had told her what he was planning before he left. She was still going over it in her mind. She thought, *Jace, if you're right and we succeed, it might end the war.*

* * *

Jana's eyes opened, and she sat up. She felt rested, the gnawing of the earlier fear now faded. She felt her confidence again and redressed. As she entered the bridge, she asked for an update. Zido answered, "I changed course to Kleis 2. We received a message from the captain of the *Wolfhammer*. It was somewhat demanding."

He showed her the message, and her analysis of it was different. *Well, my friends, what did you discover?* She then told Zido to continue to the planet before she remarked, "I'm not accustomed to being summoned. But I'm sure Captain Tucker has a worthwhile reason."

Jace returned to the ship after a couple of hours, going straight to fixing the damaged reactor containment. They removed the feeds for the dimensional shielding and discussed coming up with a better solution. Jace commented that it would come in handy, but that right now, like Eislie, he was more worried about people being harmed by the leaking reactor.

He had just finished when the secured comm channel came alive. "Captain Tucker, I presume you have a good reason for this meeting."

"When you arrive, I believe you'll agree, but I'm not doing this over the comm. This needs to be a face to face."

Jana agreed, and it was only about ten minutes later when her private scout ship arrived. Jace and Eislie were standing near the *Wolfhammer* when they heard from one of her guards, "Move away from the ship."

Jace and Eislie started walking toward the group of pirates, making Zido say, "This must be serious." Jana agreed, and they closed the distance between them.

Jace and Eislie stood silent side by side. Jana moved forward a short distance away, her demeanor not an agreeable one. "No one summons me," she said commandingly. "Why have you requested this meeting?"

Jace said, "I didn't summon you. I requested we meet. So, get off your rock a little. You're no different than anyone else in this universe."

"How dare you!" one of the guards yelled, raising his weapon. Jana raised her hand then ordered him to stand down.

Eislie quietly said to Jace, "You do know they can kill us, right?"

Jace nodded. "I just don't like people talking down to me."

Jana said, "You would do well to listen to your fellow captain. She's very wise."

Jace smiled. "I know she is. She keeps me in line when she needs me to. But that's not why we're here."

"Why *are* we here, Captain Tucker? So far, you've said nothing of interest."

Jace gave a very Terran smile. "How about that I know a way to stop the war with the Duggor?"

Jana raised her eyebrows. "I would be very interested in that, Captain Tucker."

Chapter 29

The Secret on Reothes

Jace took a few steps toward Jana. Eislie joined him, only a step behind. He stopped a few steps away, seeing the guards behind the queen focusing their weapons on them. Jace remarked, "Everyone's always pointing weapons at us. It's kind of rude."

"You mentioned a way to end the war with the Duggor. Get to your point, Captain," Jana ordered.

"No pleasantries first? Fine," Jace huffed. "Have you been to Reothes?"

"Yes. We were immediately attacked by an unknown entity upon landing. What is your point, Captain?"

Jace's demeaner was confident he rolled his shoulders back. "We've found out the thing that attacked you is called a revenant. It's a part of the Duggor themselves, created to fix a problem."

Jana gave a subtle smile. "And this is important how?"

Eislie said, "We landed on Reothes and saved some researchers. None of us were attacked, but when we arrived, I felt…" She looked at Jace. "We both felt something. It was like something was staring at us. Like it wanted us gone, but it didn't want to harm us."

"I didn't feel like it didn't want to harm us," Jace remarked. "Felt more to me like someone trying to figure out how to take me down."

"I'm just reporting what I felt. But you're right; it didn't want us there."

Jana moved closer, her voice authoritative. "You still have not told me how this incident will help us end the war with the Duggor."

Jace continued, "We were speaking with some new friends." He paused. "Well, 'friends who blow up a gravity tunnel behind you' kind of friends. And they told us what the revenant is, what it was created for. And they were surprised to find out that it didn't attack us either."

"So far you have said nothing of value, Captains."

"Yeah, this is going to sound crazy. I'm trying to think of how to explain this without sounding like someone who's been in space too long." Jace gave a long sigh. "The revenant is actually part of the Duggor. It's the combination of all of the pain and suffering the filaments have caused them."

"So, it's a weapon. Why is that important to us?"

Eislie spoke this time. "That's just it—it's not a weapon. It was meant to heal them. But something went wrong. It worked against them. And after they were forced from their world, they took over Lyri. That entity is still part of them, and it's hiding information that can help them."

"Help them how?"

"Jace is right; this is going to sound crazy. But it was made to absorb the pain those lost in the filaments were experiencing. It was the only thing that was hearing their cries."

Jana looked confused. "Pain from those lost in the filaments? What are you two talking about?"

"The Lyri weren't the first to access the filaments. The Duggor were. And the filaments aren't exactly what we thought they were. It's a little complicated. Also, it turns out starborn aren't immune to the effects of the radiation in the filaments, as we thought."

Looking intensely, Jace moved to within an arm's length of Jana as he reached out his hand toward her veil. "I know what you are," he muttered.

"And what am I?" Jana growled.

"You spent a long time in a quasi-space rupture. Or within the filaments and the radiation there. How long were you trapped?"

Jana's eyes filled with anger, but she could see the sadness on Jace's face. There was no fear either, but rather an air of concern from him. Her anger was tempered as she turned to her people. "Zido, send the remaining crew back to the ship. You may remain."

"Your Highness, is this wise?"

"I'm not sure, but I do wish to have an answer on how to stop the Duggor from destroying everyone."

Jace said, "The Duggor are being torn apart from within. There are voices crying out to them through whatever connection they have with each other. The dimensional barrier the filaments are composed of aren't enough to silence them. The entity was created to quiet those lost in the filaments."

"So, they're being driven mad?"

Jace nodded. "That thing was supposed to take on that pain, but it became too burdened and rebelled against the Duggor. It forced them from their world and then laid waste to it. Sort of like a temper tantrum."

"And you learned this from who?"

"Some of those new friends I mentioned earlier. The Ha'ak."

Zido turned to see his queen's hand shaking, her breathing now coming quickly and shallowly. Concerned, he asked, "My queen, are you alright?"

"What's wrong?" Eislie said, also concerned.

Jace pointed to the queen's veil. "Look at the glow. Seem familiar?"

Eislie covered her mouth. "Oh no. I'm so sorry."

Jana tuned toward Zido, her hand trembling as it touched her veil. "Zido, I wish to complete this meeting somewhat more privately." She turned to Jace and Eislie. "Perhaps we can meet aboard your ship."

They went inside, the computer silent as per its hardwired instructions. Eislie offered Jana a seat, but she didn't take it. Instead she asked, "Is your computer recording this interaction?"

Jace hesitated. "He usually does. But we can ask him not to."

"Please do."

Jace and Eislie both gave the command. Then Zido watched as his queen did something she never had in public. She removed her veil, glove, and arm cover to reveal the translucent blue-grey alien features beneath. "My queen, I…" he began, but she held her hand up. He remained silent as she stood there.

"Well, we know one thing for sure," Jace said. "You're a starborn."

"May I touch your hand?" Eislie asked. Jana relented, and Eislie smiled after doing so. "She's warm. Not like the Ha'ak." She looked at Jana's face. "You retained your features. That's a plus. We both started to fade away."

Jana pulled her hand away, a sense of annoyance in her voice again. "We did not come here to discuss heritage, or what happened to you in a quasi-space distortion. Explain to me what this has to do with this revenant and how we can end the war."

Jace nodded. "We need to meet with the revenant. Find out what it knows about the location of the other Duggor."

"That's it?" Jana responded angrily.

Jace shook his head. "The Duggor lost a ship over ten thousand years ago. It's been tormenting them for that long. The filament trapped them. They were never able to disconnect from the Duggor. All that screaming in their mind has been driving them to do what they've been doing. If this revenant knows the location of the lost ship, or where it might be, then perhaps we can try and bring it back, as well as those they lost. Silence those screams."

Jana looked at Jace and Eislie before turning to look at her companion. She looked back at them and said, "How can we help?"

Jace leaned back against the wall. "We're going to need a couple of ships outfitted for filament travel. They'll need to help us search." He picked up an info-pad and handed it to her. "That's everything we have. It works. The dimensional shielding we just acquired may be useful as well. We can scan that and give the specs to you later. But my main reason for asking you here is that, if we do succeed and get the lost ship back, we may need a large force to get onto the planet." Jace paused. "How large of an attack force can you put together?"

Zido was the first to answer. "How dare you!"

Jana on the other hand, briefly stunned by his request, asked, "Do you wish to take Reothes?"

Jace chuckled. "Not Reothes. Lyri. If we do this right, we may be able to take Lyri back."

"You want to take one of the most heavily fortified encampments of a Duggor world?" She shook her head. "You're insane, Tucker."

"I never claimed to be sane. But I am hopeful. And a little desperate. That emergency message Ed sent got me thinking. People know how long it takes for messages to get around, unless you're using a quantum entangled system. We also caught a Tharak message about a bounty on us. Besides, that first message will tell anyone who knows how to do math that we traveled faster than hyperspace. I'm also pretty sure the Duggor are looking for us as well, just because we're starborn. And I wouldn't put it past the Tharak to put out even a greater contract to capture us. or maybe come after us themselves."

The pirate queen now understood. "You need to do this before someone tries to stop you."

Jace nodded. "I'd love to wait, but I'm pretty sure we're running out of time. We'll need at least one ship to follow us to Reothes. Watch our backs while we negotiate with that creature." He paused. "Or bring the ship back if we fail."

Eislie said, "Wait. Preston had a ship following the *Solace Star*."

Jana replied, "He was ordered to follow the two of you."

Eislie turned to Jace. "His ship was about the same size as the *Solace Star*. If it could be fitted with the same system we have, it might be able to access the filaments."

"The *Kitsale Aura* is already partially modified," Jana said. "I had planned to use his vessel to access the filaments if you had not succeeded in returning."

"We're flattered," Jace said. "Thank you for thinking about us. Where is the ship now?"

"It's on route to Yata Beta," Zido said. "We expected you to arrive there before heading to Gilese."

Jace gave a relieved sigh. "Well, how about we head there first?" He pointed at Jana. "You can look over those specs while we head to Yata and let Preston do a thorough scan on the dimensional shielding plates. Then we can head to Reothes. After that, we'll have to play it by ear."

Jana said, "You make it sound so easy, Captain Tucker."

Jace scoffed. "I wish. But if we get this right, we'll save a lot of people. That seems to me to be worth the trouble."

Chapter 30
Revenant Revealed

It was a few hours later as the *Wolfhammer* requested permission to land on Yata Beta. Jana had ordered Preston to meet them when they arrived. Eislie also let Miriz know they were there. She had just closed the comm link with Miriz and was feeling a little subdued.

Jace overheard the conversation and understood why. "She's worried about us getting into trouble," he said as he piloted to the designated landing bay.

"Yes, she is. I told her over an open channel that we're meeting some friends at the spaceport. She insisted on doing a background check." Eislie paused. "I told her not to."

As the *Wolfhammer* landed, several people approached. One they recognized as Preston, the others they didn't know. Jace and Eislie exited the ship and approached cautiously. They were relieved when they heard Preston say, "Jana sends her regards, and has given me my instructions." He then motioned to two others next to him. "They will do a scan of the plates you mentioned. I've ordered them to do nothing more than that."

Jace gave a relived sigh. "Thank you. I don't mind the lack of privacy, but we're sort of pressed for time."

"We intercepted several messages from the Tharak and Duggor," Preston said. "They are looking for you. They've also increased their bounty for starborn."

Jace's shoulders lowered. "This isn't going to get better anytime soon." He looked at Preston. "How ready is your ship?"

Preston smiled. "I ordered the modifications before you left. There were only a few adjustments needed. We tested it before arriving."

Eislie said, "And it's working?" Preston happily nodded.

Jace closed his eyes and leaned his head back. "Good. Then we're going to follow you to the Reothes and watch our backs for the Duggor."

Eislie seemed distracted; she kept looking over toward the wall near some cargo that was waiting for another vessel. Near it, the dust on the floor shifted, but there was no one there, or at least no one that could be seen. There was a faint whisper of a conversation in the air, however, as a footstep appeared in the dust and seemed to move behind the cases. "Taylyn, report," the woman making the footsteps heard in the comm mounted in her ear.

"I've confirmed the individual they are meeting with," Taylyn said in a hushed whisper. "He is the suspected pirate who was with them when the

Karazon challenged them. I was not able to get close enough to hear their conversation. But they seem to be going over a plan."

The suit she wore caused sound and light to be suppressed in the area around her; but when Eislie looked right at her, she knew her empathic abilities would be an issue if she moved closer. "The suspected pirates are scanning the *Wolfhammer*, and the two are allowing them to do so unabated," she continued.

In the command center, Loren Diur watched over the feed coming in from Taylyn. She then tapped her comm pad to type a message to the Grand Matron. *Starborn are working with known pirate operatives. Both vessels show indications of having travelled the filaments. What are your orders?* She then spoke. "Hold for orders. I suggest retreating to a location where you can deactivate the suppression system."

Taylyn acknowledged the order and moved to an unoccupied room of the dock to allow the suit to regenerate.

"Ma'am, operator has moved to holding position," a woman at the station said. "What are your orders?"

Loren's eyes never showed fear, only a sense of duty as she read the command from the Grand Matron. With a simple nod she then said, "Stay in the area. If the subjects show signs of departure, she is to reactivate the suit and try to board the vessel undetected."

The console operator relayed the message then said, "Ma'am, the suit only has a three-hour run time. if she is onboard for longer, she will need to shut it down."

The director nodded. "The order stands. If they do leave, we need someone on board to make sure the vessel can be returned to us for analysis." She turned to her comm. "Matron, I suggest you order the apprehension of Jace Tucker and Eislie Licessien."

Taylyn sat hard in the chair of the office she was in. "I have to go with them? In stealth mode? Are they insane?" She was about to request clarification when the display of her comm in the helmet showed. *You are to accompany the* Wolfhammer *to its next location and report back. We do not want that ship to fall into enemy hands. If needed, use the override materials you have on you.*

Taylyn leaned her head back, a groan-filled "wonderful" escaping her. She then leaned forward, looking out the window to see the crew of the *Wolfhammer* still discussing something with the pirates. She then muttered, "I gave up a career flying just to do this. I really should reevaluate my life choices."

Jace looked up at the hull of the *Kitsdale Aura* as he scanned it. He knocked on it, listening to the metal resonate. "It's not the same material." He looked at Preston. "Different alloy?"

Preston moved closer. "It's press-bonded to the polyceramic, not like your ship. Our queen thought it would be more resilient."

Jace ran his hand thorough his hair. "Yeah, not sure on that. We didn't know how the energy would react when we first tested. Honestly, I like it separate."

The pirate captain chuckled. "You were testing a theory. Our design is the next step." He shook Jace's shoulder. "Someone had to be the first one to see if it works."

Eislie appeared from the ship. "Jace, they have a food synthesizer in there. We should get one for our ship."

Jace looked at Preston. "Food synthesizer?"

"Protein sequencer. It uses cloned protein and cellular compounds. It's almost like the real thing."

Eislie bit into what looked like a sandwich. She chewed, then said, "It's a little soft."

Jace laughed, then looked at Preston. "The key word there is almost."

Preston gave a quiet laugh. "I still prefer real food to the printed kind any day."

Eislie gave Jace the sandwich and he bit into it. "Yeah, that's pretty mushy." He then heard an alert and looked at his comm. "Someone's waiting for us by the ship." He checked the feed. "It's Miriz." He looked at Eislie, who nodded in silent agreement at his unspoken plan. "Preston, we're heading back to our ship. Be ready to leave. We'll give you a call when were ready."

"We'll be ready," Preston said as he ordered his crew to prepare the ship for the filaments.

Back at the *Wolfhammer*, Jace and Eislie could see Miriz standing next to Yeesen. "Hey Miriz, long time no see," Jace joked, knowing they had been there only about a week ago.

Miriz wasn't very pleased. "Who are the people you are meeting? I could barely find anything on them, and what I could find seemed rather simplified."

Eislie gently grabbed her friend's arm, leading her inside the ship. "I'll explain. Come with me." Jace pointed the way to Yeesen as well.

As the door of the *Wolfhammer* closed, Taylyn peeked from around the same cases as before. She said nothing as she waited for her chance to find out what they were speaking about.

Inside the ship, Miriz was upset. "That was the pirate from when the Karazon were here, wasn't it?"

Eislie nodded. "They've outfitted a ship like ours, and it works as well." She motioned to Jace, who handed her an info-pad. "This is everything on our ship and theirs. We want you to take it to your people."

Yeesen angrily said, "You're working for pirates?"

"No. It's a joint effort. This is much bigger than just your people."

Yeesen turned to Miriz. "Representative, we should turn them in as collaborators."

Miriz hesitated briefly before saying, "Eislie and Jace are going to explain to us why we shouldn't." Miriz was no longer playfully looking at them.

Jace said, "You have all the specs on our ship and the pirates'. And we may have found a way to end the war with the Duggor."

Both Yeesen and Miriz stood silent at Jace's revelation. It took a moment before Miriz said, "Do you mean *end* end?"

Jace and Eislie explained the whole story to them. When they were finished, Yeesen and Miriz stood silent. There was no sound for several seconds before Yeesen reached for her weapon. "Representative, I think the filaments have caused your friends to go insane."

Miriz stood still for what seemed like an eternity before she looked at Eislie and said, "You think this could help?"

Eislie nodded and said tearfully, "Yes."

Miriz said, "If you think this will help, then I'll take you to see the Matron. She'll be able to provide help."

Ed cut in. "Captains, I need to inform you that an order to apprehend you has just been enacted by the Yata government."

Yeesen aimed her weapon at Jace, causing him to say, "Why does everyone always want to point weapons at me?"

Eislie looked Miriz in the eyes. "This is why we met with the pirates. We knew something like this was going to happen. Your people don't know what we know. And I don't think they'll listen even if we tell them. That's why we're doing this."

Miriz tapped the info-pad and turned to look at Yeesen. "Stand down. Let them go."

"Representative, may I remind you that it is a high offense to disobey a direct order from the Grand Matron's office—"

Her words were cut short, though, as Miriz quickly grabbed the weapon from her. "Yeesen, I will take full responsibility for this action." Her assistant looked confused as her employer pointed the weapon at her and said, "Eis, Jace, get out of here. I'll take this information to the Matron and explain why I let you go. I'll be honest, though; they'll probably throw me in a cell for this."

Eislie hugged her. "Well, it's good you have a couple of friends who keep escaping them. We'll get you out."

Miriz's reply was muffled as she pulled into Eislie's shoulder. "You better." She then aimed the weapon at Yeesen again. "I'm sorry for this, Yeesen. I would understand if you resigned after this, but I'm letting these two go."

Jace said with sincerity, "Miriz, we owe you. Thank you."

Miriz smiled at him. "Just make it back alive so I can get you both back for this."

As Miriz led her assistant out the door, Taylyn was watching. She had also received the order to apprehend Jace and Eislie, but her other orders superseded the planetwide command. When she saw Miriz leading her assistant out at gunpoint, she rushed forward, hitting the controls to the suppression suit she wore.

Miriz felt something hit the side of her jaw, causing her to drop her weapon. She reached out to defend herself but found nothing. She quickly left the ship, and it started to lift off.

After it was gone, Miriz handed her weapon to Yeesen. "I wouldn't blame you for taking me in," she said.

Yeesen looked at the weapon for a moment, then holstered it. "Ma'am, I apologize. I think your friends are right. This is much bigger than we realize."

Miriz smiled as she rubbed her jaw. "Now you know why I trust them more than anyone else in the universe."

"Ma'am, I have so much to learn from you."

Chapter 31

The Ties That Bind

The comm of the *Wolfhammer* crackled alive. "*Wolfhammer*, you are ordered to return to Yata control to be placed under arrest," a voice ordered.

Jace huffed. "Maybe this dual citizenship thing wasn't such a great idea."

Eislie looked at him with disbelief. "We have citizenship status on three worlds. It's worked for us before." She then looked at the ships heading for them. "Well, as long as we're not causing trouble."

Jace chuckled, then hit the comm. "Yata Control, this is the *Wolfhammer*. We regretfully decline your invitation. We understand the situation but have some information that may benefit everyone. Please tell the Grand Matron we know a possible way to stop the war with the Duggor. Unfortunately, we don't have time to sit in a cell waiting for you to decide what to do. Besides, if this doesn't work, you probably won't have to worry about us anymore anyway."

Eislie remarked, "Let's hope that doesn't happen."

Jace continued, "We gave all the information on our ship and the known others to Representative Elysse. She's on her way with the information right now."

The ships fired a warning shot at the *Wolfhammer*. Jace and Eislie watched as the plasma flew by them. Jace sighed, then said into the comm, "Look, you're slowing us down. The Duggor have issued an order to capture any starborn. We're trying to save people here. Even you."

As another shot grazed off the hull of their ship, Eislie tapped the controls. "Activating tunnel field." She looked at Jace. "Let's get a safe distance away and then head out." She then took over the comm, changing to the secure frequency they used with the pirates. "Preston, if you haven't done so yet, get off the ground immediately. Have a ship meet us at the planet we mentioned."

Preston responded, "Already in the air, Captain, although the goodbye committee they sent seemed a bit heavy-handed with their fanfare. We're getting to a safe distance and using the nearest filament point to reach Reothes. See you in a few hours."

"Preston, whatever you do, don't fire on them. Just evade."

"Acknowledged, Captain. We'll meet you there."

Eislie closed the channel. "Let's lose them with a short hyperspace jump. We already know where we're going."

Jace agreed but could see Eislie looking concerned. "What's wrong?"

She looked at him with genuine concern in her eyes. "I hope Miriz will be alright."

Jace nodded, thinking about their friend. "She seems tough. I'm sure she'll work things out."

As they entered hyperspace, Jace gave a sigh of relief then loosened his harness. Eislie did the same. "Ed, how long till we reach the nearest filament point?"

"13.4 standard minutes, Captain."

"Whew, that was close," Eislie said, sounding relieved.

"Yeah. Those Yata forces really wanted us to stay."

"Why did you tell Preston not to fire on the Yata patrol?"

"We're not criminals. And even if Preston is a pirate, I don't want anyone shooting anyone else on sight."

Loren walked through three secured doors. She was accompanied by several guards, all armed. They stopped at a cell. Miriz looked up from her shallow bunk, straightening her shirt as she stood. "Did you give the Grand Matron the information I provided?"

Loren seemed unamused as she responded, "You allowed two of the most wanted criminals in the universe to escape. You are hardly in a position to joke."

Miriz smiled. "You and those like you all seem to find it convenient to declare someone an enemy as soon as it suits your purpose." Miriz looked at the guards. "Be careful around this one. You may wind up joining me in here if you don't obey."

Loren said in an even tone, "Your assistant says you disarmed her and held her at weapon point to allow your friends to escape. Is that true?" Miriz said nothing, only looking at the director with a casual glance. Loren had a hint of a smile. "I'll take your non-answer as confirmation. You have one of the most profitable businesses in this part of the galaxy. But that does not put you above the law."

Miriz said, "Or above the direct order of the Grand Matron's office."

Loren looked puzzled. "You did this freely."

Miriz smiled. "They told me what was at stake, and I believed them. When my best friend tells me with tears in her eyes that they may have a way to help, starborn and everyone, I believe her. They told me what they were doing, I won't stop them just for the sake of an order. If it saves people, I'll choose to help them and the greater good. Even if I have to sit in a cell."

Loren said softly but authoritatively, "You believe them when they say they have a way to end the war with the Duggor?"

Miriz nodded and smiled. "They wouldn't be doing this if they didn't think it would help."

Loren scoffed. "They are two of the richest starborn, criminals—"

Miriz interrupted her. "They're criminals because people like you see them as something less. Something that should be trodden on, used. They were willing to give away the Sotiral system until I convinced them otherwise. They've fought to free thousands of our people, fought to stop the enslavement of thousands of others. When they tell me they can save others, I believe them."

Loren stepped back. "We are evaluating the information you provided.

Your friends have been working with the pirates for some time. Were you aware of this?"

Miriz sighed. "I suspected they might have been. I never asked."

Loren angrily responded, "You suspected Yata citizens of willfully working with an enemy. People who have killed our own. And you never investigated or said anything?"

Miriz knew the woman's tone was meant to sway the guards flanking her, and several looked angrily at her. But she had dealt with many people in her business, some of them, people most would be afraid of. The director was no different. She, instead, smiled. "No, I never investigated. I've been running a multi-planet business, which means dealing with many not-so-honest individuals. You don't always look at what's going on behind the scenes. I'm sure the Grand Matron would agree with me. After all, she's been in power for many years."

Loren raised a brow at the representative's subtle accusation. There was a long silence before she said, "Where are they headed?"

Miriz smiled. "I gave you all the information they gave me."

"The information you provided was for the filament systems. It did not go into detail about where they are going."

"They survived falling into a gravity well. They met the Ha'ak."

"The Ha'ak are long dead."

Miriz smiled. "Apparently not. They gave them information, and they believe they can use it to stop the war with the Duggor. Maybe stop them from hunting starborn and destroying other worlds. They're hoping to bring peace to our part of the galaxy."

"They are criminals and will be treated as such."

Miriz shook her head. "They fought the Karazon with their bare hands. Won the freedom of thousands of our people from slavers. They saved me from poisoning." The expression on Miriz's face became stern. "They nearly died saving themselves from being enslaved at least twice. All of you think they're something to be used. You're not seeing what they are."

"And what are they?"

"They're my friends, true and loving. They've seen pain like most never have, and they survived. They're stronger than you know. And I'll never take away the hope they bring."

Loren motioned for the guard to step back. "You do realize that if your friends don't succeed, you will be here for a very long time."

Miriz closed her eyes. "I have faith in them. I believe they're on a path greater than any of us can see. I'll only be here for as long as is needed." She opened her eyes. There was a defiance behind them. "When they succeed, I'll be there standing beside them. Director, I understand you have a job. But don't let a blind hatred of people who don't follow the rules misguide you. They believe this is a chance to help others, not just Yata. They're looking to help everyone."

"They are reckless criminals. The only thing that is going to happen is that they are going to get themselves killed by the Duggor. Or worse, enslaved by them, like the Duggor have done to countless of their kind before. They are nothing special."

As the director walked away, Miriz muttered, "You're wrong. They're destined for something you can't even fathom."

As the guards locked the doors behind them, one of them said, "Director, she seems convinced her friends are going to achieve what they say."

The director gave a sigh before saying, "She is trying to bargain her way out of her crimes, nothing more."

The guard thought for a moment. "But my brother was returned when the Karazon returned all the slaves they had taken in the last few years. And they are continuing to bring back people who have been taken for much longer."

The director looked sternly at the guard. "You would do well to not believe everything a prisoner tells you. Most of the time they are lying." She moved closer to the guard. "Are you telling me that you believe that prisoner over my information?"

The guard said softly, "No, ma'am."

"Make sure there is someone posted. I want to know when the prisoner is ready to tell us where they went." Loren then walked away.

Chapter 32

The Revenant Speaks

Taylyn was out of breath as she leaned against the wall of the airlock. She had barely made it inside before Jace had closed the inside door. She was about to approach them before noticing the display in her helmet: *34.6 minutes to inversion.*

I'll have to subdue them before I'm forced to let the system regenerate, she thought as she moved closer to the two captains. As her foot put pressure on the deck plate, there was a squeak. The sound caused Jace's head to swivel quickly.

Eislie noticed his actions and asked, "What is it?"

Jace looked around as if silently searching for something before he responded, "Thought I heard something."

The two remained perfectly still for several moments, staring straight in Taylyn's direction. She was beginning to think the shield suit wasn't as effective as her commanding officer had insisted, but then became relieved when Jace turned forward. "Must have been my mind playing tricks on me. I don't hear anything now." She watched Eislie relax as well and returned to flying. "Three minutes to the filament point. Let's hope our backup's there when we arrive."

Taylyn moved into the hall leading back to the cabins and the hold. She decided to wait for a moment, hopefully to get a better chance to separate them. She knew she could take them out one at a time much easier than both at once.

They were moments away from the filament point. Taylyn had never experienced anything like it before, and she found herself anticipating the ride, even if it was against her orders. She watched as the cabin lit up with a multicolor display before she felt her shield suit vibrating. The field around her was moving so quickly that it was slamming into her body. The impact caused her to scream, but the suit muted her sound. However, she was loud enough to be heard by Jace before she passed out.

Jace was fighting to stay in his chair as they entered the filament, and the whole ship groaned and shook. He thought he heard something and looked but didn't see anything. He was more concerned about the ship. "What the hell was that?" he asked loudly.

Their computer responded a second later. "Captains, there was an anomalous resonance as we were entering the filament. I cannot detect the source of the event."

Jace looked at the display, searching the data. "Nothing off except for…" He then quickly unbuckled his harness. "There was an inversion detected as we entered the filament. I'm checking the reactor."

Eislie looked concerned. "If we need to punch out, we'll do that. Let's hope we're not someplace we don't want to be."

Jace agreed and made his way back to the reactor. As he went to step through the door, his foot seemed to brush against something, making him trip. He inspected the reactor but could find no sign of an inversion in progress.

As he closed the inside reactor door, the sound snapped Taylyn out of her unconsciousness. She opened her eyes to see Jace walking toward her, and she moved to get out of his way, pulling herself against the wall as flat as she could as Jace walked by. Suddenly he stopped, only inches away from her now. She remained still. Her suit made her invisible, but as Jace turned, he seemed to look right at her. Her heart raced. She was still recovering from the pain the suit had inflicted and was not at her full capabilities.

Then Jace lifted his hand and moved it toward her face. Taylyn ducked and shuffled to the side, moving as far away as she could. His hand touched the wall, but then he moved it around, as if searching. "Eis, did it sound like someone screamed in pain when we entered the filament?"

"I was too busy trying to keep us under control."

Taylyn did her best to move away from Jace, still experiencing the effects of the suit interaction with the filament. It took all her strength to shuffle as quietly as possible down the hall toward the hold. She continued to watch Jace as he searched. Then something on the display of her helmet got her attention: *Critical! Shutdown recommended in 3 minutes to avoid inversion. Auto shutdown in process.*

No, No! Don't shut down now! Taylyn pleaded silently. Then she got her chance.

"Eis, I'm checking the hold. I swear there's someone on this ship." Jace moved quickly to the back door and opened it. Summoning as much of her strength she had left, Taylyn jumped through the open door and hurried into the corner. She watched as Jace looked in her direction. She thought to herself, *I hate Terrans with good hearing.*

She remained still as Jace looked around the hold and then exited. She heard him say, "Well, if there's someone here, they must be invisible or something."

Taylyn quickly pulled out her infiltration kit and jammed it into the controls for the hold. Within seconds it overrode the ship's security for that room. She now controlled the cameras and sensors. As her timer counted down to the last few seconds, she turned off the inversion suit and was again visible. She lifted her arm. It felt like it was made of lead. The painful oscillations had stopped, and she took a relaxing breath. Quietly she said to herself, "I now know one place you can't use this damn inversion suit."

She looked at the display. *Operator has sustained injuries. Medical treatment is recommended. Blunt force trauma detected over 85% of physical body.* She leaned her head back, remarking, "Only 85 percent? Feels like a lot more." She smiled before the suit injected a pain reducer and she lost consciousness.

They reached the planet in record time, just under three hours. Preston was already there waiting for them. "Captains, it seems I beat you here," he chided.

Jace smiled. "yeah, you're allowed to get lucky once in a while."

Preston returned the chuckle. "I can send down some people with you."

Eislie shook her head. "Last time we were here, it didn't attack us, but we knew it was watching. I think the fewer people, the better."

Jace agreed. "Preston, watch the skies. Make sure we don't have any surprises waiting for us when we come back up here."

"Understood, Captain. And what do you want us to do if it attacks you?"

Jace plainly said, "Nothing. Remember, this thing dusted the entire planet. If it attacks, it's not going to matter. We'll keep a vid feed open."

The flight down to the planet was too easy, according to Jace. Eislie was feeling terrified as they neared the mountain range where they had both felt the presence a year earlier. Jace landed the ship and looked at Eislie. "I guess we should head out there. It probably knows we're here anyway." They headed for the air lock, then Jace paused. "Maybe we should grab some weapons."

Eislie was about to argue, but then looked back toward the hold. "We might as well. I'm not sure they'll be any good on that thing."

"We also don't know if there might be some smaller things lurking around."

They headed into the hold. The ship landing had jostled Taylyn awake and she turned to see the inside door of the hold open. She was viewing the suit status when the door opened. She rushed to activate the inversion suit, and she vanished from sight. She watched them grab some weapons from storage and head back through the ship. She rushed to follow them, making her way down the gantry as Jace and Eislie walked ahead of her. She could feel the numbness in her limbs from the painkillers as she followed their tracks in the soft surface.

She kept pace several steps behind them. She wanted whoever they were meeting as well as them. She planned to take them all down when they were there. Her confidence was very high until a large creature appeared at the entrance of the cave they were heading toward. Like her, Jace and Eislie froze. The creature looked like a Duggor, but there was something strange about it. Its left side seemed to be twisted, angry, it seemed to emit some sort of vapor. Jace remarked, "That's not something you see every day."

As the creature approached, Jace and Eislie didn't move. Taylyn found herself looking around for an escape. She looked down. The tracks they had made were in front. She realized she was making a third set behind them.

She was about to run but then heard the creature speak in a whispered manner, "You two have been here before. I remember." It approached. Jace and Eislie stood in awe as they watched the Duggor, one separate from the consciousness of the others, move closer. The Ha'ak had told them that it had been created to lessen the pain of those lost in the filaments. They also told them that the revenant had turned on the Duggor. Its actions in destroying the

Duggor home world had made the Duggor desperate, and they took over Lyri and the Daak homeworld to find an answer.

"We have been for many years," the creature continued. "No Duggor can step home until the others are found. All must suffer until we are whole."

Jace had to say something. "That's selfish. You're punishing innocents. What about the people they're attacking?"

"We hear their screams; we feel their pain. All must suffer. You have traveled the filaments, but you cannot hear."

Jace muttered, "Well, this went downhill fast." He turned to the revenant. "Why must others suffer? Your people have destroyed entire planets and species for something you willingly did."

"You are of Terra. You should understand. Your people suffered a similar fate. The Ha'ak gave us this and it destroyed us. Your people were changed by them, and then the Gel twisted and abandoned your world. You of all people should understand our pain."

"I'm not sure I do. I am who I am. It doesn't matter where I'm from. Your people enslave any who have Lyri in them. You took their home. The Daak—"

The revenant quickly moved forward, aggressively interrupting Jace. "The Daak deserve punishment. They would not aid us. They are like us. They have lost others like us. They would not help. They abandoned themselves. We cannot forgive."

Jace angrily responded, "Bullshit! You think you feel pain? Yes, I can understand. But I can't understand why."

Eislie asked, "Are you sure antagonizing it is a good idea?"

Jace looked apologetic. "No, it's not. Right now, I'm trying to figure out what it wants."

The creature heard him and answered, "We are in pain. All who caused this must suffer."

Eislie said, "Why? Why must all others hurt just because you are? Jace is right; that's selfish."

"We are—"

Jace interrupted the creature this time. "You are stupid, selfish assholes is what you are. Pain is a part of all life. It saves us from harm, teaches us, because it isn't what we need. Both our people realized that long ago. My people continued, forgot who we were, and became something else. Hers too."

There was silence. Taylyn's eyes were wide in surprise.

Jace looked at Eislie. "It's afraid. They hurt themselves and now they're trying to blame others."

"Insolent!"

"Yes, I am. I am the sum of my past, you moron. And even though I know you can kill us, I'll ask one question."

There was silence before the revenant responded, "You are arrogant and combative, but you do not attack. Why?"

Eislie said, "Why haven't you attacked us?"

Jace observed, "The Duggor may be one mind, but I think they're fighting internally, the same way we do when confused." He now addressed the revenant. "You destroyed lives, destroyed worlds, but now we're here confronting you, and you're afraid. And I think I know why."

There was a moment before the creature spoke. "Confused. We are afraid."

Jace said, "Huh. Stubborn. Proud. Sound like another planet we know?"

Eislie's eyes widened. "Earth."

Jace smiled and stood tall. "We have yet to see the Duggor kill starborn or any Lyri, but you've enslaved them and used them. I'm surprised you've never asked for help."

There was a pause, and then the revenant said, "We need help. The pain needs to end."

"We can try, but no guarantees. If we do, you'll stop the war?"

There was a long pause before the revenant answered, "Yes. We will reconnect to the whole."

"Well, then, where do we start?"

"We know of another race, the Ha'ak, gone since the times of our leaving. They were on Lyri."

Jace responded, "We met them. That's why we're here. We know about the ship, and about the others of your kind who are lost in the filaments. We were hoping you could help us find them. Maybe even get us close so we can try and bring it back. Bring your people back."

The revenant moved closer. "You would release the vessel? Allow those held within to return?"

Jace nodded. "That's what we were hoping. But we need to know where the ship is. Do you know?"

The revenant stepped back for the first time since they arrived. "I will tell you what I know."

.

Chapter 33
The Missing Ship

The revenant explained as best as it could where to find the lost vessel. It was known as the *Eidolon*, and Jace and Eislie were doing their best to show the creature the maps they had. As the information displayed on Jace's comm, Taylyn was standing closer to him. She was doing her best to keep her eyes on the timer for her suit's power source, but she was more interested in the maps. *We don't have any of this information*, she thought to herself. *How much have they been holding from us?*

She leaned in closer for a better look. She had to move as Jace turned quickly, as if looking for something, then was relieved when he said, "I think this planet is making me jumpy." Taylyn had been warned about the empathic nature of those from Gilese, but what she really worried about was those with Terran senses. They were more heightened than most similar life forms, with better senses of smell, taste, touch, and vision, especially when it comes to movement. Terrans were always the ones you hoped weren't after you during the Alliance training sessions. Some of the cadets she had served with complained when they allowed Terrans into combat and stealth programs. Everyone knew there was something in Terrans that made them what they are.

Taylyn moved closer and could see the comm display. She then watched as Jace changed the display to communicate with someone. "Preston, do you have an updated map for the Teserin sector?" she watched him say. "I can see it on the map, but I don't have any details."

Teserin sector? That's several clicks and a half outside the galaxy. We've just started exploring that area, Taylyn thought to herself.

Preston was about to reply when Jana ordered him to do whatever the captains of the *Wolfhammer* command. He swiftly obeyed. "Here is the current data, Captain Tucker."

As Jace's comm loaded, he could see the extended map the pirates had provided. He happily showed the revenant the information. "In this the area?"

The revenant paused to think. "It is close to where I sense them. They are disturbed by my connection. I cannot clearly hear them; they are all screaming at once."

Jace stepped back. "If you need a moment, I understand. I can't even imagine what it's like to hear something like that and not be able to tune it out." Jace then turned to see Eislie's eyes. She seemed to be in pain. He moved closer. "Are you alright?"

Eislie shook her head. "You're lucky you can't feel it. He's in a lot of pain."

Jace turned to look at the revenant before returning to Eislie. "Why don't you go back to the ship? I don't think our friend here is going to attack me." He looked at the revenant. "At least, I hope not."

The revenant seemed almost relieved. "You are trying to save my people. I will not attack the three of you. Especially since you have also experienced the pain of the filaments."

"Three?" Jace said, narrowing his eyes.

Taylyn was stunned and took a step back from the revenant, her voice betraying her as she whispered, "Can it see me?"

Jace's senses went into overdrive. The entire trip there, he could have sworn there was someone else onboard, but they couldn't find anything. He looked down to see a footprint appear in the soft soil, and he said, "Whoever you are, I can see you."

Taylyn had thought about remaining still, but as the timer on her suit was now indicating she had only ten minutes before shutdown, she decided to reveal herself. As she seemed to appear from nothing, she said, "By the magistrate of the Yata defense council, I am placing you all under arrest."

Jace did his best to not laugh and politely responded, "Sorry, we have to decline. We're busy right now trying to save the galaxy." He pointed at the revenant. "You can try and arrest him if you want, but that thing pretty much toasted this planet, so I'd be careful."

The revenant said to her, "If you are here to stop them, I will destroy you."

Eislie smiled. "Whoever you are, I'd rethink what you're planning. We're trying to help him. So, if you're going to insist on arresting us, well…"

Taylyn was surprised as the revenant was suddenly standing before her, close. She froze. "You are not of Lyri, but you use the inversion like them," he said.

Jace looked at the back of the agent's suit. "Hey, that looks similar to the regulator we installed on the reactor for filament travel." He reached up and pulled out the control core. He was surprised to see numbers counting down. He held it to her face. "Countdown to an explosion, or something else?"

Taylyn said nothing, allowing the counter to reach zero. They watched as the whole system shut down before frying itself. Taylyn rushed to take it off her back when the suit itself started burning as well. Eislie rushed forward to help her out of the material. Jace complained, "I don't think she knew the system was designed to do that."

"Are you alright?" Eislie asked. Taylyn looked down to see parts of her skin torched. She hadn't felt the pain yet; she was still running on adrenaline.

Jace stomped on what remained of the material. "Not gonna get anything out of that. Is she hurt?"

Taylyn was in shock. She had been told the system would delete itself, not thermally destroy itself. She looked at herself, starting to feel the pain of the burns she had suffered. She was now standing pretty much naked, and she tried covering herself.

Jace handed her his jacket, then said to Eislie, "Let's finish up and get back to the ship." He turned to the revenant." Do you think the information you have is correct?" The revenant nodded. "Okay. Listen, if we don't find anything, we'll bring back the data and try again."

They all watched as the creature moved back. "I believe you will not fail."

"We'll do our best. Hopefully we'll find them before the others hunting us find us."

Taylyn said nothing as she boarded their ship. She was surprised to hear their ship's computer say, "Captains, I do not recognize this individual. Is there a threat?"

Jace and Eislie rushed the woman to the med bay. "Ed, activate table one, and include the restraints," Eislie said. She removed Jace's jacket carefully, finally able to see the injuries the woman had. She heard Jace mutter, "Guess I'm getting a new jacket."

Eislie told the computer to do an injury analysis. The computer responded, "I am detecting second and third degree burns on her arms and upper back. Indications of spide radiation damage to legs and torso. This patient will require several hours of treatment."

The pain from her injuries finally caught up with the agent and she groaned as Eislie gently pushed her to the table. "Relax. We're going to heal you. We're not monsters."

Taylyn glared at Jace. "I want him out of here."

Eislie, frustrated, said, "Jace, get out. She's pretty much naked here."

Jace nodded. He turned but didn't look at the agent. "If you attack her, or in any way harm her or this ship, I'll throw you into space myself." He paused. "I'm pretty sure they didn't tell you that suit would burn you alive, did they?"

Taylyn said nothing as Eislie administered a painkiller. The agent felt her body relax and the searing pain subside. She heard Eislie ask for her name, but she remained silent. She was surprised when the restraints activated and she found herself now held to the table. "Relax, I'll take them off in a minute," Eislie said. "You keep moving around. I don't want you harmed by the regen veil."

"If you think helping me will make me ignore my orders, you are wrong," Taylyn said, trying to stay conscious.

She was startled when the computer spoke, "Ma'am, I do not know your name, but if you harm either of my captains, you will not survive the return trip."

Taylyn gasped. "Your ship is sentient?"

Eislie nodded. "Yes. And a good friend, so I suggest you behave yourself."

Eislie placed the regen veil. around Taylyn. She did her best to make the woman comfortable. "Are you sure I can't convince you to tell me your name?" she asked.

"How about idiot? I hear that's a popular one back in most governments." Jace walked in. "I figured you'd have her covered up by now. I just came to check you were alright." He put his hands up. "Not that I don't think you couldn't handle her."

"She's in pretty bad shape. That suit would have killed her."

"I know. It's a dead man's setup. Or a dead person's setup. I'm an equal opportunity insulter."

"You've been awfully antagonistic recently. Is everything alright?"

There was silence as Jace gently pulled Eislie close. "Her being here is proof that there are people still trying to hunt us for the wrong reasons. It's getting annoying." He said loudly enough for the woman to hear, "We're giving filament travel to everyone, and I mean everyone. If we play things right, it should end the war with the Duggor. If you have a problem with that, you're stupider than I thought."

The woman made a hand gesture toward the two that neither recognized. Jace looked at Eislie. "Did she just flip us off?"

Eislie nodded, then placed her head against Jace's shoulder. "We never get any respect."

"I was just talking with Preston. They're going to take her off our hands."

"We can't. They'll kill her," Eislie protested.

"Preston and Jana both gave me their words. She'll be returned to an Alliance facility after another ship arrives. It's going to be a couple of hours before they get here. Preston's going to follow us in the filaments. We're lifting off in a minute. Just wanted to make sure things were secure. And I wanted to give you a heads-up that I'm sending a message to Captain Wehen. I think we'll need an ally, even if he says he's not. We have to try and stop this. Maybe he'll understand."

She gently moved to touch Jace's arm and could feel his muscles tighten. Eislie wasn't in much better shape. Her heart was racing as she thought of attempting something no one had been able to do in nearly ten thousand years.

Chapter 34

The Crazy Plan

Preston stood on the flight deck of the *Wolfhammer*, listening to Jace explain where he thought the Duggor vessel was. "I think it's here, maybe. The creature down there was as accurate as it could be. I was really waiting for it to slash the hell out of us. That thing seemed a bit unstable."

Preston crossed his arms as he leaned back against Jace's command chair. "So, you think it's there?" Jace nodded, but the expression of concern in his body language was disconcerting.

Jace said, "Is Jana listening?"

"She is. And she has asked why you are concerned."

Jace slowly walked across the flight deck. "Because we have limited time. Because this might kill any of us. Hell, because we may never find the damn ship. That and the way we left Yata Beta and Miriz behind. Not to mention that we probably have not only Yata but the Alliance calling for our heads by now."

In his implant, Preston heard Jana say, "Preston, Jace is correct. There are orders to immediately apprehend or disable the *Wolfhammer* and its captains. The Alliance has issued a level seven, category one order to all vessels."

"What?" Preston spat, then looked toward Jace and Eislie with something they had never seen in their friend. Fear. He told them what Jana had relayed.

Eislie quietly said, "That's a kill order," before sitting down in her chair. She looked at Jace then looked away.

"Wonderful." Jace kicked the rear wall of the bulkhead. "That means every idiot with a ship is looking to cash in. I'd probably be looking for us as well. That means we've got less time than I thought."

Eislie looked at him. "Then we're really going to do this now?"

Jace nodded. "We don't have a choice." He then looked toward the med-bay. "Ed, how long till that woman can be moved?"

"1.2 standard. I do not recommend moving her before that, due to her injuries."

Jace asked Preston, "How long till that other ship arrives?"

"About half a standard."

They both watched as Jace paced the small hall to the back of the ship. He went back and forth several times before stopping and said, "My guess is that they know we're working with the pirates, and they'll probably be following any known ships. Especially if they suspect they have filament capability. Yata is close. My guess is that you sent a ship from there."

Preston looked confused until he heard Jana again in his implant. "Tell Captain Tucker that there were two dispatched from Yata Beta and two from Julion. The closest was Yata." He relayed the message.

"Shit. My guess is they're being followed or tracked. Hell, they may even have someone with a similar undetectable suit to that what that woman was wearing."

Preston said, "That means we may only have half a standard to be ready to leave."

"Less. I don't want her on board," Jace said flatly. "We have no idea what kind of training she's had. If she does something stupid while we're in the filaments, none of us may make it out."

There was silence for a short while before the computer said, "Captains, I believe I can have the patient ready in under ten standard. If we move her to the *Kitsdale Aura* we can enter the filaments ahead of them and possibly find the vessel. We would not be in this vicinity to possibly be captured."

Jace slowly turned to look at the control panel that held their friend. "Ed, are you telling me you want to leave the pirates here to face a possible slaughter?"

There were several seconds before the computer responded, "Captains, I have calculated the possibility of the Alliance or Yata security response. If several ships were dispatched by the pirate queen, then only a few more were possibly dispatched by Yata security forces. And the Alliance does not know exactly which direction we headed. The odds are that any force that was sent will be smaller than anticipated."

Jace said to Preston, "I don't like the idea of leaving you to fend for yourself against whatever may be coming. Hell, there may not be anyone either."

In his implant, Preston heard, "Preston, do as their ship's computer suggested. It's the best option as per my own calculations as well."

Preston huffed then smiled. "My queen thinks your computer is correct."

Jace asked Eislie, "Whaddya think?" Eislie gave a shallow nod and Jace gave the order. "Ed, have that woman prepped to leave in ten. We'll transfer her over. Also, work out a course to where we think the Duggor ship is." He got up and started toward the med-bay. "We might as well be ready to run out of here while we can."

* * *

"Subcommander Helles, what is the new heading of that pirate ship?" the captain of the *Della Mar*, a woman named Ullo, asked.

"Ma'am, they are still heading toward the same system."

The commander walked up to Ullo. "Ma'am, the estimated course is toward a restricted planet, Reothes. The Alliance has restricted all ships from that area." The commander looked worried. "And it is within Duggor space."

Ullo tapped the armrest of her chair before standing. "Thank you for the update. Keep me posted on any course corrections. I'll be in my private office."

The commander acknowledged the order and took command. Her subordinate approached. "I've never seen Captain Ullo worried before. These fugitives must be dangerous."

The commander stared into the screen before her. "I've read the report. We're after two starborn who have developed something dangerous. They even incapacitated one of our best undercover agents. We had a signal from her that went dark immediately after it activated."

"Two starborn?" the subcommander asked. "It's not those two in that Takloh ship, is it?" The commander nodded. The subcommander thought for a moment. "But didn't they save thousands of our people? Why would they turn on Yata?"

"Subcommander, remember that you are loyal to this ship and its crew. You have taken an oath to protect all who serve it and our world. Do I make myself clear?"

"My apologies, commander. I did not mean to imply anything less than that." She returned to her seat, but in the back of her mind she was still thinking, *I'm not sure we're doing the right thing.*

Back in her office, Ullo activated a scanning device. When she heard the alert from the device telling her it was secure, she sat down and activated the small screen on the desk. "Security code Janas, seven, host, one, four, sixteen. Open a secure priority channel, Gessler encryption." Within seconds the screen displayed the Yata security forces emblem on a wall. Several seconds after, Loren Diur appeared. "Captain Treels, report," she said tersely.

Ullo took a breath before answering, "We've confirmed the location of the beacon before it deactivated. The ships appear to be on the same course."

Loren looked to the side for several seconds before returning to Ullo. "How long until you reach the estimated destination?"

"Less than one standard. Have you heard from the other ships?"

Loren placed her hands with great control on the desktop. "Yes. They have confirmed the same suspected destination as you have. Reothes."

Ullo sat forward. "Director, Reothes is a restricted planet. I have not been briefed on why." Loren just sat quietly, and Ullo continued, "Director, I am responsible for this ship and its crew. I am also aware of who I have been dispatched to apprehend. I need to know—"

She was cut off. "Captain Treels, I remind you that you serve the great people of Yata Beta, no other. I have been briefed on your brother's return by the actions of the two starborn you are being sent to find and capture. Do not let that cloud your sense of duty."

Ullo held her anger back. "Director, I have heard other reports that the two we are trying to capture have also given us the information on filament drives freely and willingly. Why would they run from us?"

"Captain, Reothes is a restricted planet for a reason. That world held vast amounts of life over ten thousand years ago. It is now a barren wasteland according to information from the Alliance and our own reconnaissance. There is nothing living there. It is a world of barren dust."

Ullo looked confused. "Was there a natural disaster?"

"No, Captain. On that world is a weapon the Duggor created, one that forced them off their own world. It destroyed everything living on that planet. And it's still active."

The captain sat in surprised awe. "Why would they go there if it's still active?"

"We have reason to believe they came upon some information about it while they were inside a gravity well."

"They survived being inside a gravity well? How?" Ullo couldn't believe what she was hearing.

Loren sat back. "Captain, they willingly gave us the information on filament travel. Something worth trillions of shil. And they immediately headed out to that world. That means whatever they found is worth more than what they gave us."

Ullo was still in disbelief. "Why would they give up something so valuable?"

Loren's stare hardened. "Captain, we believe they may have discovered how to control the weapon. If that is the case, those two would have exclusive control over an extremely powerful weapon. When you add the ability of filament travel, they could possibly control the entire galaxy."

Ullo shook her head. "No, I can't believe that. I've read the files on both."

With a practiced tone Loren sat tall. "Captain, may I remind you that they have killed a seasoned agent of my department. You have your orders. If you are not willing to follow them, I'm sure some in your crew would be willing to."

Ullo sat up straight. "Yes, ma'am, I understand. I will bring them in as ordered." The screen went blank, and she sat motionless for several seconds. Then her shoulders leaned forward, and she placed her face in her hands. "Goddess, I pray she is wrong."

Chapter 35

Disobedience

Ullo sat for a moment after her session with Loren. Her orders to destroy and kill the crews didn't sit well with her. As far as she could tell, those two had done nothing but good since they had escaped their prison. The captain had read the reports and knew their punishment hadn't fit the level of the crimes they had committed. "Why do they want them dead?" she muttered to herself.

As if by design, her personal comm notification gave an alert: *Incoming message from the* Aquaese *Coul*. "That's Wehen's ship," she said, looking down in contemplation. "I wonder what he wants." She opened the message and a video started.

"Hello, Nanaan. It's been a while." Ullo felt herself smile. "I heard from our intelligence that you were sent after the two starborn."

"Word travels fast when a level seven threat is issued," Ullo whispered to the air.

"I'm on my way to Reothes. I suspect that's where they're heading. I've forwarded the information on filament travel to my superiors. I understand they've done the same for your people."

She had been involved with Captain Wehen several years ago but had decided to continue her career in the Yata space corps. She knew him well enough to know that there was something concerning there in his stare.

"Nanaan, listen to me. I've learned they're working with the pirates."

"Well, you just confirmed that they're criminals," she muttered.

"They're trying to stop the war with the Duggor. Nanaan, they aren't bad people. They were punished for being what they are. I believe, deeply, that they're trying to stop the war with the Duggor. Whatever you've been told about them working with the pirates, and about them being dangerous…" He paused for a moment. "Actually, they *are* dangerous, but just not in a criminal way. They're trying to achieve something. They're looking for a ship the Duggor lost within the filaments. They're hoping it will stop the Duggor from attacking. Right now, I believe them. They sent me a message explaining everything. And I'm sharing it with you."

An image of Jace Tucker appeared on the screen. "Captain Wehen, or whoever is watching, we need you to understand. We don't have much time…"

She watched the entire video, understanding more and more. Finally at the end, she hung her head low, questioning in her head whether she should do what she was now thinking of doing.

She was alerted by her commander that they were nearing the target point. The ship dropped out of hyperspace nearby the planet Reothes. They could see the *Wolfhammer* disconnecting from another ship, while a third one floated close by. "I want them all scanned. Now!" Ullo ordered.

Moments later, she entered the bridge. "What's our status?"

The commander relinquished the command chair. "Captain, we've confirmed two of the vessels, the *Wolfhammer* and the *Kitsdale*. We do not have identification on the other one. It's likely a pirate vessel. We know they are working for the pirates. The *Wolfhammer* and *Kitsdale* appear to be moving away." She called out to the crew, "Ready all weapons."

Ullo glanced over, the recent communication still fresh in her mind. "Subcommander, have the ships armed any weapons?"

"No, ma'am. They appear to be leaving the unidentified ship on its own. There appears to be no movement from the vessel."

"Sounds like a trap," the commander said out loud.

"Commander Brunna, I doubt they would leave a fully staffed ship as a trap. Open a comm." Once she had, Ullo called out, "This is Captain Treels. Identify yourselves."

"Captain, the *Wolfhammer* and *Kitsdale* have left sensor range. Shouldn't we chase after them?"

The captain was hesitant. She couldn't stop thinking about Wehen's message.

"Captain," Brunna said impatiently, "we have direct orders to capture or destroy the *Wolfhammer* and that other ship. If you are not willing to obey those orders, I will ask you to relinquish command."

Ullo looked at her. "You want to take command of this vessel? Under what authority?"

"Under the authority of Section 39 of the Security Act. If I feel you are unfit or incapacitated in fulfilling your duties as captain, I have the duty to intervene." She moved closer to Ullo. "Currently you are disobeying a direct order from the magistrate."

Taking a chance, Ullo briefly explained the message she had received. Brunna responded, "May I remind you that they killed one of our operatives?"

"May have killed. I'm about to find out for sure." She tapped the comm. "Unknown vessel, do you have an injured Yata citizen onboard?"

Several seconds later, the screen for the comm came alive. "Yata vessel, the agent you sent to capture and kill our allies is alive and well. We ask that you allow us to return her to you. We have done our best to heal her injuries your equipment caused." Several members of the command crew looked around at each other before the pirates continued, "We have been ordered to not attack you by the captains of the *Wolfhammer*. They only wish to return the agent you sent so that she may receive proper medical treatment. They have asked that you allow us to go on our way afterward. We ask that this be a mutually beneficial event for us all."

The captain took a moment before responding, "Please dock on the upper bay. A medical team will be waiting for you."

"Disregard that order!" Brunna yelled. "Fire on that vessel!"

The crew never moved, only looking at the captain. She sighed. "Security, please escort Commander Brunna to her quarters. I am having her temporarily restricted there for the time being."

"Captain, you are disobeying a direct order from the magistrate!" Brunna declared.

The captain nodded. "I know. And if anyone wishes to lodge a formal complaint, they may do so now." There was an uneasy silence from the rest of the command crew. The captain turned to face Brunna. "Leanna, I don't want to put you under arrest. I know you think these people are criminals, but from what I've learned, it seems that the magistrate is lying to us."

"How can you say that? They killed an agent of ours in cold blood."

"Then why did they heal this agent, then ask one of their own vessels to stay behind to return her to us?"

"It's...it's a trick."

"If it is, I promise I will relinquish control of our ship to you. But for now, I'm going up to meet the medical team."

When she arrived, the pirates were standing within the causeway, while two of their crew brought a gurney with the agent into the docking bay. "She received severe burns from this device," one of them said, handing over what remained of the pack to the medical team. "Captain, we are at your mercy. We ask that you allow us to return to our ship, and we will leave peacefully."

The captain took the medical scanner and scanned the agent. Her eyes widened. She then turned to face the pirates. "Thank you for returning her to us. You may leave peacefully. Know this, however; the next time we meet, you will not be walking away." The pirate smiled and nodded as he closed the door.

The captain turned, following the medical team, "Commander, you may yet have a chance to take my place," she muttered to herself.

Chapter 36

Search and You Will Find

"We've been searching for hours. This was the location the revenant said the ship would be," Eislie said as she piloted.

Jace nodded but continued to search on the smaller screen while the computer did a broad search. He tapped the comm. "Preston, any luck?" He then turned to Eislie. "It's good we found out we can communicate while in the filaments."

Eislie continued to fly while they searched. Traveling within the filaments was still new to them, even though they'd now done it a few times.

Preston said over the comm, "*Wolfhammer*, it's been over six hours since we reached the suspected location. We should consider that possibly the information we received was wrong."

Jace sat back in thought before responding, "I doubt it. That thing wants this to stop. It had every reason to tell the truth. Maybe it just had the location wrong."

There was a long pause. "It's your call, Captain."

Jace stretched. "Were you able to reach your queen?"

"No. Since we've entered the filament, we've had no communication. She did warn that this might be the case."

"Alright, keep trying. I'm still hopeful we'll find the damn ship." He returned to the small screen and continued searching. Several minutes later he rubbed his eyes. "Been staring at this screen for so long, things are getting blurry." He looked at Eislie and saw that she appeared tired too. "Let's go a little longer, then find a place to punch out. This multicolored flashing is really starting to get on my nerves."

Eislie chuckled. "Let's hope we don't have to start from the beginning again."

Jace groaned. "That would really suck. I mean, can you imagine what it would be like to…"

Eislie looked at Jace as he paused. "What is it?"

Jace tapped his screen. "I thought my eyes were blurry, but a blurry spot usually moves. This isn't moving."

"Where?"

Jace pointed to the lower part of the screen. "There, a short distance away. That blurry spot hasn't moved at all. Let me have the controls for a minute."

Eislie switched the flight controls to Jace as he hit the comm. "Preston, I'm increasing speed. I think I see something." As he did so, the spot started to grow, filling the screen as they got closer. The ship gave an alert as sparks started to fly from the front of their ship. "Warning, dimensional and quasi-space collision detected!"

"I got it, Ed," Jace said as he backed off the throttle. "Can you discern the size of the anomaly?"

"Approximately 2,200 meters on the long axis, and 700 on the vertical. Captain, it has a regular shape. Not like any quasi-space incursion I have ever seen."

"That's about the size for a Wrent-class vessel." He smiled. "You wanna bet that's what dimensional shielding looks like inside the filaments?"

"You mean the shielding we took was from a Duggor ship?" Eislie said.

"Yep. I thought it looked familiar, but I couldn't put my finger on where it was from. Damn, now I wish we hadn't disconnected the shielding." He tapped the comm. "Preston, did you outfit your ship with that shielding we brought back?"

"We were able to install some on the front half of our ship. We weren't on planet long enough to finish."

Jace thought for a moment. "Yeah, us too. We disconnected everything until we found a way to connect it better. Can you use what you have?"

"Checking. I would have preferred to test this outside the filaments."

"Agreed," Jace said. "At least it seems we've found what we were looking for, even if we can't touch it at the moment."

Nearly an hour later, Preston said, "Captains, I believe we can now activate the system. What is your plan?"

"I'm thinking the shield could be used to pierce or maybe somehow resonate with what's in front of us. I'm kind of shooting from the hip here, though. I don't want to put you in harm's way."

"No worries." Jace heard Preston give the order to his crew to activate the dimensional shielding. He and Eislie watched as the front half of the ship blurred and blended into the energy strands of the filament.

"Preston, keep the comm open," Jace said into the comm. "Right now, you look the same as the thing in front of us. Well, at least half your ship does." He sent along a live feed from their own ship's camera.

"That *is* an unusual sight, captains," Preston said as the *Kitsdale Aura* moved toward the anomaly. They watched it slow and contact the other shield. They suddenly stopped, then a moment later they started to move again. "Looks like we've got the frequency right. Moving forward. Sending you a feed of the inside as soon as we have one."

Seconds later an image appeared. "Shit, that's a big ship," Jace blurted. Eislie's eyes were open in surprise.

Jace could hear the excitement in Preston's voice. "It seems we've found what we were looking for."

They watched as the crew of the *Kitsdale Aura* suddenly shifted forward in their seats. That made Jace concerned, but he didn't know why. Then there was a blinding flash, causing the sensors of the *Wolfhammer* to overload.

They also lost their feed from the *Kitsdale*. It took a few seconds, but their sensors came back online. The screen showed smoke and sparks within the cabin. "Shit, something blew," Jace said, pounding on the comm. "Preston, we'll dock and give you a hand."

Preston came on the screen. "Belay that. We're alright. The main power feeds for the dimensional shields blew, that's all."

"Anyone hurt?" Eislie asked, concerned.

Preston shook his head. "We had already evacuated those areas. This isn't my first time using unproven technology. We're currently on secondary systems, but we'll have main systems back online in a few minutes."

Jace then noticed something. "Look at that," he said to Eislie. The shorting of the *Kitsdale*'s dimensional shield had also shorted out the one on the Duggor ship, and it was now visible, inert and floating sideways.

It was another hour or so before they had locked down all the issues with the *Kitsdale Aura*'s systems and had the main feed running again. Eislie admitted she was getting a weird feeling from the ship, "like someone over there is watching us." They docked with the Duggor vessel, and Preston with several of his crew joined them. Although the sensors said that the vessel they had connected to had an atmosphere, they decided to be on the safe side and wear breather masks. Jace paused as his hand hovered over the door release, but eventually he pressed it.

The outside door opened to reveal a dark airlock. There was still power to the shields on the Duggor ship, but the engines were offline. A quick scan revealed that it had jettisoned the spide core and was now running on a secondary fission reactor. Preston remarked, "This is a big ship."

Jace opened the inside door of the Duggor vessel and stepped inside. The hair on the back of his neck stood on end and he froze. Preston moved forward with a scanner. "Seems deserted."

Jace put his arm out to stop him. "Scan it again."

Preston did but found nothing. "What's wrong?" he asked.

Jace looked around. "It feels like someone just walked over my grave."

Eislie hesitated as she took a step, visibly shaking. "Jace, I don't want to be here."

Preston was about to reassure her when he noticed that his own crew also seemed to be backing away. "Charl, what is it?" he asked.

The woman shook her head. "I'm with her, I don't want to be here. There's something really wrong here. Something feels very angry."

Preston looked at Jace. "She's a heavy empath, like your partner."

Eislie said with urgency, "Preston, scan that far hall again. Now." He did but found nothing.

Jace said, "Preston, do you have a quantum beacon on you?" Preston waved to one of the others, who handed him the device. "Activate it and drop it. Let's get back to the ship."

"What is it?"

Jace shone a light down the hallway, revealing a large shadow. "A shadow normally goes away when you shine a light on it."

The group rushed back toward the airlock. As Jace closed the outer door, he disconnected the docking clamps. "Eis, get us the hell away from this ship, now."

Shortly later they were connected to the *Kitsdale*. Things had calmed, but there was still a lot of speculation over what they had seen. Preston chided Jace and Eislie, "You all just have ghost ship nerves. It happens to us pirates all the time."

One of his crew joked, "Then why did you run too?"

"Because Jace made a good point. We've seen what a dimensional shield can do. Maybe there was something there that had a similar effect. Anyway, we left that quantum beacon. We'll always know where the ship is now."

Another crew member said, "Let's just tow it."

Jace smiled. "The engines aren't active. We can't restart them. And we can't move it by ourselves; it's too big. Even together we couldn't pull it fast enough to travel well with it."

"We're near the Teserin system," Preston said. "Maybe there we can find a ship powerful enough to do the job."

Jace looked at Eislie, then back at Preston. "Actually, I have someone in mind."

Chapter 37

Someone Call for a Tow?

They saw Jana's face on the outpost display. The flurry of activity behind her was an indication of the resources she had called in to accomplish the task asked of her. "It was good fortune you found the vessel intact," she said to Jace on the other screen. "It's possible that whatever you thought you saw was simply out of phase with the filament."

Jace shrugged his shoulders. "We could've worked around that. The problem is the size of the ship. Even extending the tunnel field wouldn't allow us to move a ship that size."

Jana thought for a moment. "None of my ships are large enough either. If we had time, we could build one."

Jace agreed then said, "There is one person we know that has a ship with powerful enough engines. But he'll need an escort. I'm pretty sure they'll be watching him."

The queen raised an eyebrow. "Your engineer's ship?"

Jace nodded. "We need to get a message to him and have him meet us here. We have a beacon on that ship and have been tracking it. Although, now that we've blown out the dimensional shielding, I hoping it won't start to degrade."

"That is a valid concern, Captain Tucker. I'll instruct my people to relay your message. I will inform you when he is on his way."

"Thank you. Now, what about the other matter of the fleet? If this works, we're going to need them."

Jana smiled. "I have amassed several hundred vessels, including Alliance and Consortium. Once I told them who was requesting the aid, of course. It seems you two have somewhat of a following, even among your enemies." The look Jace and Eislie gave each other made her chuckle. "I am aware of your lack of interest in leading. But it may be something you will have to consider."

Jace sighed. "Jana, I'm concerned about the people on those ships. It's something the Ha'ak told us." He told her how the Ha'ak had modified the planet, and that perhaps the entire surface was now flooded with spide radiation.

"That is a fair point, Captain Tucker," Jana replied. "I will inform all in the fleet that only those with over sixty-five percent Lyri DNA will be able to explore the surface once we have been victorious."

"And if we do this right, no one will have to fire a shot."

"I hope you are right, Captain. Even with this size of fleet we are at a disadvantage."

"Yeah, me too." Jace looked at Preston. "Do you have any tunnel coil cabling?"

"Yes, several spoons. Why?"

The queen answered for him. "Because he is planning on lining the Wrent cruiser and powering it with the reactor of the *Wolfhammer*."

Jace said to her, "We're going to need tow pads and the mounting hardware as well."

The queen smiled. "That facility has the supplies you need. I was planning on using it for a disassembly station."

Jace chuckled. "We're in a spaceship chop shop?"

"I'm glad you find that amusing, Captain Tucker," Jana said with a hint of warning in her voice.

Jace gave a dismissive wave. "Hey, your place, your rules. We're just interested in one ship." He pulled up an image of it. "My other concern is the filament itself. The ship got stuck because it couldn't leave the exit point."

"That is what trapped our dreadnaughts the last time."

"Exactly. At the exit points, the filament seems to pinch closed. The entrance and exit are always the hardest to navigate as well. That's why only smaller ships seem to be able to use them."

Jana moved back to her console. "Preston, the three of you plan out how to outfit that vessel with the coils system. I will inform you once their engineer is on his way, and we will coordinate with you once you leave for that ship. I expect a full data pack on everything."

"Yes, my queen," Preston and the other pirates all responded.

Jace shook his head before saying, "Let's get to work."

Several hours passed and Arren arrived in record time. Jace and Eislie couldn't stop smiling, seeing their old friend giddy from riding the filaments in his own ship for the first time. When he stepped off his ship, Eislie greeted him with a hug. "Eis, you and Jace are so lucky to be able to do this," he said, a smile plastered on his face. "It was amazing. It travels faster than any ship I've ever flown on. I don't have the words to describe it." Then he turned a little more serious. "It's too bad it's coming under these circumstances. The Alliance and everyone else have issued a level seven for you and the *Kitsdale*."

Within moments, all the pirates, including the crew Jana had provided for Arren, were assembled in the docking bay. Above the console was an image of the Duggor Wrent cruiser. "We attach the anchors here, here, and here," Jace said, indicating the spots. "We'll run the power through our back hatch."

Arren interrupted, "No, you won't. That secondary panel in your hold won't handle the power. That stunt you pulled with that scout ship was probably maxing out your field generator. My ship has an auxiliary connection. Remember, it's designed to tow or push ships. You don't have the power on that little ship of yours. Even if you combined them, you won't be able to power the field."

"Arren, if we connect the field coils together, we can use both our systems—"

"You don't have the hardware to regulate the systems together. You need one system. And my ship is the only one that has that capability right now. I'm not going to argue with you anymore. It has to be my ship."

The large screen of the facility came alive, showing Jana in her command center, surrounded by monitors. "I'm afraid your friend is correct," she said. "My resources have detected several dozen ships heading toward your location. It seems they may have retrieved the data from one of our ships that was damaged."

Jace asked Arren, "You're sure your ship can power a field that big?"

Arren replied with a smile, "I designed it to tow a Wrent class. It'll handle the job."

Jace looked around. "Okay, then let's move the cabling to Arren's ship and we'll head out."

The dock of the pirate outpost was a flurry of activity as they moved the supplies to Arren's ship. After loading they ran through the plan once again. "We place the anchors on these areas. We run the tunnel coils along this axis. The power gets connected and running. The *Kitsdale* and we will run point. We'll connect tow lines to take the strain off the engines of *Ciaimose*. We'll do the install." He looked at Arren. "Sorry, old man, but we're built for this environment. I'm not sure the Sotiral suits will handle the exposure for as long as we have to be out there."

Arren looked annoyed but could see the sarcastic stare Jace gave him. "I'd be better inside anyway, hooking up the power feeds. None or you know how the systems run." The old engineer waddled over to Eislie. "If we work this right, we'll only have to make one run."

Jace motioned to Preston to contact Jana. Once she appeared on the screen, Jace said, "We're heading out. We don't have a way to contact you inside the filaments, so give us at least six hours to get things set up and underway. It should take us another eight to bring the ship to the exit near Lyri."

Jana replied, "That gives us about ten hours to get the crews equalized, ready, and nearby. We'll make sure not to encroach too far into Duggor territory. We'll be ready for you when you exit. If you need the support, you'll have it."

They signed off. Jana sat at her control console, her hands working the controls with furious speed and accuracy. "Zido, I need your assistance!" she yelled.

Her loyal assistant appeared almost instantly. "Yes, my queen."

"Ready the *Blue Viper*. I want you to handpick the crew. Make sure they're all starborn able to walk the surface of the planet. We'll also need at least several other ships ready for surface combat. I fear Captain Tucker is correct. We may be able to drive the Duggor from the planet, but we'll need to hold it as well." She stood, placing her veil over the side of her face. "Zido, Jace and Eislie have expressed no interest in leading the starborn who return. Right now, I'm the only one qualified to do so in the interim, but honestly, I share their hesitation. I may rule the pirates, but I'm not sure I could rule a world."

Chapter 38

The Hour of Fate

Several hours passed before the Duggor ship again came into view. "It hasn't moved much," Jace said with a hint of concern. "I'm hoping what you sensed on the ship and my reaction were just a fluke. The only other ship we've been on was that Lyri scout ship about a year ago. That ship was smaller, and we could see in there. This one has almost no lights. It's kind of creepy as well, but I can't quite figure out why."

Eislie replied, "Maybe it's because you know people died in there."

"Maybe, but we're still going to have to go back onto that ship." He reached over, touching her arm. "You can stay here. I'll go over."

Eislie nodded but said nothing. When Jace switched over the flight controls, she quickly took command. "Eis, it'll be Preston, me, and three of his people," Jace said as he went back to put on his environment suit. "You stay here in case I need a fast way off the ship. You can also coordinate with Arren."

It wasn't long until Jace returned, his helmet in hand. He caringly walked over, giving Eislie a kiss on her head. "I'll be back in a bit. If we get this to work, it might end the war with the Duggor. Maybe they'll stop hunting us, maybe not. I don't know." He turned to look at her. "We gotta try, right?"

"Yes. Maybe we'll get some peace and quiet." Eislie was semi-hopeful as she landed the *Wolfhammer* on the front of the Duggor vessel. "Magnetic clamps on. We're secure." She switched the screen to look behind them and could see the *Kitsdale* and Arren's ship landing as well. The extra holding clamps protruded onto the Duggor ship.

"He wasn't kidding that his ship was made to recover something like this," Jace muttered before tapping his comm. "Preston, I'm heading out. If you have someone ready, I'll meet them outside our ship, and we can head to the back of Arren's ship after we unload the anchors."

"How many of the anchors are on your ship?" Preston asked over the comm.

"We have ten. That's all we could fit. We'll use those for most of the front. The ones you have we'll use toward the rear." He put his helmet on and headed into the airlock. "Eis, keep the engines warm."

Eislie switched on the ship's lights; not that it did much, except even out the brightness of the light in the filament itself. She was concerned about Jace. Neither of them had been outside in the raw elements of the filaments themselves, especially wearing only an environment suit. She watched them before quickly running back to put her suit on. She kept her helmet nearby.

A little over an hour later, Jace was complaining as he pulled the third run of the drive coils. "Couldn't you find something heavier?" he teased Preston.

The pirate cheerfully responded, "We can steal some heavy ones. You want me to take a quick hop out and back?"

The laugh through the comm made Eislie smile. She needed something to take her mind off the feeling of something watching them. It felt like something very angry. She tapped the comm and said, "Maybe get something with a logo on it next time." Jace smiled, but when he saw the look on her face, he asked what was wrong. She shifted uncomfortably as she looked into the screen. "I'm feeling the same thing as last time. How much longer do you think it'll take?"

Jace asked Preston, "What's the status of the connections in Arren's ship?"

Preston in turn tapped his own comm. "What's the status of the power, Julsin?"

Julsin replied, "We're connecting the second-to-last run now."

Arren grumbled, "Everyone's in such a rush. It takes time to properly connect coil power." The old engineer looked at the pirate. "It'll be about half a standard, then we can test the integrity."

Jace said, "You hear that, Eis? About half an hour. How are you holding up?"

"I'll be okay. I just don't want to be here too long."

Arren shuffled out of the small area. "Are you alright, Eis? You're not looking good."

Julsin said, "This happened when we entered the ship before. Yin and Gomez had a similar reaction. Jace did as well."

Arren tapped his comm. "Jace, Eis doesn't seem to be doing very well. Julsin says you had a reaction to the ship as well. What's going on?"

Jace shook his head, his response lacking its normal sarcastic tone. "I was doing fine ignoring the hair on the back of my neck standing straight out until you reminded me. Just get those connections hooked up."

Arren stepped back and asked Julsin, "What's going on?"

"There's something in the ship. Anyone with a high empathic sense is feeling it. It's whatever is on that ship. I'm not empathic, but even I know whatever it is it doesn't want us here. Let's get these last connections done and we can get moving."

"There, connection secure," Arren said as he closed the panel. Julsin pointed at some marks from a previous incident and Arren replied, "It's nothing. Had a connector blow." He headed toward the control room. "Tell them to get on board their ships. I want them ready to run if something goes wrong."

He brought up the reactor power. It took a few minutes for Jace and the others to board their own ships. Arren did a countdown, then brought the power up slowly. The coils energized. "I'm not getting any reverse feedback. That's a good sign." He tapped the controls. "I'm going to try and move the ship. Hang on, everyone."

As Arren brought up his engines, the Duggor vessel could be heard creaking, but it was also moving. Arren tried maneuvering but the reaction of the ship was sluggish. "Damn, this thing's heavy. Preston, Jace, I'm going to need some help moving this thing. I can push the ship, but steering is another matter."

Arren did his best to center the ship within the filament. He felt the side of his command chair when the Wrent class hit the boundary of the filament tunnel. He watched as a chuck of the outer hull ripped away and floated by his ship. "Slac, it's bigger than I thought too." He turned to Julsin. "We're going to have to figure a way to keep it centered. Otherwise, it'll get torn to shreds while we're flying." He powered down, tapped the comm, and said, "We need to have a meeting. This isn't going to be as easy as we thought."

Jace shook his head. "I was wondering when something was going to happen. It's been too easy so far."

Preston chimed in, "We have a pool going on how long it would take for something to go south. We'll head over and meet. Jace, you should join us."

Eislie turned her head, looking at Jace. He could see the look in her eyes. She didn't want to be there. Especially not alone. Jace moved closer. "Why don't you come with me?"

Eislie shook her head. "I'm not leaving the ship. One of us needs be here in case something goes wrong."

"You're not alright, are you?"

Then the ship's computer interrupted. "Captains, I must inform you that we are accelerating. Current speed is 10.6 meters per second and increasing."

"But we don't have any engines running, do we?" Jace asked before hitting the comm. "Hey, we're getting an acceleration reading. Is anyone else seeing that?"

Preston, looking at the piolet, said, "He's right. Speed's increasing exponentially. We're at about 11.1 meters per now. Arren, are your engines running?"

"I'm shut down, but I'm seeing it too. We shouldn't be moving."

Seconds later, the energy filaments around them started to distort. It took a moment before Arren realized what was happening. "Jace, Preston, this part of the filament must be near a heavy gravity body. The tunnel is being distorted, and the gravity is affecting the ship. We're accelerating toward the opposite side of the tunnel."

He looked back at Julsin. "We don't have much time. I've seen this before. Had a ship pulled out from hyperspace by something similar." He pressed the comm. "Everyone, I'm starting my engines. I'm going to get us going a little faster, get us away from the gravity well. No one should be outside. I suggest everyone stay inside until we get clear."

They all felt the surge as Arren hit his engines, and the filament started to move around them. Jace sat, his environment suit still on, as he watched. "Arren, I thought you said you can't control this thing by yourself."

"When we get up to cruising speed, I won't be able to. But I can nudge us. I'll do my best to keep us as centered as possible. I just want to get us away from that heavy gravity."

Julsin asked, "How come we've never encountered this before?"

Arren exhaled and thought for a moment before saying, "The ship's shields were probably dampening the gravity's effect. My guess is that since it didn't seem to be moving, it might have been in equilibrium. We messed that up by shifting it." He looked at his display. "I'll get this far enough away from that area to no longer affect it, then we can make a new plan."

About an hour later, the ship was moving slowly through the filament, and they were no longer feeling the pull of the gravity well. Arren said, "From this point forward, either use the comm to communicate or dock your ship with mine. I don't want anyone outside while the ship is moving."

The *Wolfhammer* being the smallest ship of their ragtag fleet, they elected to ferry everyone to Arren's ship. They docked with the *Kitsdale* before moving to the *Ciaimose*. Once everyone was onboard, they started working on a plan. As the ship continued to move, several faint shadows appeared on the outer hull of the Dugger vessel. When Ed went to look at them, though, he found nothing. Concerned, he informed everyone. "Well, whatever they were, they're not there now," Jace said. "Keep your eyes open, Ed."

Gomez had accompanied Preston on the *Wolfhammer*. Both he and Eislie kept their arms wrapped around themselves as they walked onto Arren's ship. Seeing Eislie in this condition, Arren rushed over. "You alright, Eis?"

Eislie shook her head. "It feels like something's watching us. Something very angry. Scared."

Gomez added, "I keep feeling a chill, like something clawing at me."

Jace shook his head. "Can't get hair on my neck to go down. I'm working through it, though. I'm good to go."

They went through the plan that Arren had thought up, then got ready to set up their ships. Arren pulled Jace along back to the *Wolfhammer*. "You can use the support struts here," he said, pointing to the new crosspiece in the cargo area. He turned to Preston. "You use the docking clamps on your ship to attach. Your ships will have to work together to guide the Wrent. I'll power the coils and push."

Jace looked around. "It can't be that easy."

Arren smiled. "Flying shouldn't be an issue. It's exiting where we're going to have to get creative. This is a big ship, but from what I've seen in the data, we should be okay, as long as we don't hit the sides or collapse the filament on ourselves."

As they continued to plan, none of them noticed the wall along the small hallway darkening. The shadows seemed to converge on Jace and Eislie. Jace was standing right in front of Eislie when the air behind him shimmered. He froze. There was a collective gasp before everyone in the cabin went silent. No one moved. The only sound was the computer seeing the event and saying, "Captain Tucker, are you alright?"

Jace said nothing, only staring at the ghostly hand protruding from his chest grasping at Eislie. Gomez nearly fainted. Eislie was staring at the thing behind Jace, her eyes open in terror.

It took a moment before Jace's expression changed to one of anger, his Terran ancestry kicking in. He grabbed his chest, spinning around and pushing at the specter. His actions seemed to contact the entity, pushing it back. "What the fuck?" he growled. "Get off me, whatever you are."

The ghosts stepped back, their expression turning from anger to fear as they moved away. Eislie wrapped her arms around Jace, holding him tightly. The look on Jace's face turned to rage. "I don't know what you are but get off our fucking ship!"

They all watched as the entities quickly moved away in fear, several moving along the walls and floor to the ship below. Eislie spun him around, making sure he was alright. "Geez, what the fuck was that?" Jace said, still checking for a hole in his chest.

Arren, shaking, leaned on the nearby console. "Gods, protect me and them from whatever that was." Preston, meanwhile, stumbled back with his hands shaking. His eyes were wide, but he said nothing.

Several minutes went by before Jace said, "Okay, we've got a ghost ship carrying real ghosts. Let's just get this thing out of here. Drop it off and let the Duggor fucking deal with them."

Arren stumbled as he walked. He said to Jace, "I've never been so scared in my entire life, and I've lived a long time."

Chapter 39
Running the Gauntlet

"Zido, how many ships are ready?" Jana asked as she sat in her captain's chair.

"871, my queen. But by my calculations, we only have about a third of the Duggor fleet's firepower."

"I'm aware of the situation. If we don't engage the Duggor directly, we may have a chance." She looked at her display. "They're underway. I'm tracking the quantum beacon. By my estimation they will arrive at the Lyri filament point in about three standard hours." She looked around at her crew. "Zido, are the ships crewed with enough Lyri lineage to survive the radiation of the planet?"

"Yes, my queen."

"Then let's get underway."

A short while later, Jana sat in her private office, reviewing the data from the previous filament runs of Preston's ship, when there was a knock on her door. Zido stood in the doorway. "My queen, I have the tallies of the weapon capabilities of all vessels."

She waved him in. As he handed her the info-pad, she noticed him looking at the screen. A smile graced her face. "It's incredible, isn't it? Preston's ship has more than seven times the speed traveling the filaments, and that's just from conservative runs. The *Wolfhammer* has gone even faster, although a bit more recklessly."

Zido chuckled. "Well, they do tend to be running away from danger more often than our captain."

The queen gave a quiet laugh. "They have been in some rather harrowing situations, haven't they?"

Her commander smiled. "Yes, they have. It is unfortunate." His expression hardened. "When they initially attacked us, they caused the death of several hundred of our people. I wonder when you will be extracting compensation for those deaths."

The queen's expression also hardened. "You think I've been too forgiving."

Zido stood tall. "Many of those who lost someone they cared for want retribution but have not spoken up. I, too, will abide by your decision."

"Technically we attacked them first. They were merely trying to escape. The deaths of the others are as much on our hands as it is theirs."

Her commander nodded. "Of course. I meant no disrespect."

Jana gently touched his face. "Rest assured that if that wasn't the case, I would have killed them myself." Her hand slowly dropped away as she stood. "They've worked with us while asking for no compensation, no real demands. They've given us the secrets to filament travel willingly. And, right now, they're risking their lives to try and end a war that has affected all starborn and us. I'd say they've compensated us generously for their previous actions."

She walked toward the door, motioning for Zido to follow. "If those who want compensation are still filled with bloodlust, I ask only that they not act in anger, and to understand that these two are what all starborn could be. I will not stop any from seeking vengeance." She paused. "But I will caution them that if they do decide to act, that they prepare for the consequences if they fail."

A chill ran down Zido's enhanced spine. "People who act against them in anger do tend to meet unfortunate ends."

The queen smiled. "That, my dear Zido, is an understatement." She opened the door. "Make sure all ships are ready to fight when we arrive. I'm sure the Duggor will respond. But we must not engage the Duggor until we're certain the *Wolfhammer* and the others are near enough to achieve their goal."

Zido gave a shallow bow. "Yes, my queen. I will see to that personally."

On the bridge of the *Blue Viper*, Jana sat in her command chair as they exited from hyperspace. She watched as the screen filled with the ships of the rest of her fleet. She pressed the comm. "To all ships, remain in formation. If the Duggor approach, do nothing. No one is to fire on any Duggor vessel until the order is given."

Several hundred responses came back. Lido processed them quickly. "The fleet awaits your order."

The queen nodded. "Stay near the filament point, and be ready. I'm sure a fleet of this size has gotten their attention."

* * *

Arren was grunting as he maneuvered his ship, his hand slamming on the comm as it started to drift. "Preston, you need to move more to center. You're swinging the back end of this thing like a raza whipping its tail."

Preston complained, but Arren just kept working the controls. Jace, on the other hand, said, "You had to mention raza, didn't you?" Arren raised his brow. He had forgotten about the raza attack that had nearly killed Eislie and Jace back on Charon. He was about to apologize, but thought it was better to leave it alone.

Suddenly Preston was on the comm. "Arren, my calculations show us about an hour out. How's your ship holding up?"

Arren looked over at Julsin as he examined the displays, his finger tapping one in particular. Julsin said, "Problem?"

Arren glanced at him. "I don't think so, but the external panel seems a little warm." Arren then realized he had only repaired the panel, not upgraded it like he had promised Jace. The temperature reading was high, but not like when it blew out, injuring him. He looked at Julsin. "Go get a direct reading. Let's make sure it's correct."

The pirate jumped from his seat, grabbing a monitor. "We should probably tell them."

"Check it out first. Let's not worry them if we don't need to. Right now, let's stay focused on getting this thing where it needs to go."

Julsin agreed, going back to check the power panel feeding the tunnel's coils, draped across the Duggor ship. He scanned it and, surprised, muttered, "471? That can't be right." He hit the nearby internal comm. "Arren, it's well above the safety limit of 250." He watched it climb again, now to 473.

Arren sighed, muttering at the ship, "You better hold together." He then got on the internal comm and said to Julsin, "We'll throttle down a bit. I'll let them know." He tapped the external comm. "Hey, everyone, we're running hot. I'm going to slow down a bit."

He heard the acknowledgment from both ships guiding the Duggor Wrent along the filament. On board the *Kitsdale*, Preston said, "Let's hope it's not enough to make the drive coils fail. That would be really bad for all of us."

The *Ciaimose* slowed, but they were still on schedule. Jace was piloting, taking over from Eislie who needed a rest. She was still feeling the effects of the ghost onboard the ship they were hauling. He could see her pacing and sensing something. "Still getting the shivers from the ship behind us?" he asked, trying to sound confident.

Eislie nodded. "It's not like before. It's a mix of fear and I guess you could say hope. Sort of." Jace chuckled nervously and she said, "What is it?"

"I'm just hoping Jana gets there before us. Not that I don't trust the Duggor, but I don't think us popping out of a filament point with this ship is going to be as welcome as I had hoped."

"She's not there to take the planet back, is she?"

Jace shook his head. "I only told her that. I mean, maybe. But to be honest, it was more to keep the Duggor off our asses."

"We should tell her after this works."

"Nah. Some things are best left unsaid. I don't want her to know I used her as a threat for not getting caught. Let's leave it alone." He then looked at the display. "Arren, looks like we have about twenty standard before exiting. How is your ship holding up?"

On the comm they heard, "Still running hot, but not as bad as before. I think being in the filaments draws more power. I've already compensated for the issue. But we have another problem."

Jace nodded. "The exit, I know. Can your ship handle the surge as we're exiting?"

"It's not my ship I'm worried about."

Eislie sat up suddenly and hit the comm. "Arren, the hull of that ship is polyceramic."

Preston said, "You're thinking about the discharge, aren't you?"

Jace nodded. "We didn't think about that, did we?"

Arren stared at the comm. His ship could withstand the surge on its own, but something this massive was something he had only considered once they'd been underway. "Jace, Eis, I can disconnect the feed lines a second before we exit. There should be enough charge to get the ship through. And my ship can handle a larger surge than either of yours."

"Arren, we can't do that to you," Preston said. "Let's slow down and think about this for a minute."

Arren turned to Julsin. "What was the temperature of that panel when you checked last?"

"Around 270."

Arren smiled. "Jace, Eis, Preston, let's keep going. I'll rig the system to disconnect. The charge should go back onto the Wrent. It'll probably blow a hole in it, but since there's nothing living on it, it should be fine."

"That's a cold way of looking at it, but he's not wrong," Jace remarked, making Eislie stare at him before he looked back. "It's us or the other ship. And since it doesn't have an active power system or spide system to worry about, it should only suffer superficial damage."

Eislie sighed and bit her lip before saying, "I hope you're right."

Chapter 40
Arrival

The crew of the *Blue Viper* remained busy as a large Duggor fleet approached. The Duggor had mobilized more than half their entire fleet after seeing the pirates and others idle near the filament of the stars that Lyri orbited.

"All ships, do not fire first," Jana said. "I repeat, do not fire first. Allow the Duggor to attack." She turned to Zido. "Any indication of the quantum beacon?"

Zido shook his head. "I am scanning, but the last indication was that they were nearing the exit."

"Keep searching. I'm hoping to stall until they get here."

It was only a few moments later when the Duggor opened a comm. "You are trespassing in Duggor space. Leave now or be destroyed."

The pirate queen waited before answering. "Duggor, we are not here to attack unless provoked. We are seeking a peaceful end to the war and for your abductions of starborn."

The Duggor fired anyway, the shot glancing off the shields of the *Blue Viper*. The ship rocked and Zido yelled, "Shields fluxing but no damage. Should we return fire?"

"Well, you figured out the lead ship fairly quickly," Jana muttered before saying to Zido, "No, hold fire unless they destroy one of our ships." She hit the comm. "I repeat, we are here under peaceful conditions. I ask that you do not fire on our vessels."

There was another shot, once again glancing off another ship's shields. Jana ordered, "Hold your position." She then watched as all of the Duggor ships took up position before a different ship on the front line, but remaining a short distance away. She said in amazement, "Hmmm, they might actually believe me."

* * *

On the *Wolfhammer*, Jace was having difficulty maintaining steering. The ship was shaking violently as they neared the end of the filament. At one particular spot, the ship lurched and they could hear the upper right stabilizer being ripped off. "Dammit, this isn't as stable as I thought it'd be," he said as he worked to regain control.

Eislie pressed the comm. "It's getting bumpy up front. How are you doing, Preston, Arren?"

The *Kitsdale* was experiencing the same turbulence. "*Wolfhammer*, we've switched to cables. We disconnected from being directly on board. How's your ship, Arren?"

There was a delay before Arren responded, "We're getting thrown around here. I've sent Julsin back to check the connections. Once he's back I'll have him take over piloting, and I'll set up to shut things down."

He turned to see Julsin walking into the command deck. "Panel's warm again. We probably shouldn't put too much stress on it."

Arren nodded, then pointed to the controls. "You take over. I'll get us ready to disconnect."

Julsin smiled. "I can do that, old man. You just fly."

Arren, annoyed, responded, "Sit down and fly. You don't know this ship like I do. I built the damn thing." He then got up and pushed the man into the command chair. "You can fly, right?"

Julsin smiled. "Better than you, old man."

Arren scoffed, "We'll see."

He walked down to the engineering room and went to work, grumbling as he loosened several large power connectors. He rigged a pull line to pull them all out safely from outside the door. Once he was ready, he tapped the external comm. "Jace, Preston, I'm ready. We're about four seconds behind you. Give me a countdown for exit."

Eislie answered on the comm, "We'll give you a count, but are you sure this will work?"

Arren smiled. "As long as the capacitance in the drive coils stays steady, we'll be fine."

Jace said, "Fingers crossed."

Eislie then started the count. "Exit in ten, nine, eight, seven, six, five, four, three, two, one."

The *Wolfhammer* exited the filament point, and the charge on the ship flashed brightly around them. The *Kitsdale* was next. Seconds later, the leading edge of the Wrent appeared. Arren could see the stars of normal space and pulled the cord to disconnect the system. Moments later there was arcing inside the connector room, and then Arren heard an explosion from the rear of the ship. He knew exactly what had happened; it was the same panel that had blown earlier. *The coils!* he yelled in his mind.

As the midpoint of the Duggor ship reached the exit, it started to slow. Within moments, the exit doorway of the filament started to collapse. Arren was knocked on the floor, and then he heard it, the hull of his ship being forced against the Duggor vessel, and the filament itself tearing apart the top part of his ship. He closed his eyes. His last words on the comm were, "Please, let there be just enough to get these lost souls back home."

There was a bright explosion as the back half of the Duggor vessel and Arren's ship exploded. Jace and Eislie shook their heads in disbelief before Jace pounded the comm. "Arren! Arren, are you alright?" They heard nothing. "Arren! Are you there?"

The ship's computer scanned the area. Ed could see that the last quarter of the ship was crushed, and debris was floating where the *Ciaimose* was connected to the Duggor vessel. The entire area had been crushed into a thin metallic frame protruding from the Duggor Wrent.

Jace called out to the *Kitsdale*, "Preston, are you finding any life signs?"

The crew of the *Kitsdale* was also looking for their other crewmember in the wreckage. They had yet to find any signs of life either, and were calling on the comm as well. The flash and energy of the explosion was noticed by the pirate fleet, and several ships rushed toward them to assist in the search. Then Ed told them the grim news. "Captains, I cannot find life signs for Arren or Julsin. But I am detecting biological remnants that match their DNA."

Eislie started sobbing, hiding her face, while Jace fought back a tortured look as he made the call. His voice broke as he said, "Preston, we've confirmed that Arren and Julsin didn't make it."

Preston pounded his fist into the console, his voice unsteady. "I understand. They were good crew and friends."

"Yeah. Let's hope they didn't die in vain."

Jana was monitoring the conversation. She remained stalwart but had to measure her words as she spoke. "Captains Tucker, Licessien, Elis, we have been monitoring your communications. Do you need assistance?"

There was a long delay before Jace replied, "We're safe for the moment. How is the other situation?"

Jana had expected to see the Duggor attack, or at the very least head toward the vessel. Instead, they were silently floating in formation before them. She tapped the comm, but as she was about to speak, the Duggor came onto the screen. "You are all starborn. Starborn have made us whole."

Jana stood, muttering, "They did it."

Zido moved to stand next to her. "They said they are whole. What does that mean?"

Jana solemnly said, "It means our friends did as they promised. They brought those missing back home. And hopefully, brought all starborn home as well." She steeled herself before she spoke on the conn again. "Duggor, these people have attempted to bring home your missing. Were they successful?"

The Duggor no longer sounded threatening as they responded, "Yes. We are whole."

"Duggor, you have taken a world from our ancestors. We are here to reclaim it. Take your missing and leave. We do not wish a fight, but know that even though we are outmatched, all of us here and now were a part of this plan to bring back your missing."

Jace and Eislie were watching the comm as Jana spoke, Jace remarking, "Let's hope they do this peacefully. I'm not particularly in the mood for a fight."

"We cannot return home," the Duggor responded.

Jace tapped the comm. "Jana, let us speak with them."

She nodded before saying, "Duggor, one of those who orchestrated this endeavor wishes to speak with you."

Jace and Eislie came onto the screen. "Duggor, we spoke with the one you left behind. The one who drove you from your world. It gave us hope that you might return there. Allow us to take some of your ships with us to speak with it again."

They watched as the Duggor nodded and several ships moved toward them. "We await your return."

Jace tapped the comm, changing the channel. "Preston, do you want to come with us?"

The captain of the *Kitsdale Aura* responded. "Captain, we are already setting a course."

Chapter 41
Equilibrium

The *Wolfhammer* landed on the surface of Reothes, followed by two Duggor vessels. They made sure to land near where they had before, only to find the revenant was waiting outside. When the figure approached, it walked past Jace and Eislie to meet the Duggor face to face. The revenant bowed, opening its arms before standing. It then turned, approaching Jace and Eislie. "You fulfilled your agreement," it said. "I am grateful." One of the Duggor touched the revenant on the shoulder, and all including the revenant said in unison, "We are grateful for the return of our world."

Eislie smiled, reaching out to hold Jace's hand, the two standing in silence.

The Duggor spoke again as one. "You have healed us. We return your world to you. It has been left as it was when it was taken."

Jace bowed his head, an expression of sorrow and annoyance on his face. "We are not the ones you took the world from. The Lyri, who used to live here, are now gone. Not to mention two of our own, including one very good friend. They paid a heavy price to heal you."

The Duggor bowed. "It is unfortunate that some were sacrificed to achieve this goal. But you have helped us, as you have helped many before. You say you are not Lyri, but you hold yourselves to the same teachings as they. Your friends will be remembered by us as those who gave their lives to heal us. We will assist you in reintegrating into the world that was lost. It is but only a small part of the debt we owe you and all starborn."

Jace seemed to relax. "You know, I've been called many things, including a starborn. I understand that it was a term for all beings whose planets were lost to them. Your people would be considered starborn, but they were never seen as lesser as us." He looked at Eislie. "My partner and I are from different worlds, but we don't see anything wrong with that. We agreed to help you, hoping to get back a world lost long ago by both our ancestors. Have a wonderful life. Welcome home."

Eislie pressed her comm. "Preston, we'll be up in a few. Let's head back to Lyri."

When they arrived, Jana was waiting for them in orbit around the planet. She was monitoring the highway of Duggor ships now moving back and forth from the surface. She monitored the Duggor all leaving buildings and facilities they had built, taking what they could quickly carry. When the

Wolfhammer slowed in a matching orbit, Jana said over the comm, "I take it your plan worked."

Jace nodded. "Yep. They're leaving. They said they'll help us reclaim this world since we helped them reclaim their own." He looked out the portal window. "Has anyone gone down yet?"

"No, I ordered them to wait until you returned." She sighed. "I guess it's time we set foot on a long-forgotten world."

Jace nodded and looked at Eislie, who started their decent.

It only took a few minutes before they landed. The gravity felt light to Jace and Eislie, but a quick scan around found a planet that looked like a paradise. The plant life looked strange to him but almost normal to Eislie. They opened the door and started down the ramp. The moment Jace's foot touched the surface, he felt off-balance. It took a moment before his senses equalized. Eislie had a similar issue, grabbing onto Jace and the strut of the stairway before she got her bearings. Jace started to walk, his feet no longer feeling unfamiliar on the surface. It almost felt like home.

Nearby, Jana stepped from her ship flanked by guards, all armed. They all seemed to hesitate as they touched the surface. Even the pirate queen didn't seem immune to the effect. She walked up to Jace and Eislie as they stared out over the well-kept park. "Captain Licessien, Captain Tucker, you look well. You don't seem to be affected by the high radiation levels."

Jace smiled. "It feels weird standing here, but also normal. Does that make any sense?"

"Your statement makes sense, Captain Tucker. At least for you, that is."

Eislie said, "He's right. It's like we're supposed to be here. It feels like we did something we were asked to do." She turned to Jace. "Is that what you're feeling?" Jace nodded.

Jana looked around and watched the Duggor leaving. "I never thought I would be standing here. The sensation you're experiencing is the planet itself. The energy here is a part of all starborn. Did you know that most Lyri had incredibly long lives? That's why most offshoots have long lifespans as well. Except for Terrans, that is." Jace gave an annoying glare at her, making her laugh. "Have you ever felt yourself drawn to a section of the sky, no matter where you were? A need to look up at the stars?"

Jace remembered when they were at Miriz's place, and back on Earth, where both he and Eislie had found themselves staring up at the same point.

Jana's stance softened as she replied, "I have found myself doing the same. In fact, all starborn have been known to do so. It's the planet calling to them to return. Most don't listen, of course. They just want to explore. That sensation is the planet welcoming us back. The Ha'ak knew of the phenomena."

She walked forward, standing before the entire group, before saying loudly, "We are all starborn. We are all children of Lyri. And we have returned."

***

It was a day or so later, as Jace was moving supplies to the ship, when Preston stopped by. "You're leaving already?" he said. "We have so much to learn about this world. I'm surprised."

Jace chuckled. "Well, we have some things to fix. Some people we left behind."

Behind him Zido approached. Preston saluted him as he neared. "Captain Tucker, your co-captain will be along shortly. The negotiations with the Yata government have gone well. It seems the Alliance and they have dropped the kill orders on the two of you and Captain Elis."

Jace looked at Preston. "Bet you're glad to hear that."

Preston nodded with an ear-to-ear grin. "It'll make things easier when I do finally leave. I am a ship's captain, after all."

Zido updated Jace on the remaining actions of the interim government being set, reminding him that they will need clearance to land. Jace remarked, "Just like every other planet."

"I also wish to inform you that Representative Elysse has been reinstated, with a full pardon and compensation from the Yata government."

Jace rubbed the back of his neck. "Yeah, we're heading there first. She kind of went to jail for us. It wouldn't be proper for us to not show up and see how she's doing." Jace thought for a moment. "Oh, and take back control of the Sotiral manufacturing. They kind of stole that from us."

"That has been negotiated for you as well. You merely need to show up to fill in the paperwork and sign an agreement to place a facility here on Lyri as well."

"So that's why she likes having you around. You're very efficient at getting things done."

Preston looked fearful for a moment but turned his attention to Eislie as she walked up pulling a small cart of supplies, as well as local fruits and vegetables.

"Oh good," Jace said. "Food we have no idea how to prepare, what it tastes like, or how it'll make our systems react."

Eislie gently tapped his head with the paperwork she held. He looked at it with surprise. "Wait, this is a citizenship declaration. Where did you get this?"

Eislie laughed quietly, looking at Jace. "All starborn are being given citizenship. Including us."

Zido nodded. "The queen has ordered it. That means all who are citizens may be aided by the resources of this world." He leaned in, saying in a quiet voice, "Try not to monopolize them too much."

Jace laughed, then looked at Preston, then at Zido. "Thank you. Thank you for all the help."

"Captain Tucker, our queen plans to establish a filament trading outpost on the nearby moon," Zido said. "She does hope to see you there when you have finished your other business."

Jace looked at the cart Eislie was pulling to see a metal canister with Arren's name on it. He touched it gently before looking her in the eyes. "We're heading back to his home world."

Eislie said, "They were going to give him an official delegation, but Jana felt it may be best for the two of us to take on the responsibility. His affairs stated that if he died before compensating us, he be forgiven."

Jace nodded. "He did more than he needed to. I'm willing to honor him with that." He looked around. "We'll head to Arren's home world first, then go see how Miriz is doing. You don't think she'll mind, do you?"

Eislie raised an eyebrow at Jace. "Yeah, I know when to shut my mouth."

"Goodbye, gentlemen," Jace said. "We'll see you sometime."

Zido responded with, "Hopefully you will return soon."

Jace thought for a moment. "I told the Duggor we're from different worlds, but that we don't see anything wrong with that. The queen said we are all starborn, children of Lyri." Jace looked back as they walked up the ramp of the *Wolfhammer*. "Who knows? Maybe this planet does feel a bit like home."

Chapter 42

Returning Home

It only took a few hours for the *Wolfhammer* to reach Rosta. They had placed the small metal canister containing Arren's remains in the hold. The container was made from the material of the ship he had built, per his wishes. When they landed on the surface, they were met by a delegation from the planet's government. Jace and Eislie had no idea what the protocol should be but remained respectful. They were surprised when only Arren's wife, Malain, whom he hadn't seen in years, was the one to greet them.

They had known Arren for only a few years, but he had lived for nearly 900. She explained that all Rosta, in their later years, go and try to make amends to all those they have harmed. She said that Arren had had a lot to answer for in his profession. He had two sons, Bala and Jenti, who they had already met. They were on their way back to the planet, but it was taking some time.

"If we knew, we would have picked them up," Jace said.

Malain shook her head. "No. It would not be proper to burden you. You were some of those he harmed. He asked for your forgiveness. Besides, they will arrive in a few hours."

"I don't want to seem ungrateful, but we forgave him a long time ago. We would have been honored to bring them home for this."

Malain smiled. "You have already honored him by returning him yourselves. The ceremony is in a few hours. Please rest. If you need anything, please ask."

The two got caught up with several people, sharing their stories about adventuring with Arren. When his sons arrived, the entire room went silent. Jenti approached Jace and said, "It is good to see you again."

Jace did his best to keep his composure as he shook Jenti's hand. "I'm so sorry he's gone, but he saved a lot of people."

Jenti bowed. "We can only hope he saved more than he harmed."

The rest of the conversations were more subtle as everyone gathered outside. They filed behind a small cart with the canister. Jace and Eislie were asked to join them, which they happily did. The walk was only a short distance from the building. Jace was in awe of the view before him. The small green ocean far below was breathtaking. As she looked out over the scene, Eislie had tears rolling down her face. "It's a beautiful place."

Jenti walked through the crowd, accompanying the canister, stopping at each person and bowing. Some bowed back and said, "He is forgiven." When he stopped before Jace and Eislie, Jace said, "We forgave him long ago. He owed us nothing. He was a good man."

Jenti bowed. "You returned him home. We are grateful for that."

Eislie said, "It was our honor."

When he finished going through the crowd, an official from Rosta briefly met with Jenti. He then took over as Jenti moved to pick up the canister. "I have a letter from the people of the planet he helped. I have been asked to read it aloud for all.

"The one known as Arren aided us in a time of great need. He gave his life in the service of ending the war with the Duggor and allowing us to return home. We wish to honor his sacrifice. We, the people of Lyri, make Arren Jestial a citizen of our people. May his light shine like the stars."

Jace could feel the tears on his face, but it didn't stop him from commenting, "I'm going to miss him." He felt Eislie nodding against his shoulder. He was startled when a woman next to him grabbed his hand. He turned to look at her and could see the innocent questioning in her eyes. When he heard, "You are Lyri?" he didn't know what to say.

There were suddenly dozens of eyes focused on them. It wasn't difficult, as they were taller than everyone there, but it still felt unnerving. They both stood there as the official walked up to them. Jace could see Jenti looking surprised at the canister he held. He didn't know what was happening, but it became clear as the official spoke.

"You are Lyri? The Lyri have returned to their world?" the official asked.

Jace nodded. "Yes. He helped us end the war with the Duggor, which has allowed anyone with Lyri in them to return to the planet."

The official said, "There were billions of people on that world."

"He helped us heal the Duggor and bring the people of Lyri back. He had also stayed behind to help us save billions more when we were protecting Oppa."

The official looked at Jenti and nodded. The man took the canister to the edge of the rocks and opened it, pouring the ashes out, the crowd silent. The ashes swirled and fell into the green ocean below. He put the cover back on and handed the canister to the official. He bowed and approached Jace and Eislie. "We thank you for sharing his redemption with us."

Eislie's voice cracked as she said, "He was our friend. It was our pleasure."

The official held the canister up. "He will be honored as a hero, not just redeemed."

There were conversations all around as the people of Rosta returned to their day. Jace and Eislie stood silently, looking over the water. It was a while before they headed back to their ship. A heavy sadness weighed on them as they closed the door. Eislie held Jace, rocking with him for a time before they returned to their control chairs. The only words said were that of Ed: "Captains, I will miss our friend."

Jace said softly, "So will we, Ed. This was harder than I expected." He looked to Eislie and said, "We could stay a little."

Eislie shook her head. "No. As much as I want to, I don't know if I could."

Jace tapped the engine controls. "Yeah, I know what you mean."

It was a few hours later when they arrived on Yata Beta. They were both concerned about Miriz. She had gone to jail for letting them escape. Both were surprised to see her assistant, Yeesen, still in her employ. She led them to Miriz's office, where they could hear a spirited conversation already taking place.

"I told you, we've already increased production of the Sotiral systems to almost 200 percent. The facility on Arlain was just opened; I have another opening shortly." Miriz disconnected and leapt from her chair, rushing over and hugging Eislie. They held on to each other for a short while before she released Eislie and grabbed Jace. "It's good to see you both," she said, her voice muffled as she nuzzled her face into Jace's shoulder. "You look like you've had a rough time."

Eislie nodded. "We just got done saying goodbye to Arren."

Miriz's eyes turned sad. "I'm so sorry about what happened."

Eislie smiled with a tear rolling down her face. "Considering I almost lost two friends, I think we made out okay."

Jace said, "That's true. How many people are willing to get thrown into a cell for us?" The stares of both women made him remark, "That didn't come out like I meant for it to."

Both women started to laugh. Miriz said, "He's learning."

A few days later, Eislie was in Miriz's office on the comm with a contractor scheduled to arrive on Lyri. "Lacki, I'm speaking for Mirizali on this. You must ensure all Sotiral systems are active before heading to the planet. The whole surface is like that." She looked to the wall. "I swear they're going to get themselves killed."

She looked at the clock. It was nearly past lunchtime, yet Jace and Miriz hadn't returned. She had asked to stay behind, near the ship, in case the contract signing for returning the company to Jace and her was a trap by the Yata security council. She was relieved when the door opened and she saw Yeesen place a satchel on the chair near the door.

A moment later, Miriz walked in, Jace following close behind. "You just had to insist on them leaving production the way it was on Yata, didn't you?" Miriz complained.

"Miriz, you have three shifts working now. The last thing you told me was that you were either going to have to build a new facility or close down your ship parts division and retool it. I didn't think either was a good option for you."

Miriz looked at Eislie. "He's very stubborn, he doesn't take commands well, and honestly, he kind of strongarms things."

Eislie rose from the chair and walked up to Jace. "I know he's stubborn." She then kissed him. She smiled before turning to Yeesen. "Was there much trouble getting in to see the Grand Matron?"

As Yeesen was telling Eislie about the encounter with the guards, Miriz had watched Eislie casually kiss Jace, and she decided to do the same. As Miriz neared Jace and moved up to kiss him, Eislie put her hand over Jace's mouth, and Miriz's lips landed on the back of her hand. Seeing Miriz's surprised expression made Jace bellow out laughing so hard, he began hyperventilating. Eislie looked at the back of her hand to see the lipstick on the back, which made her start laughing. Within seconds, everyone was laughing, including Yeesen.

When everything calmed, Miriz sat at her desk, an expression of feigned disappointment. Her only words were, "You win again."

Jace shook his head. "I may have to find a way to convince the two of you to tell me about this competition between you."

Eislie and Miriz seemed to think for a moment before Eislie told him again, "When you're older, we'll tell you."

Jace ran his hand down his face. He looked over at Yeesen and asked, "Do you have any idea what this is all about?"

Yeesen shook her head. "Not a clue."

Jace took a few moments before he shook his head. "The way things are going, I may never find out." He walked to the cabinet and opened it, pulling out a bottle of white rum Eislie and he had brought from Earth. He looked around and asked, "Glasses?"

Miriz pointed to the cabinet to his right, and Jace quickly found four glasses. He poured rum in each, handing them to Miriz and Eislie. He grabbed the other two for himself and Yeesen, who asked, "What are we celebrating?"

Jace held his glass up. "We have the company back under our control. Notwithstanding the additional paperwork for the facility on Arlain, it seems they're up and running. And I heard from the Grand Matron that the agreement for making the systems on Lyri was finalized."

Miriz raised her glass. "Here's to other people doing all the hard negotiating instead of us for once. That made all this possible."

Eislie said, "I was just on with the contractor, surveying the area for the plant on Lyri. He was concerned when he saw the radiation level." She turned to Miriz. "It's about 120 percent above lethal."

Yeesen's eyes widened. "That's pretty high."

"There are places on the planet where it's over 600."

Yeesen nearly choked on her drink. "That's insane. Can the systems handle that radiation density?"

Miriz smiled before pointing at Eislie and saying, "Her designs can handle up to that and more."

The rum disappeared from Yeesen's glass as she gulped down what was left. "I didn't know you made them that powerful," she said. "I've seen some images. The planet looks beautiful."

Eislie chuckled. "Sounds like you want to visit." Then, a curious and mischievous stare filled her eyes as she looked toward Miriz. "What about you, Miriz? You want to go see Lyri, ride the filaments?"

Miriz's eyes went wide. "You mean ride along with you in that ship of yours to a planet that could kill me?"

Eislie shrugged as she snickered.

Yeesen quietly said, "I'll go. I've never ridden in the filaments. Plus, how many security personnel can say they survived being on Lyri?"

Miriz said, "I just returned from prison, and I'll be taking a ship that was stolen by prisoners and reconditioned so it can fly faster than most known vessels. Sound familiar? Maybe I'll even have time to find a cute partner."

Jace slapped his forehead, dragging his hand down his face and making Eislie laugh. She simply replied, "You can try."

Several hours later, they were at the nearest filament point. Jace said, "Hold on, we're going in."

Miriz and Yeesen watched through the small portal windows as the cabin lit up with multicolored light. Yeesen remarked, "It's beautiful."

Jace snickered. "Yeah, but after a few hours it gets to you. It's like being inside a boat on a cruise, but the air around you is moving the same way."

Miriz sat down. "I would love to feel that. So, it's six days to Lyri. What do you suggest we do?"

Eislie smiled. "Miriz, this isn't hyperspace. The trip will take us a little over four hours. We're taking a straight run."

"Okay, so we have four hours to fill."

Eislie smiled at her. "We're taking a yellow line. Someone needs to fly it manually. That would be Jace."

Miriz pouted. "That's no fun."

When they arrived on Lyri, the landing took longer than anticipated. The new government had only just been established, and there was still some confusion over arrival protocols. It was nearly twilight before they were given clearance to land near the facility. Miriz put on a Sotiral system, as did Yeesen, and they stood ready in the airlock. As the door opened, Miriz held her breath.

As the warm air touched her, she felt it against her skin. As she walked out, her footsteps were slow and deliberate. She was well aware of the effects of spide radiation, but she also knew the abilities of the shield suit she was wearing. As her feet touched the ground, she paused, smelling the sweet air and the unknown fragrances.

Yeesen stepped out after hesitating, the starlight falling on her. "It's warm," she said.

Miriz watched Jace and Eislie secure the ship and meet up with some of the locals working on the site. Reaching down, she dug her fingers into the soil taking some of it into her hand. She was rubbing it between her thumb and palm when Eislie walked up. "How are you feeling?" she asked.

Miriz looked around, then at the dirt in her hand. "This is where we're all from, isn't it?"

Eislie smiled. "Most of us, yes."

"I can only imagine what it feels like."

"It feels a little like home."

They continued to the partially constructed building and went inside one of the protected areas. As night covered the site, Miriz and Yeesen again put on their Sotiral suits and walked outside with Eislie, while Jace went to get some food. Miriz sighed, saying to Eislie, "So this was what it was like to have to wear a visor on Yata."

Eislie nodded. "Kind of like this, yes."

Miriz smiled. "It's beautiful here. What's the housing situation?"

Eislie sighed. "The Duggor rebuilt everything. We're just waiting to have a unit assigned to us."

"So, you're staying?"

"We'll get a residence and think about it. Both Jace and I want to go back to Gilese."

As Jace walked up with food, he said, "I got some local stuff and some normal stuff." He held up some rations, making Eislie laugh. "Still don't know how some of this food will react with us, although it hasn't been an issue so far."

Miriz watched as her friends turned to look up at the sky. Eislie said, "There are so many stars." She looked around to see a few others looking up as well. Most weren't wearing protective shields, and she could see them all staring out into the stars.

"Why are they all staring at the stars?" Miriz asked.

Eislie said, "Can't you hear them calling?"

Miriz looked up. She could see the stars clearly, more so than ever before. At that moment, she thought she could hear something from the stars above.

ABOUT THE AUTHOR

Stephen brings over three decades of experience in technology, engineering, and sales to his storytelling, creating a unique blend of analytical precision and boundless imagination. His passion for writing science fiction and fantasy spans even longer, beginning with role-playing games and personal short stories where he first learned to weave technical knowledge with vivid creativity.

Known among friends as someone who always has a story to tell— usually sprinkled with adventure and wonder—Stephen has an innate ability to find magic in everyday moments. His storytelling philosophy centers on the belief that life itself is an adventure, and that the addition of magic, whether literal or metaphorical, can transform any experience into something extraordinary.

After years of crafting tales for personal enjoyment, Stephen decided to share his imaginative worlds with a broader audience. He is the author of *A Fairy's Light* series and *Legends of the Starborn*, inviting readers to see life through his characters' eyes, where adventure awaits and life is always better with a bit of magic and adventure.

OTHER BOOKS IN THIS SERIES

Legends of the Starborn includes:

<u>Wolfhammer</u>

The original story that set the two starborn on their galaxywide adventures. Along with their ship, the Wolfhammer, controlled by an artificial life form. All thrown away, but no one could dream what two people and a fearless AI in a small, unassuming ship were capable of.

<u>Filament</u>

After discovering they could access the network of stellar filaments, the Wolfhammer crew is working to find a way to enable everyone to travel through them. The only problem is that there are people already waiting to take it from them.

<u>Vengeance</u>

While still working on a way to travel the filaments safely, Jace and Eislie find out that their former jailer has set a bounty on their heads. When they attack, Jace watches Eislie apparently die as she is blown into space. When Jace finds out Eislie is not dead, he risks his life to get her back. Heading to the very planet, and those looking to enslave them both.

For more stories and other things please visit:

www.wolfhammer.com